A Memory of Forever

A novel by

K. L. Caldwell

PublishAmerica
Baltimore

© 2005 by K. L. Caldwell.
All rights reserved. No part of this book may be reproduced, stored in a retrieval system or transmitted in any form or by any means without the prior written permission of the publishers, except by a reviewer who may quote brief passages in a review to be printed in a newspaper, magazine or journal.

First printing

ISBN: 1-4137-1721-7
PUBLISHED BY PUBLISHAMERICA, LLLP
www.publishamerica.com
Baltimore

Printed in the United States of America

Acknowledgments

For Grandpa Clifford Querl and Grandma Arlene Querl, a pair of "soulmates" if ever I saw…

And as always, with great thanks to my patrons, Billie Lee Rein and Steven C. Rein, and others who've donated to the cause…

And to those who have found, or are searching for, that soulmate…

K.L. Caldwell

My love…

*My love is the wind upon which your laughter is carried
My love is the stones upon which you may cross the streams
My love is the boat upon your desires are ferried
My love is the sky-blue background of your dreams.
But your love is where my life begins and ends
Your love is the beating of my heart
Your love is the deep cool waters I swim
Your love is the glue that keeps us from coming apart.*

Anonymous "Soulmate"

1

HERCULENIUM, ITALY 79AD

H<small>IS WAIL OF DESPAIR</small> drifted, like a steamy smoke dissipating, up into the snow-like flakes of gray ash. Julius coughed and spat, tears streaming, then raised his fist to the dark noonday sky.

"*SWAN!*" His voice haunted the air for several seconds, but when it was gone, and only the snap—rackling of cooling lava could be heard; he hung his head. "Where are you?" he whispered.

The ash colored his black hair white, and his once green eyes were red and smoky. His toes were beyond burnt, and his wrap was peppered with black-edged holes from the falling pebble-sized rain drops of red molten lava.

He had no desire to return home, to live, to breathe in the poisonous air, but a fluorescent river of liquid rock pushed him back to the road, and he could not abandon all hope. So he walked, eyes braving the sulfuric air for her shape amongst the shadows and the dead. He passed his neighbors expansive property, where once twenty-three human beings had lived, and where now only a wind-blown pile of darker ashes marked their existence. He did not know who had torched their home, or the rest of the plague-ridden homes, but it didn't matter. He knew it would all be erased, cleansed by Vesuvius' fiery judgment.

Several ten-foot marble columns marked the entrance to their villa; a small but reputable manse deserving modest regard.

Looking up through the constant rain of warm gray powder, he saw a white roof instead of red. Along the stone pathway a last rose bush was just on fire, and he knew this would grieve Swanlake's heart. He passed it and went up the fifteen steps, then froze. He drew his short sword, strangling a hope that soared into his chest.

One of the two doors was open, and he spied a marring of his own footprints as he crossed the threshold. He turned left, down four ash-covered marble steps, and surveyed the dining room. Since all the servants had died, the large room had become ghostly, and every surface was covered by the all-invasive gray powder. But it was too quiet, and the hairs on the nape of his neck bristled, sore muscles tightening in readiness.

He swiped a heavy bead of sweat off his grime-streaked brow, and went with his hope-steered instincts; "*Swanlake?*"

"Julius? Julius!" Her voice was an echo in his mind, a dream-voice warbling through the villa, bouncing off the walls.

He ran for her, room to room, down the hallway, cursing the luxury of his large home, then doubling back through the empty servant's quarters, bursting through a kitchen door—

"Julius!" Swanlake couldn't help exclaiming when she saw her husband.

The hope in his chest now strangled him and pushed a lump into his throat. "—Swan," Julius croaked at last. Moving forward, they met fast and hard, and he held her too tightly. Her laughter was the music of his soul, and they clung together, bony rib to bony rib, but hungry for nothing.

He wanted to burst forth with speech, to explain his joy, his utmost happiness at her being right here right now, but his voice was choked. He stared into her portals of heaven, so blue, so clear and revealing of her Gaulish ancestry. She was an equal contrast to his own slender build, but her beauty far outshone his own. Her blonde curls, when loosed, seemed at constant battle with the native black hair. In her face he could see the features of the sun and moon, alabaster and fire. He knew her anger by the gold flecks that alighted in her blue skies, and her passion as well. Her delicate brows slanted upward, not quite joining together in the middle if one were to look long and closely. Today there were stains on her magnolia cheeks, and her dusky ringlets escaped from a frayed head coverlet, tumbling and untidy, though to him, beautiful. He had seen her at her worst since the last of the servants died, which was a week ago, and he thought no less of her. She had blossomed in their fight to survive, and her strength had more than once brought him back from despondency. They enjoyed each other, as if they were children pretending to play house, with all the perks of being adults. How he loved her.

Swanlake reached up, long naked fingers, and caressed the smooth skin at his temples, then leaned forward. "Julius," she breathed into his mouth, then took him in her arms. "Thank the Lord."

He felt her tremble, as she did on the night of their wedding. "Swan," he sang gently. "I've searched you out in every corner—I saw you in the smoke—in the piles of the dead—"

"Shhh." A soft index finger pressed his lips into silence.

It was all coming on him now; believing her kidnaped and raped by the wandering rogues that had come with the plague and fire; seeing her ghost in the smoke-filled alleys, or her bones sticking up out of the cooling lava; a memorable trinket in a sticky puddle of blood. He began to tremble with her.

"Shhh, my love, we are once again; we are alive and as one. I am okay." Her lips touched his. "I've not been harmed," she lied.

He saw her look, and knew the latter to be untrue. "Who took you?" His concern was immediate, as was his assumption. "Was it that pig Mathius? By Remus I'll write a history to skewer he and his for ages and into Hades! I will—"

Her finger and her smile stopped him again. Swanlake's laughter filled the kitchen. "Was not Mathius, lover, or any other we know of." She knew his hatred for Mathius.

Beneath their feet the earth moved and shook. The marble floor cracked, and pots not already shattered did so now.

He steadied her, then looked into her frightened eyes. "We must leave this doomed city. Quickly, or perish!" A kiss.

"What of Father? Who will bury him?" Her blues eyes filled with golden fire, then were extinguished. Small diamonds rolled down her soot-stained cheeks, leaving ivory trails that marked their passing. She knew the truth of her own question. More tears.

He kissed them away, trying to ignore the growing rumble below. "God himself will bury Alexander. Now, we must save the little one—"

Her hand shot to her belly, and a flash of guilt coursed through him until he saw that a new fire arose in her blue skies.

"Yes. We must leave!" she said with new purpose.

Julius stayed near, not letting her out of his sight. He sat on their bed, wiped the liquid from his blistered feet, and put on a new pair of sandals.

The soft leather straps reminded him of the last summer festival, where he'd won the sandals with his history of the quarry owner's family. He'd won another prize, but gave that award to Swanlake's father, for he could take no credit for that story. He had only to revise and edit from Alexander's firsthand account, which the whole province had heard, or had heard rumor of. He had first heard the tale six years ago, during his papermaking apprenticeship under Alexander, but long after he'd fallen in love with Swanlake.

"We can't take the pillow, my love." He gave her a sad smile. "It's too big..." It would be difficult to leave behind.

"But—" Swanlake started, then laid the extra long pillow down, a hand caressing it in fond memory.

His thoughts went back to the sad saga of Swanlake's birth, and her mother's death, twenty-three years ago tomorrow.

It began on the fifth day out of Rome, heading back to Herculenium. The skies had loosed a downpour upon young Alexander, and a very pregnant Serena Lorenzetti. The roads had long since turned to a clay mush, and they'd lost their ox and cart to a flash flood, which almost took them. In all Alexander's twenty two years there had never been such a storm, but he knew he had to keep them both moving, or be swept away. When Serena tired, he would carry her on his back. Their shoes had long been stolen by Mother Earth. They traveled like this for days, like two tiny ants lost in the Garden of Eden during a thunderstorm.

A MEMORY OF FOREVER

On the eleventh day Alexander noticed his young wife's growing silence, which near dusk turned to soft, pain-filled whimpers that broke his heart. She tried to hide them, but he knew and decided to stop at a lake filled with swans.

She refused the last of the soggy bread and moldy cheese, and Alexander tried to distract her. "The swans are beautiful, no?" There were more than a hundred of the gracious birds on the lake.

When he turned back, he saw the pain in her expression, even as she tried to smile. "How is it with you, Serena?" Alexander prayed it was the cramps, or the child kicking.

"Truthfully?" Serena waited for his nod. "I ache, my love. I think we shall be one more within the hour." Her exquisitely delicate features tightened, and she whimpered in pain, gripping his hand with a strength he hadn't known she possessed.

"Lay back, my love." He set his outer wrap beneath her.

A cold crooked stiletto entered the flesh at the base of his spine, then continued upward. He'd felt this fear reaction only once before, when he'd been alone on his uncle's small fishing boat, taking on water, slowly sinking into the shark-infested waters. The great beast, larger than the largest fishing boats and with teeth the size of a man's head, had come to him that day and looked into his eye in passing. He was that afraid of losing his Serena.

Shaking off the feeling and the memory, he came back to her, and searched for some measure of hope in her eyes, which were the color of an afternoon sky, dotted with flecks of sunlight that flickered to life whenever emotions ran hot or cold.

"Dry clothes for the babe—" Serena huffed. "Strip off my underclothes...see if I bleed..." Another series of agonizing explosions penetrated her stomach. She could not hold back her scream this time. Preening swans stopped, and looked on.

He tore open the oiled leather pouch and brought out the only dry cloth they had, and then stripped off her underclothes. He gasped in horror, tears blurring the crimson tide that washed out of her small body. "My love?" It was too much blood, he didn't say, but she understood.

"Watch for the babe—Xander!" She screamed the last.

Her arms shook, and she grew pale before his eyes. Goose flesh covered her entire body, even the taut-belly skin that only three weeks ago he'd caressed lovingly. He came between her legs and watched her open, trying to ignore the hot rain that fell down his face and salted his lips. Then he saw it, a toe. A foot!

"Push, Serena! Push! I see a foot! Push—push!" He reached into her and found the other foot, and gently, instinctually, brought it to the other, and pulled very slowly amidst her screams.

Then, just as fast as it had begun, it was over, and Alexander was smoothing back delicate blonde curls. "We have a baby daughter, Serena—A baby daughter!" He was bursting forth new tears.

Serena smiled weakly, struggling to see, and Alexander quickly placed their daughter in her bosom. He watched Serena delight in the tiny gem, then went to the water's edge to wash his hands. He looked back often, worried, for there was too much blood on the ground beneath his wife, and she too white.

When he returned, Serena's hand cupped the child's small head, but she was facing the lake. Eerily the swans had gathered at the shore, and were watching in silent worship, drawn by some mysterious electricity in the air above Serena and the baby.

"Swanlake," Serena whispered, the fire leaving her eyes, the child beginning to cry at last. Her hand fell away, limp.

Alexander fell, sitting down beside his wife, his friend, his confidante and lover. He took her limp hand in his own, and held it until a square in the heavens opened. A golden light shone down upon the three of them.

"Swanlake..." he heard her whisper, and he saw a ghostly mist rise up into that dazzling light.

Through his tears of grief and pain, Alexander picked up their child and pushed her into the bright golden beams. "I name thee Swanlake! Hear me, my departing friend and lover, for she is as thee last spoke! In her name my love for you will always be!" The rays blinked away in acknowledgment, and he gently lowered his baby girl. "Swanlake, such a beautiful name," he told a crying Swanlake, bringing her close to his warmth.

couldn't help to the people still on the land, still suffering. "What is there to live for? Even God has put us to the cross—"

"I live for you, my love, to wake in your arms. As long you are with me it will be okay, for your love is my only true source of life and happiness." He was grateful for the gloom. Their tears fell unseen.

Her hand went to his face. "My love—" And she didn't hide her sniffles.

"Shed not a tear, my Swan. We must swim further into the bay. I don't think the mountain has loosed all its anger yet—"

Something large splashed into the water nearby and nearly toppled their small haven.

"You see? Cry thee not, kick thee fast!" Julius played, and heard her music, and felt better for lifting her spirits.

They were heavy and weightless at the same time, even having shed their clothes. There was no way to know how far out into the bay they were, or how far down the bottom was. There was no night or day, only a constant gloomy darkness. How long they'd been like this, he couldn't say. Julius had ducked out from under their protective roof twice, searching above through stinging eyes, then cautiously breaking the surface, only to be suffocated and choked by the thick ash, which hung about impersonating the very air they needed to breathe.

He sensed her waning spirit, and decided to divulge a personal story. "Remember the pools of Napoli? When your clothes disappeared, and you hid behind the statue of the virtues, trapped, pleading with your female friends to hurry and get you another wrap?" He knew her honey-colored brows were knitting together, having been drawn into the question.

"How did you know of this? I've never told you of this?"

He saw as she drew near to him, her expression go from query to suspicion. "Nay, I've never told you of this, Julius," she added

"Twas I who moved the curtains." His words were met with silence, and disbelief. Julius gulped, thinking he may have made a blunder in revealing this secret.

"You? *You! Scoundrel* you are, waiting like a weasel in the tomato patch! Ouph! And what! perchance! did you see whilst I hid behind the virtues?"

"I saw many virtues blush and disappear, I do guarantee." Julius moved to the aft seat, further from her, knowing that her smile sometimes hid a wrath, from which he could not now run from. *Uh-oh*, he thought, as her hands left their balancing task. "Swan, you must assist me in keeping the balance or we'll perish! Serious!"

"The seas are calm, you weasel, and your arms have strength enough. Besides, I'll need both of my hands to deliver the punishment for such deceit and perversion

"Nay, deceit yes, but perversion..." Julius couldn't help but laugh "...we are both of guilt, and for which I do claim my defense, for it was you who stirred my blood to such a heated moment that I cannot be, uh, therefore culpable, uh, what' re you doing? Swan!" Julius nearly let go of the boat, before realizing that he had to keep both hands up and was trapped.

"I have the weasel himself. Fret not, my love." The fires danced in her blue skies, and should light suddenly appear, he would have been hypnotized, as was her effect on him during these escapades.

"But how is thy—" He wasn't sure how to ask her, wondering if such activity was unpleasant after—

"Fret not, my love, my weasel, for it will not hinder your just deserves."

As her flesh covered his own, he saw her smile, and knew he had done his part.

"My love?" Julius checked to see if she was awake, and whether she felt that beneath them.

"Julius?" Her voice trembled.

"We must flip the boat back over! I think we can breathe now, but there's something."

"I know, I felt it. Hurry, Julius."

He knew it was not a difficult thing to do, especially with two people, but if they didn't do it properly, the boat would sink. The water beneath him heaved upward, cold from the depths, it came from—

"Push!"

Sunlight blinded them, and they both sucked in fresh oxygen, and she was light and up into the boat.

Julius struggled, feeling the pressure wave, knowing that this was the last moment before a great shark swallowed a man whole. He'd heard the tales from a few legless survivors. The jaws snapped behind him, but he rolled over the edge, into the boat.

Infuriated, the great white beast exploded out of the sea, following Julius into the boat, teething with great triangular saw blades the wooden bow, throwing the aft into the air. Julius looked into its huge black orb, and as he slid towards the room-sized mouth, struck at it, scratched at it, which drove the beast mad with fury, but made it jump away from Julius and the boat.

Swanlake screamed, having been thrown into the water when the beast had jumped onto the boat. The whirlpool pulled the boat away from her. Something swirled the water beneath her. "Julius!"

He spotted her instantly, and shrugged off his fear and jumped into the water to stop the boat from being sucked into the beast's wake. In the cage with the beast he knew that each kick, each splash, each foot moving, striking the water, was a dinner bell to the white devil.

There she was— *"Swim! Swim faster, Swan!"*—but five meters away. He *jumped* into the boat and ran towards her. The swells had grown, and he lost her in a valley, then found her on a hill. "Hurry!" He searched out the sea, but not for her. "Grab my hands!" he shouted, reaching down just as a swell raised him and lowered her for a few precious seconds, then brought her back. He found her delicate wrists, but saw her eyes widen in fear. Behind her shoulder, past her naked buttocks, down into the deep and surprisingly clear ocean, the white-gray shadow. Like that of a large sinking ship, but not sinking, rising, pushing the water to a boil around her. Then he saw that pink room surrounded by jagged white edges, and that she was already in it, and that she knew this. He bent down, nearly into its gaping mouth, and grabbed hold of her upper torso and pulled her out and over his own body, closing his eyes and praying, until he found himself at the bottom of the boat, with her in his arms—

"Are you okay, my lovely, wet, sea nymph?" Julius asked victoriously, before seeing a strange light in her eyes, and the dark blue color of her lips. A shiver racked her body, and through it his own. "My love? We are safe and still together, no?"

She smiled bravely. "I love you more than God, my Julius, and know this is my truth for I am going now to meet Him, Who I will ask for your life—in the coming days..."

"Oh no!" He felt it upon his numb legs, a liquid warmth that was her life, seeping out over his own. He could not bring himself to look, instead kissing her delicate purple lips and holding her tightly, slightly atop her. "Oh my love—we shall go together into the light, I swear. When last thy eyes cloud, I shall jump into the mouth of the evil beast that has robbed us, and it shall choke on me and die. I swear this be true." He kissed her again, and she blinked, then gulped. His teardrops fell freely upon her lips. "Drink my sorrow."

She gathered in her last strength and met his eyes. "May our souls meet and know each other from here to forever—if you wish it—" She gulped. "Would you just hold me close, look into my—eyes and speak kindly to me in this last silence together. I can't feel you—Julius?"

"I am here, Swan. Feel me?" He squeezed her half-body tightly and looked into those oh-so blue skies as they blinked—blinked—blinked—a soft smile bidding him adieu—then began to cloud over. He refused to accept her passing for a long while. His voice, always reliable, left him as he looked up at the sky, that, for a moment, parted to reveal a sliver of golden sunlight. A finger shot down to the little boat, and as she was given, so she was now taken. The parallel ending did not touch him kindly.

Tears of pain and anger and rage and loss and love blurred his vision, stole his wind. No whipping seas surrounded him, No clouds. No sound. Just he and her lifeless half body, until finally he could breathe, and with this, he roared to the heavens something intelligible only to himself. And to God.

A MEMORY OF FOREVER

It grew dark quickly, but Julius cared not, so long as he held onto the pillow in which her body had been placed. Her blonde strands covered his face, and the evil beast had long since cracked the bottom of the boat, so that water was up to his ears.

He could hear it toy with the wood, rub against it, but he just lay there, holding her, his salt mixing with the seas. He moved only to stay above the water, and to hold her a while longer, every—so—often looking into her cloudy skies, which had milked over long ago.

He was prepared for the long slow death brought by the water, or the fast, agonizing death brought by the white shark. He prayed for the later, so he could wedge his bones into the beast's mouth and choke it to death.

Cold seas soon filled the boat, lifted it and dropped it, as he held tightly to her form within the pillow case. He spoke to her of their dreams, their future, as if life was just begun. The sound disappeared as they went under, cheek to cheek.

So this is it? Julius thought to himself, no longer afraid.

"Swan," he whispered to nobody, the boat gliding out from under them, the current taking him and her to some unknown destination, like two feathers afloat on a summer breeze. He at last breathed in the ocean, gripping Swanlake to his chest, until his shakes became still, and the water no longer burned his eyes.

"Julius?" He heard her whisper, and opened his eyes, not knowing they'd closed. *Where is the cold water? The beast? Swan?* "It is I, my love?"

"*Swan! Swan!*" he yelled in the blackness. A panic enveloped him. He had to find her. A golden flash quieted him, soothed him.

"Where am I—where are you?" He heard her music.

"Find me, Julius, find me," he heard, then was completely taken away from wherever he was.

2

FLORENCE, AZ
PRESENT DAY

BLOOD DRIPPED OFF the side of the snitch's nose. The haft of a rusted iron shank stuck out of his left eye, the sharp business end deep within the skull. The side of his face and the tips of his eyebrows were frosted with dust. He had fallen on his stomach, and had not moved much, only twitched. The point of had been made by the Chicano prison gang; dead rats tell no more tales.

The prison recreation yard was deathly quiet. The tin roof could be heard expanding under the Arizona sun, like the groans of an old submarine passing twenty fathoms. The sound of shotgun shells being jacked into the barrel resounded off the bricks. Four large walls, eight feet high and topped with another six feet of fence and razor wire, surrounded a square yard the size of two football fields.

Dutch Giovanni was on his stomach, staring into the one cold blue eye that suddenly softened, and turned a milky white color. Some force gripped his guts and twisted his consciousness. Amidst twenty other hard core convicts he started to shake, and the once forgotten fears started to finger him in the chest. Even in this dry desert. It wasn't this dead man in front of him, or the killers laying down next to him. It was—

"Vato? Hey, essay, ain't 'chu seen a dead rat before?" Munchi said, then gave his comrades a look.

Dutch sucked it in for a moment, pushing down the fear brought on by the salty scent of the high seas. "Can a mo-fo go to the bathroom?" He smiled at Munchi.

"Hey—hey—that's too much info. Gee, and I'm right behind you, so do me a favor—" one of the killers said playfully.

"Look! Gee's turnin' white, he's gotta go so bad." A few convicts smiled or laughed, understanding.

But he didn't have to go to the bathroom, he was trapped in a world of deja vu that swirled out from the dead snitch's eye. He lost his name, and for a moment, a new language rifled through his thoughts. But he knew danger, he knew the "Eastside Killers" were watching him, yet this was all secondary to the terror induced by the rolling cement beneath his fingers. Images flooded his memory that wasn't his memory.

Oh, this is too crazy, he thought to himself in English.

"Anthony Rodriquez, Dutch Giovanni, John Lopez, Carlos Garcia, and Pedro Gomez, stand up! Place your hands behind your head and walk slowly to the wreck-shack," the loudspeakers ordered.

Four tower guards with Mini-14s aimed at the two hundred-plus inmates on the field tensed, then adjusted to follow the men walking towards the small one room building.

"Dutch?" George Haloway hissed. He was Dutch's road dog and didn't want to see his friend get blown away. "Go on, man, they're calling you."

"Just my luck," Dutch whispered to himself, trying to shake the surreal sensations and unreal apprehensions. He pushed up from the hot cement, dusted himself off, and looked once more— "Jewel." It was a whisper in his ear. Did the lips move? He bent down and looked closer at the delicate shade of blue, and feminine shape— "Julius." He spun around. A cop in the tower fired a shot and chips of cement bit into his bare legs.

A MEMORY OF FOREVER

"Quit fucking around, Dutch!" George Haloway hissed. "They'll blow you away, man!"

But he wasn't hearing. His hands shook as he looked up. Blue. The sky reminded him of something—something warm and tender and inviting—something he loved.

"Last warning, Inmate Giovanni!" A bullhorn.

Then it was gone; the butterflies, the chills, the shakes, the sense that some evil beast stalked him, the fear of being near or in the ocean. It was all gone, and he started walking towards the recreation office—they call it the "wreck shack"—by the yard gate.

What had happened to me? he asked himself, trying to remember all the sensations, jotting them down in a mental notebook for future reference. He was usually fairly coolheaded, except for the one fear. No experience as overpowering as this had ever come upon him, except one time many years ago, but that was fear generated, and he was just a kid. A skinny little runt. Now he was wiser, bigger, and if needed, much more tactical and offensive. At six-foot-two, two hundred twenty-five pounds, he'd have a better chance in the ocean than he had when the shark attacked him ten years ago...

Inside the wreck-shack he did the routine, took off his shorts, shoes, shirt and socks. Bent over, spread 'em, wink and cough, get dressed, handcuffed, and sat down in a chair.

"I did not do it. I do not know who did it. I want an attorney if I need one."

Lieutenant Franco pshawed, and stared at Dutch. "Think you're smart eh?" Franco threatened.

Lieutenant Franco was a heart attack waiting to happen at fifty years old, and over two hundred and sixty pounds on a short stocky frame. His demeanor was like that of a charging rhino protecting her calf, or a snake sidling up the tree to offer you a poison fruit. His lips were thick and protruding further out than was natural, and his teeth were crooked, yet sparkling white. Thick fleshy chins hung below his solid square jaw. His eyes were made of the darkest green, so that if you looked at them from a distance, they looked black. But no matter his outward appearance, and lazy slow stride, he had things going on upstairs, and was as streetwise as any nark. There were rumors, and facts, and coincidences, and "accidents," and other manners of happenings, which befell inmates who had pissed or dissed the LT.

"I was just trying to be clear, L—T." Dutch had made sure to pronounce every word, as did most other inmates who had been around Central Unit the last six months, when a fish had been convicted for an assault on another inmate. The black inmate, not too well versed in the English language, had tried some Ebonic type slang, and the county attorney took it as a confession. "I din't d-it" sounded close to "I did it" on tape. Now all the inmates either didn't speak, or made sure to pronounce every word slowly and precisely.

Cell Block four was one of the third oldest four-tier units in the Arizona State Prison system, and although it'd been condemned many times for various reasons, it was packed full. The cells were slightly smaller than a small bathroom in a home, and there was a sink/toilet, and a bunk that folded up against the wall, and one steel desk, and one small light bulb. The fronts were bars, and beyond that, if you were lucky enough to get a cell on the west side, was a view of the recreation yard and South unit and the Special Psychiatric Unit, which sometimes provided a show, and a beautiful sunset. During the summer the entire unit was an oven, as it was this day.

Two officers escorted Dutch back to his cell, and a keyman, behind a separate barred enclosure where inmates weren't allowed, pulled the lever for cell 15 on the fourth tier. "JOHN RUN."

"Closing!"

Dutch stripped down out of his sweaty workout clothes after they uncuffed him and left to pick up the next inmate. He started filling up his small sink immediately, because the whole unit would be locked down, and therefore, they wouldn't be allowed to use the showers. It was a bird bath or nothing. He was lucky to get that, because he knew that some of the Chicanos were in the holding cells down in the basement, where one could be forgotten and starve to death.

He unstrapped the bunk and let it fall, then took out his manual typewriter, preparing to write a few pages. He had to hunch over the board because the desk was made for somebody no taller than five-five. For a while he stared at the keyboard, then at the white sheet, hands poised over the plastic concaves, waiting, thinking, willing the story to emerge as it always did for him. Words never failed him, they were like ants to a summer picnic basket left unattended, slipping through unseen holes, but always appearing.

He was born Dutch Salvatore Giovanni, son of Salvatore and Heidi Giovanni, some twenty-nine years ago on a dark street four blocks away from Los Angeles County Hospital. Antone, Salvatore's brother, had delivered him, and his first namesake.

"Dutch!" Antone exclaimed, and seemed to blame Heidi for not bringing out a black-haired Italian. But Salvatore, and soon all of the family, had fallen in love with the handsome baby.

Ten years later, Dutch lost his father to the ravages of the chemotherapy, which had been used to fight the multiple organ'dcarcinoma that invaded his body. The chemo was like shooting a bullet into a bullet wound to dislodge the initial bullet, and if the cancer didn't get you, the chemo would.

At sixteen, Dutch found himself taking the rap for a burglary his best friend had committed, though he'd witnessed it. Loyalty and friendship meant more to him than freedom. His father had taught him this much: "Mind his own business, and don't be a stool pigeon," his father had warned him many times. There was no way in the world that he was going to rat out his best friend. His only friend. He practically owed him his life.

They had met at Long Beach, when Dutch had found himself being sucked out by a powerful riptide that had nearly drowned him just moments before. John Hinckle had paddled up on a slim surfboard and helped him get back to shore, where Dutch's mother was engrossed in a novel.

He was shaking from fright and from the cold and from what had touched him while he was in the water. Something had nipped at him, like a lion licks the fur of its prey before tearing it apart. There was a long slice on the backs of his calves, parallel to the horizon, and a rub rash from something scraping its rough skin across his thighs.

"Wow, man, were you attacked?" John pretended to ignore the shaking and the tears.

"I think so." Dutch sniffled. "Something grabbed me, and scraped or bit me while I was under." He looked at John, who was about his age, and started to calm down a little and smile at his own luck and bravery.

"Wow, man, I would've shit my pants, dude! What's your name? I'm John. Hey, wanna go play some video games at the pier?"

They were best friends from that point on, as far as Dutch was concerned.

From that day forward he never went ,near, or swam in the ocean, or any pool that was too big, or didn't have anyone swimming it with him.

A week after John got his first car, a metallic brown '66 VW bug, they were both in trouble. John's mother was a bartender at the local cop hangout, so the blame was put on Dutch. He spent an hour in a police holding cell, where they had set up a mock lie-detector test, which Dutch was told that he failed. He confessed to the burglary of the sporting goods store next to John's mother's bar. A few months later he was fighting for his life.

Dutch was the only white, in a dormitory filled with Chicano and black gang members. There was one other crazy white dude, who Dutch thought was playing the loco role to keep from being extorted or sexually assaulted. Dutch fought for the first two months, and was constantly in trouble with the counselors, until the blacks and Chicanos left him alone, and even accepted him.

Not once, even when he was in the hole for twenty-four hours, did he think about ratting his best friend out.

He exploded to six feet two inches, added thirty pounds of muscles, and his hair darkened to a sandy-blonde, which gave him an overall appearance that was beyond the boy who had went into the warrior camps. When he walked out of the gate, he was a man going on eighteen.

He graduated a year earlier due to the Youth Authority's high school system, and their philanthropic attitude regarding graduation rates, and the high school grades, of "their" kids. A good graduation rate showed the public that they were actually doing something for the younger generation of unfortunates. He was whisked through a school year in six months, but it was of no consequence. His parents had insisted that all his previous education be had in private schools, so he was far ahead of what they were teaching seniors in high school.

Two years of college passed by when his mother was killed in a freak accident, while getting off the city bus. Dutch quit school that week, stunned, and watched days slip by, while his own family fought over a small, but sizable estate. Barracudas came out, feeding on anything not bolted down. Surely it is not true of all humankind, but it was there that day, in the eyes of his own family; greed. Leeches, smiling with their puckered mouths, tiny hooks hidden but ready to dig in and suck. Greed and lust and materialism and flashes of anger between family members and some deep-seated and mysterious hates lingered about the rooms and halls of the once happy home that he and his mother had shared for nearly ten years. He was perpetually ashamed of what he saw that day, just moments after he had tossed earth upon her grave. Was every garden so savage when the eldest plant dies? All the others draining the nutrients of all the withered and brown leaves, which float to the ground and become the soil in which they, too, will grow, and die. While he was weeping in the shadows were they not scheming about who got the couch, the stereo, the TV, the brass sculpture, the bed sets, and even her wedding band. He stayed distant, accepting their facades and soothsaying, keeping to himself in small recesses only he knew about. Tears fell and thoughts crushed him from within. He remembered all the times that he didn't listen to her, or mind her, or when he'd told her he hated her in childish anger. He hadn't really had the chance to say goodbye, for he always thought she'd be there, at least for another thirty years. These guilts fell upon him, but something was opened up in him, like a wound, like a distant calling that he didn't understand. At last he locked himself into the bathroom where his father had chosen to die, put his head under water, and cried, saying her name into the water, begging for her to come back or to acknowledge his presence. "I love you, Mom... Do you know that?" he'd cried. There was no response. Just the sound of roaches outside the door eating up all the food they'd brought for him.

He felt emptier than when his father died, because he'd known that he was going to go away, and had time to say goodbye. He still expected his father to come home from the welding shop, rumble in his baritone voice that he was home, and swing Dutch around in the air, all the equipment on his father's tool belt rattling. But when she died, it was an instantaneous flash upsetting the balance of his life, tearing a huge piece of his everyday life away. There would be no more home and "Hi, Mom? How was your day?"

Responsibility heaped upon his shoulders, like boulders, crushing his once carefree life of school, studies, and the indefinite search for the elusive perfect woman. The distinct need to continue that search grew stronger the moment his mother had been buried next to Salvatore Giovanni.

At the morgue he was given her effects, including the family heirloom; a small ring with a circular-shaped emerald. He promised himself, and her, that the right woman would be fit to wear the ring. He fashioned it on a gold necklace and never took it off. After seeing how the vultures circled, around anything of value, he was glad he had put it out of sight. This band would fit his wife...

The need to venture, to be rid of these familiar bonds, called to him in the breeze that blew across the back patio of the Covina Hills home. He looked around the small backyard. The house was fifty feet above most others in the "hills." Interstate 10 ran over Kellog Hill to the south. On clear days he could see the Pacific Ocean to the west, and the Angeles Forest to the east. To the south was the heart of Los Angeles, and the many suburbs captured within its county boundaries. There was much to see, if the smog alert was low enough that you could breathe and see outside. It had grown dull upon him, this middle-class suburbia. He had the urge to fly away. It was strong enough to make him jump into the air and take to the winds.

He took the ring, all the cash on hand, and said goodbye to one aunt and one uncle, then began searching for something missing from his soul.

Three weeks later, he was face down in a ditch, hiding from the police, puking on the dry Arizona dust of an unfinished highway, praying that the cops would overlook him. The pleas went unanswered and two feet landed upon his back. Cold steel bracelets snapped around his wrists, clicking tighter and tighter, until they bit into the tender flesh.

Once again he was struck with a blinding flash that would leave him dumbstruck and wanting behind steel bars and concrete walls. It was as if someone were playing a cruel game with his life, obstructing him, moving him, but never killing him. Pride had kept him from calling home for help, until he finally saw that they were talking seriously about putting him into a prison for just being a passenger in a stolen car, but it was already too late—

"But he wasn't a passenger," the state prosecutor charged.

"This man, Dutch Giovanni, came to our law-abiding state with a criminal record, stole goods from a store, and stole vehicles from you, then ran from a police officer and endangered his life, as well as many others on the road that night. You heard the officer tell you that he was in fear for his life. I submit to you that Mister Giovanni came to Arizona with the intention of taking advantage of our trusting Arizona lifestyle—"

"Objection!" Dutch's public defender said. The judge nodded. The twenty-four-year-old prosecutor was working on his thirty-second straight conviction, make that thirty-three, when the jury came back.

"We the jury find the defendant guilty…" the foreman started. Dutch hung his head as the foremen pronounced him guilty on every count. He was now a thief, an assaulter, and transporter of stolen goods. He wondered if maybe he was guilty, thinking back to the fateful night. His only guilt was that he didn't rat first, while Rick had started snitching the moment they put the handcuffs on him.

The day before his twentieth birthday, after a year in county lock-up, Judge Cates sentenced him to twenty years. The same day a woman had been sentenced to four years probation for killing a man while driving under the influence. Dutch hadn't harmed a soul, or even tried. A month later, Dutch was sent to a maximum security prison unit affectionately called "The Walls."

The Walls served as a housing unit for hard core convicts, murderers, lifers and inmates with over fifteen years, prison gang members, and other aggressive or dangerous men. There was seven cell blocks within the walls. There were four older units—CB 1 thru CB 4, and two newer units—CB 5 and CB 7. CB 6 was strictly death row, until they moved the row to the Special Management Units, which were total segregation type units. No sun, no contact, no nothing. The westernmost part of the unit was the recreation field. Inmates were allowed to go out three times a week for one and a half hours. Lately they were locking the yard down and denying inmates any type of recreation. Too many assaults and stabbings, due to a lack of mutual respect. This was created by the constant lock-down periods, which acted to bolster a man's self estimation, as if the bars would always be there to protect him.

The first three recreation periods he came out prepared to battle. That was the convict way. New inmates, or fish, were first tried before they were allowed to stay. Even if you were beat down, so long as you fought back, you would be accepted as a convict, crimes permitting. But in Arizona, he found that the practice was not strictly enforced, as it was in the California systems.

In Arizona, the race roles were completely reversed, the demographics completely opposite, with whites outnumbering blacks three to one on the yards, sometimes ten to one. The Chicano population was probably the largest of the three main races, but white and Chicano gangs were equal in power and usually stuck together during times of duress and agitation, from either the blacks, or the prison guards. But every convict steered clear of Head of Security, Lt. Franco, if he was smart and wanted to survive.

Lately the prison administration had been building these new cement and steel isolation cages, and calling these 31 million dollar warehouses, Special Management Units. Then they started trying to fill them, but there weren't enough "bad" inmates to fill them up, so the prison officials started making inmates gang members, or associates of a certain "Security Threat Group." These units had to be filled, because housing inmates in these cells meant that the prison administration would get more money allocated to its fiscal budget, as each inmate housed in a SMU was worth approximately 40 thousand dollars, while normally housed inmates were only worth around 25 grand.

So if an informant, or some inmate who just didn't like you, came forward and said they saw you speaking with a suspected gang member, this was reason enough for the administration to reclassify you and throw you in Ad-seg at SMU I or II. If you renounced your nonexistent gang membership, and told them what they wanted to hear, you could be released to the yard where you were an instant target. If you didn't snitch, then you would be in the hole indefinitely, watching a TV, eating sack lunches, unable to ever touch family members or go to funerals, or do art, or anything else they didn't think you should be allowed to do, since the pretext of this housing was that you were the "worst of the worst."

For seven years Dutch tried to make his time productive, to dream, to plan, and look towards a future. He stayed in shape, read many novels, studied different styles of fighting and combat skills, and wrote short stories. Many guards and even wardens didn't like the fact that a convict was trying to be something better than they could ever be, but he ignored them or tried to show them how to do what he was doing, just so they'd note his humble attitude.

He looked at the sheet of typing paper, thinking of the past, the very recent past, trying to recall the feelings he'd had out on the rec-field. When he was sure water had rushed over him, thick with salt and oddly familiar scents, and a subconscious threat of filling his lungs—he shut his eyes, and thought about that warmth, like hot syrup, flowing over his legs, the cold object in his arms—felt the sting of cold sea water, then saw the pale white face surrounded by a halo of golden curls, blue eyes alive with fire, lips red as the living blood now swirling before his face, clouding his vision. He realized the cold object in his arms, like a stone, was the half body of this beautiful living woman, whose name he tried to recall. This woman whom he loved. What was left of her he held, wrapped in a pillow case, only her head out of it, lips upturned in a soft smile. Her mouth opened as if to speak, to tell him something of great—

"I don't know what's wrong with him, sir—he was kicking his feet, all soak and wet, eyes rolled back in his head. Spooky stuff, if you ask me, LT." The new guard was telling Franco.

"They make sure he wasn't faking it?" Lieutenant Franco asked. He was skeptical about anything any inmate did, but this was almost too perfect, too much like a setup. He knew he was being watched, but wondered if the FBI could have contacted Giovanni to have him assist in the setup. But inmate Giovanni didn't seem the type to rat.

"The nurse said he was having a seizure of some sort, that his reactions were all off. I guess that's why they called the hospital," the guard said, while Franco wondered about coincidences and possibilities.

Dutch Giovanni was important to Lieutenant Franco, not only for the job specification reasons, but because of something even more important. His life depended on Giovanni's well-being. Their blood types matched up, and Giovanni was disease free, and Franco needed a liver transplant. His years of hard drinking had nearly destroyed his liver, and now he needed a replacement. It wouldn't be the first time he'd harvested an inmate's organ, but it would be the first time he did it for himself.

He and Doctor Brown had the perfect operation going at the County Hospital. Brown would look at prisoner medical files, match blood types with that of prospective buyers unwilling to wait the years it took to get an organ, then Franco would have the inmate taken care of.

He'd planned on taking care of Giovanni in two weeks, when he was planning on taking his month long vacation. After twenty years, he deserved as much. *Inmates are scum,* he thought to himself, watching the ambulance leave the prison grounds through the front gates. He turned and watched the new guard walk to the yard office. Something about the new man, Franco suspected from behind his mirrored sunglasses

He was thrilled, otherwise, looking forward to the interrogations and cell searches, on account of the death of one of his snitches. It gave him a sense of power to invade the inmates' personal stuff, even the nude photos of wives and girlfriends. Sometimes he'd take the pictures to fuck with their head, or leave the nude photos on the floor, to let the inmates know that he knew. But tonight would be utterly special, like those days that he'd have an inmate hit.

Someone was going to pay dearly for killing his snitch. They knew better, and would have to be taught a lesson, be made an example of. The suspects were all in the dungeon, a small secret place beneath cell block 4. *They'd all be getting hungry about now,* he thought with a smile, and watched the rays of the Arizona sun jump off of the roof of CB 2, and then disappear.

A MEMORY OF FOREVER

He took out a Camel-non and lit up, then started walking towards CB 4. He wondered if that pussy of a deputy warden would show tonight. Last time they conducted "interrogations," the puss had puked his guts out when one of his boys had gotten a little too nasty. *I'll have to remember that tonight*, he thought with a smile, then stepped on his butt and went down into the dungeons....

3

Remembering

She was telling him something important. White lights blinding him and she disappearing and water evaporating, being sucked out of one lung, then the other, and air rushing in as fast as the water was gone. He had to remember—

"He's convulsing again—*oh my God!*" A nurse screamed as she was sprayed with an almost endless stream of water from the inmate's mouth. It wasn't the fact that he was puking on her, she'd been puked on before, but the liquid coming out was so cold and there was so much. Her finger was punching the code alarm button that should be bringing all of the night staff into the room. "Doctor!" Doors banged open, and Doctor Brown ran into the overnight room.

—but something was distracting him. It felt like he was choking on something large, as if he'd just been electrocuted—

"Grab his fucking tongue!" Doctor Brown shouted, still disturbed by the soaked nurse. He knew if she didn't get a hold of the tongue the inmate would choke to death, and he wasn't ready to— "*Dammit!* Grab hold of the fucking tongue—what the hell's a matter—here—" He pushed her shaking hands away from Dutch's opening and closing mouth, thrust a long finger in, felt for the thick muscle, and pulled the tongue out in one swift motion. "Goddammit, Nurse Flour, when I say grab the tongue, grab the fucking tongue! I've seen you do it a hundred times—"

Nurse Flour burst out in tears and ran out of the room, just as Doctor Bob Hazel was coming in. He turned and joined Doctor Brown in watching Nurse Flour stride away, her hands over her face.

Bob Hazel, one of the only neurologists in Pinal County, turned to see what was going on with his new patient. He found Doctor Brown checking the vitals. *We should have at least three nurses, even on the night shift*, Doctor Hazel thought to himself, steeling himself to write the administrative board about this deficiency that would cost lives sooner or later.

"Can you believe that nurse? Geez!" Doctor Brown said as Doctor Hazel looked at the chart.

"What happened?"

"He was having another one of those seizures—choking on his tongue. Nurse Flour was soaking wet. You'll have to ask her what else happened," he explained. Doctor Brown was trying to downplay the urgency of the situation. It was bad enough that he'd had to bring in Doctor Hazel. *A damn cowboy boot-wearing doctor*, he thought to himself disgustedly. "He seems fine now. He's all yours."

Doctor Hazel gave a questioning look to his fellow doctor, who suddenly turned and walked out of the room, as if nothing had happened. He hadn't liked the doctor since he came to work here six months ago, had known his type the moment he saw him, and wondered what he was actually doing here in the desert. He was a carpetbagger, a falsely pretentious grifter who had been given a doctorate to be false and cunning at a higher level. That he should be working on the same night shift, whether he was a doctor or not, this was an annoying, disconcerting fact of life.

Doctor Brown checked to make sure his office door was locked, although he was one of only four staff here at the County Hospital. He had to make sure—

"Listen, Lieutenant Franco—"

""Don't ever say that name on an open line, you idiot!"

He hesitated before trying to explain. "I think you might want to find another donor—"

"Listen, Doc, as soon as he's conscious and medically able to move, I want his ass right back here and I'll take care of it! Deal? Right, Doc?"

"Yes, sir, I understand." It could work, if he stayed late and waited until Doctor Hazel went home. Nobody cared about who signed inmates in or out. Then, if something happened on the prison yard, he couldn't be connected.

"Good. We'll have an incident next weekend, so you have all your shit together, Doc, okay."

"Yes, sir." He placed the phone in the cradle and hung his head. He ran his long surgeons fingers through his greasy black hair.

It would be five years tomorrow since he had been forced under the thumb of the lousy prison guard. He felt suffocated and subjugated. The day the fat lieutenant had walked into his office with an ominous smile, and pictures of he and his seventeen-year-old stepdaughter, a deal had been struck; the lieutenant would supply victims and a buyer, and the doctor would supply the surgical skills necessary, and medications needed, to transplant organs into certain rich and powerful individuals who were too important to wait in any federally regulated waiting game. There were catches, such as the fact that he basically had to do whatever it was that Franco wanted. He had killed two of the inmates right here at the hospital with a lethal injection. Franco had had some powdered soap put in their food, and they came to the hospital with severe stomach cramps. They never went back. He didn't like that part of the deal.

In the patient overnight room Doctor Hazel shined a light down into Dutch's pupils—

"*What's goin on!*" Dutch bolted upright.

Bob Hazel nearly tripped as he stepped backwards, watching the man whose pupils wouldn't react to light but who could sit up and talk.

Dutch fell back into the softest bed he'd slept on in seven years. "Swa—Swan..." Dutch moaned, chains rattling against the steel rail of the hospital bed.

"Mister Giovanni?" Doctor Hazel queried. He stepped forward, looked for signs of consciousness, but found none. He lifted an eyelid and played the beam back and forth. Neither pupil adjusted. "Hmmm? That's odd?" There should have been some reaction.

Nurse Flour walked into the room. "I'm sorry—Oh, Doctor Hazel. I thought you were Doctor Brown—"

"Speaking of Doctor Brown, he said I should ask you to tell me what happened prior to the convulsions." He saw her look away, embarrassed. "No need to be shy, Nurse Flour, we've known each other six months." He gave her a *you can tell me anything* smile, and waited.

A moment later she slumped down in the chair and told him about what happened, and what she thought about it, and how it had been the most unnerving thing she'd seen in all her years as a nurse.

He handed her a handkerchief, thinking about the paper he'd be writing on Dutch Giovanni, the man who could talk while having no detectable pupil reactions. First he wanted to see what was going on inside the patient's head. He looked around the empty room, sensing something was missing, but not able to put a finger on it.

"I want to run an MRI and a CAT-scan, nurse. ASAP." He was done with the sympathizer role.

She looked up, surprised at the change of tone in his voice, then nodded. She knew in a few weeks this would all change.

Her flaxen hair flowed behind her, slightly darker, in the water. He knew he wasn't supposed to be here, the wedding not yet planned or known about, but he couldn't help himself. She had been the moon in his day and the sun in his night, always present in his thoughts and dreams and oh so fine desires. He'd written her many anonymous poems and stories, expressing his love for her, his wish to be by her side always, but she had never given him a sign that she had liked them, or had even received them, though he knew she must have. Today he was going to deliver his latest story.

He visited her father's house many times a week to learn the craft of making paper. It was an art form in itself, which had been learned

A MEMORY OF FOREVER

by Swanlake's grandfather, and passed down to her father, and now him. He felt a great pride at being allowed to learn this craft that went hand in hand with his future as a writer. He arrived after studies every other day at the Lorenzetti house, walked through the courtyard that separated the main house from the courtyard, and was greeted with a heavy paddle, and a vat of wood pulp.

There were large vats, and small vats, screens and presses and drying boards of all sizes, and many other tools that were needed to make quality paper. Older women, who were paid with coin or paper, were always stripping bark and shredding the wood with forklike tools, until the wood was a pulpy mush, which was then thrown into the boiling water. Sometimes the water was dyed with colors. He had been allowed to make a few practice batches, using the old drying boards and excess pulp.

But today he was planning on delivering a story of a wedding, and there was a feeling of excitement in his belly, and his hands were a little shaky. He hoped she would be there this time, when he slid the letter and golden silk ribbon under her door. He so much wanted to see her face as she read this....

He crossed the patio and large plants in front of the kitchen window, then turned left, entering a long hallway that led to her room. He checked both ways, making sure he was alone, then bent down and slid the package under her door.

The door opened, trapping his hand. "And what might I ask is this?" Swanlake held onto the edge of the letter, which she had grabbed as soon as she saw it come under the door. She savored her long-planned victory, but knew it was far from over.

He stammered for a moment, turning a variety of reddish colors, as he tried to regain his composure. "I was only asked to deliver this letter—"

"Then let go." She smiled at him.

Ever since she found out who was delivering the poems and love stories, she had begun planning a way to catch him in the act. But she had also started to watch him, and found him quite handsome. She knew he had a good future in writing, obviously, and a paper-maker as well. She saw his young shyness, and quietude, but once given the stage, he exploded like a flower accepting the sun in the early morning. His words and plots drew rapt attention from the young students, and she knew, from many of her friends as well. His voice rose and fell, just like her father's did, when he told the stories. Soon she found herself longing for him to be speaking only to her, to have his full attention, to feel his touch, even though that was forbidden until her father approved. *I will be seventeen years old in two days*, she reminded herself, *and I will be married shortly thereafter*, she vowed, staring silently into his unsure hazel eyes. She loved him.

"Is this not mine?" she teased.

Does she know, he asked himself, then, with great hesitation, let go of the letters. He started to turn, surely expected in the workshop, but longing to be in her presence for a moment longer. He looked one last time at her lovely face, the outline of her breasts under the garment—

"Please, stay while I read this. Let me see, 'Two Loves Joined Forever'," she taunted him, still pretending to be surprised and at the same time, biting her tongue to keep tears from flooding her eyes. "Please, wilst thou tell me who may be my secret admirer, so I may deliver an answer back to him this time? I would be forever grateful, Julius.

He could not deny her, and nodded, while cursing his stupidity and lack of words, standing there like some dunce in a corner of the classroom, watching his love and not being able to speak. Was he not a writer of histories, a poet, an orator of—

"Would thee read to me this story, for my throat is dry and I fear I may become sick if I were to read this aloud?" she asked.

Her eyes, so clear and bright and anxious, penetrated his very being. He had no answer to her stare, simply putting out his hand and taking the papers.

"Come, let us retire to the reading room. There is drink if thy lips become parched." She watched him swallow.

Never had he been alone in a room with Swanlake, that she knew of, and especially while reading words of intimate bearing. He didn't know if he would last through it, but deep inside he was glad the subterfuge would be over, for once the words passed his lips and landed upon her ear, she would know the true author of these stories.

"Swanlake?" her father called from the courtyard. "Have you seen my apprentice—Julius?—he was supposed to be here today to help with the new batch."

Julius thought for a moment that he would be saved. He could put this off for yet another day when he was feeling much braver, and had something better to offer her, maybe drink a little wine before coming to her—

She saw his face brighten, even at the excuse of having to go to work in place of reading to her his words of love, and she was having none of that. "I have him here, Papa, and I must have him read to me the newest message from my secret admirer."

"Uh-oh," Alexander Lorenzetti said to himself, a secret smile playing on his lips, causing the wrinkles at the corners of his eyes to lengthen and multiply. He knew who the admirer was because it was the paper and the writing of his young apprentice that his daughter had brought to him many moons ago. It was paper that he had sold to a certain family, who had a certain son he favored as an apprentice. He had let his daughter find out who it was on her own, with no help from him, and knew that she was the lovely spider and Julius the helpless fly now.

"Have him back within the hour; we need the sun today," he called back to her.

Julius was prepared to hand her back the perfectly wrapped letters.

"Relax, Julius. We're not engaged in some lovers' embrace," she teased, enjoying watching him flush. She grabbed his hand—he felt the instant spark and magnetic connection, as she reached out and nearly dragged him to the reading room.

The room was a small and very personal room, with only two chairs and a reading bed packed with cushions and pillows. The ceiling was quite low, so that when you went in, it was as if you were in a different world, closer to the story, without distractions from the big world outside. There were no windows, which added to the effect. Against the walls were shelves of books and loose-leaf papers. There were Chinese dragons against one wall, drawn on long sheets of thick Asian paper, at least a century old. These were hung from the low ceiling, so that they blocked some of the more political books that were not open for any visiting guests...to read.

She guided him to one of the chairs facing the reading bed, where she pretended to fall into the deep pillows and turned to face him with a brighter smile than he'd ever seen on her perfect lips.

"Well, wilst thou sit and read, or sit there dumbfounded?" she teased, giddy with excitement, anxious to hear his newest story of love, because she knew the subtle inference was that the two lovers were he and her, and this made her blood warmer than should be in the presence of a young man, in a room alone....

"Let me drink first," he said shakily, pouring some of the tart grape juice into a small clay cup. He took a drink, then set the cup gently down on the wood table. There was nowhere to run, he knew, then undid the yellow ribbon, which she reached over and took.

"This will look lovely in my hair, but that's probably why he sent it. What do thee think, Julius?" she asked, twirling the long silk ribbon through her like-colored hair.

"Yes, I'm sure that's why, though anything would look beautiful in thy hair, Swanlake." He hid his stare from her eyes, which he knew, were locked onto him. He cleared his throat, after a moment, then began. "Two Loves Joined Together." He gulped.

4

Part of the Story

"I watched thee today, a natural wonder that once again stole my heart, a bolt of lightning that drew my eye amidst dark clouds and pale skies yonder. Like waves pushing and pulling, my heart was taken in by thy gravity, pushed and pulled, swaying with golden locks, falling into the slightest glimpse of blue eyes flecked with fire, yet I know our planets have aligned before, and now draw closer together. If only thee had knowledge of my love and never-ending tenderness, which I should bare for all the world to see, if only thine eyes would rest favorable upon my not-so-handsome face. I know we are destined, and soon we will no longer face the nights alone without each other's bosom for comfort, but instead, like pods of whales, we shall swim together within our sea, united, in day or night, in sleep or wakeful being. We shall create untold histories, memories of such lightness and love, and songs of such passion and joy, that the Gods above shall envy our love, and our knowledge of each other, of the endless nights of passion and love and whispers and unbroken promises, our knowing of every curve and mark of each other's body, and our knowing of the thought that enters the other's mind before it has arrived on the tongue. This is us, me and thee, two lovers in the coils of forever and beyond. Two lovers joined.

"Swanlake, my galaxy of colors, thou art the star I see each night in my dreams, together in the heavens, written in the book of God as part of a whole. Our names take up but one line; eternal lovers. A caution written in blood next to our name; Never to be separated.

"And if ever tears of sadness should befall thy pillows, I will be there to dry them, to bring back that sweet smile, to walk for hours holding thy hand, mile upon mile, for it is my pleasure, no, my aching need, to have thy happiness surround me, for all the days and all the nights.

"And if ever blood flows from thy flesh, my heart too shall bleed, and I shall ache and be in pain as thee are in that dreaded moment, for we are linked in heart, mind, body, and soul.

"Close thy eyes, my soft feathery Swan. Feel my tender caresses, like ripples on the surface of the pond, my lingering breath upon thy soft petals. We must embrace in front of all, reveal our love to the world, in the Holiest of all ceremonies, for my true love is equal to none, like white doves, gentle and strong. Let them see us, our hearts beating like wings of the hummingbird, in sync with one another, bouncing light as air to the next flower, tasting, discovering and collecting our never-ending memories.

"Walk with me, my forever love, my day and night, my life-giving breath, my poem in the clutter, and be mated to my soul. Let my words be as a trowel, searching out every space, every vein, every hidden place in: thy heart, so I may fill it with my essence, and thee shall be, always and an eternity, connected to my soul.

"After our wedding I shall whisper in thy ear a promise of such truth and devoted passions, that thee shall fall faint, but fear not, for in my arms thy body will fall, never touching the ground. Bend close, my love, let me feel the pulse of thy life as my cheek slides close against thine own…"

"Are thy eyes closed?" he asked, looking up from the story. He saw tears in her eyes, but she put up a hand to calm his worry.

"My eyes are closed, are they not? Continue, Julius, please," she whispered. "My heart shall break if thy voice is not in the air…"

"Yes. Keep thy eyes closed." He looked at her, his heart full and near to bursting out of his chest. He felt himself become faint, and realized he wasn't breathing, so entranced by her beauty.

"Do not tease me, Julius," she implored.

He looked at the small diamonds rolling down her pale cheeks, and though this stirred him to protect and console her, he also saw that she looked content and happy.

"See us, thyself in virgin white gowns that flow with the warm spring air, thy perfume scenting the air from Naples to Rome, thy beauty on the lips of every living being. I will behold thee in this way until the day I die. Hear my praises, for they are whispers among the thousands, who have come to bear witness to the joining of two loves, forever, thee and me.

"And once bound we shall burst heavenward, escaping to a plateau that none other have seen, for it is our mutual bond, our connection of past, present and future, signified by this golden ring I now place upon your finger, which binds thine own heart to mine own." Julius bent down next to the couch, gently lifting her small hand with his shaking hand, and slid the ring onto her finger, hoping she didn't mind silver. He saw that she was starting to open her eye.

"Do not open thy eyes yet," he whispered, and started to lift the papers to begin reading again, but didn't need to. He knew them by heart. His eyes were captivated by her smile, by the dew catching on her long lashes, small puddle at the heart-shaped curve of her lips. He longed to kiss her, but knew he must first finish the story.

"Now that thy heart is bound in love to mine, I shall let thee in on the secret of our never-ending love, for it is as sweet as the heat flowing through thy senses, threatening to overpower even the simplest thoughts, and burn them in the fires of our impending passions that linger about in both of our minds." He paused for a moment, still holding her hand. "It's the simplest promise, not complicated by the strings of society, or guilt of the past, and things that never last. This is the promise I give to thee; We shall forever be, thee and me, hand in hand, in the dark and in the glow, we shall be together, like two heads on a pillow."

Swanlake opened her eyes and looked at him kneeling before her, then at the most beautiful silver ring she'd ever seen. She touched his face gently with her fingers. "I've known my heart for many moons, my love."

"I am yet done with this poem," he said shakily, though there was much relief flooding his body and mind knowing she would not reject him. "My Swan, my love, thee have had my heart from since I first knew love, upon paper I have given myself to thee, with these words that are my life, my souls fluid, my very essence. So I ask thee here now to consider joining souls in this life, and in the next, for if not, I shall be forever sorely vexed, and my heart shall wither inside me and I shall die without ever having thee in my arms..."

He had not planned it, but the ending brought a smile to even his own lips, and tears were falling from his eyes, even as they ran down Swanlake's face. He brought a trembling hand and placed it against her right cheek, even as she had hers upon his. At the touch his hand steadied, and he leaned forward.

She closed her eyes again, letting, not being able to stop, a heated flush that flowed through her body, to the places she knew forbidden to reveal, but ever so wanting him to pierce the whirlwind of desires and fire, give her some measuring stick with which to hold onto, to center her, pin her solidly to the ground of this dizzying world. The walls spun as their lips touched, and the aura of their body heat mingled, and he reached out with his free hand, meaning to steady them, but his hand fell upon her thigh and she moaned...

"Doctor Hazel!" Nurse Flour called out. Her forehead wrinkled in worry, as she stared into the darkened room, where the patient was laying within the MRI machines cylindrical tunnel. She swore to write the FBI another letter about there not being any guards around tonight. In all her twenty years working as a nurse, she'd never seen what she saw this night, had never been shaken to tears of actual fear.

Her thick white nylons swoosh-swooshed as she walked to the glass door of examination room. She'd been monitoring him from the small computer and data storage room, which was separated by a large window, where she could watch the patient's feet, and see the flickers of lights as the machine went back and forth. When she heard a voice was when she stood up.

She saw his feet moving. "Oh my God. Doctor Hazel!" He could be a serial killer, and they'd taken the handcuffs and shackles off due to the sensitivity of this particular machine.

"Where am I? Hey? What's going on?" Dutch asked. He couldn't move his head, his arms, or his legs. "What the hell's going on?"

"Don't move, sir."

He heard a door open and shut. "Hello?" Nobody answered.

He started to panic, testing the nylon straps, and recognizing the taste in his mouth. The Tyrrhenian Sea. He rocked, and something clicked and he started to roll out of the small tunnel. He looked around with his eyes, then pulled his arm free of the strap, then the other, then reached up and yanked off the plastic frame that his head had been strapped to.

The room was dark, except for light coming from a small room behind a window, and a few indicator lights, some blinking green or red, on the large machine. He knew he was in a hospital of some sort.

"Hello?" *Where are the guards, and who had spoken to me?* he wondered, feeling a cool breeze, then realizing he was wearing one heck of a flimsy hospital gown.

He walked to the door and opened it, expecting at any moment for guards or cops to rush him. He felt free. This was the first time in nearly a decade since he'd been outside of a prison without a pair of handcuffs on. A clock on the wall told him it was nearly midnight. He turned right, down a short hallway, and walked to the end door. He pushed against the bar, and felt the warm air of an August night. He smelled freedom, not caring that he was half naked and barefooted, and stepped out into the parking lot. To the east was the glare of high-powered fluorescent prison lights, so bright they could be seen miles away, or light up the backyards of the prison town.

He saw a truck, and remembered what George Haloway had told him about how easy it was to hotwire one, and then he was opening the door, leaning in and yanking out the wires. Green on black, touch the red wire. The motor came to life instantly.

"You learn something in prison after all," Dutch whispered to himself, then threw the truck in gear and rolled out of the lot, and out of town.

He checked the rearview mirror every thirty seconds or so, and, when the headlights approached, he would hunker down in the seat until they passed. He swore each one was a squad car. As he drove he was improvising a plan. He had to get clothes, identification, money, and leave the country. He had to get out of Arizona within the next six hours. He saw the lights of Phoenix and depressed the gas pedal a little more, dreaming of France or Italy.

He sensed that if someone were to speak Italian he might just understand it, (*Capire*) which was why he was leaning towards that destination.

"I'm flipping out," he whispered aloud, but thought: "*Sto impazzendo, sto perdendo la testa.*" "Yeah, exactly," he said, not realizing he'd thought in old Italian.

Agent Dawn Carroll stared intently into the dark sky, through the windshield of the surveillance van. She saw no beauty, in fact, she was seeing red. The temperature in the vehicle had risen twenty degrees since they had watched a hospital-gown-wearing man walk out of the rear exit door—and she swore—hotwire a truck and drive off. Her senior partner, Special Agent Bob Striker, had overruled her want to apprehend, or at least question, the man. That was the last straw. She had loosed a tirade of insults, threats and the truth about the incident, which had happened two weeks earlier, and steam, which had been building for two weeks, had finally blown.

At five-foot-four, a hundred and twenty pounds, she was no match for Agent Striker physically, but her words struck him like body blows and gut punches. He couldn't help but revisit that night, trying to find his fault.

After a "Twentieth Anniversary" surprise party for one of the upper level administrative supervisors, Agent Striker had come on to her. They were both sloppy drunk. A typical Arizona fed party. In D.C. agents didn't let go as much as they did here in this dust pit of a city. She had hated being assigned here after four years of college, and a year of training at Quantico. She had been trained to be a supervisor, but when she came here, she found a macho-maniacal desert town pretending to be civilized, where men still ruled, except when a woman front was needed. She knew that was the only reason why a woman governor had been allowed to be elected. What the public didn't know was that there were many more positions that were more powerful than the governorship, many of which are not elected positions, but appointed seats, like the director of Arizona Department of Prisons. Behind the scene there was an undercurrent of the rich elite who spun things to their liking, whenever it suited their interests, or that of their friends'.

That night they were in the parking lot behind her apartment building, when he leaned over and kissed her on the mouth, forcing his thick, soaked in Jack Daniel's, tongue past her lips. She'd had no choice, under his weight, but to play it out until he backed off and she could get out of the car, then she felt his fingers rough inside of her. She could not figure out how he'd gotten his hand up her skirt and past her panties without her feeling it, even though she wasn't feeling much of anything after the party. She felt pressured and assaulted, not being able to stop him without some violence, and thinking that if she did try to stop him, he would think she was a prick tease, or a frigid tramp who let him get this far, then cut him off. In the back of her mind, like a blinking neon sign, was the ever-present thought that if she did try to stop him, it would turn into a rape. But it would be an "acceptable rape" that would never be called a crime. She could hear their questions: "You let him put his fingers inside your vagina? You let him put his tongue in your mouth? How many fingers? Did you object when his hand went past your panties?" She knew the story from countless investigations, and was thankful she was drunk, because the humiliation was so great. She was becoming that which she detested: She was sleeping with her own boss. The seat went back and instead of fingers entering her, it was his manhood thrusting up into her, bruising her, giving her a friction burn, while she endured his dirty talk. Then when he was done, he wanted to go inside of her apartment and "make love," he'd said. She felt like a whore, and when he was finally off of her, she told him to fuck off, and got out of the car and ran into her apartment. Early the next morning, he showed up at her door with flowers, wanting to come inside and fool around, and she told him to fuck off again.

For two weeks they kept silent, she rejecting him twice, and he thinking she just wanted a one night stand and let it go at that.

Now they sat in the van: she very red-faced, the small pockmarks from childhood acne very visible, feeling the humiliation of him being inside of her body once again, burning her from small feet to the tips of her auburn-colored hair. Her Irish green eyes were open, but not seeing. Bob Striker sat in the back of the van, looking out of the tinted window, with the headphones on. He wiped the perspiration off of his bald head, which he shaved daily, and sucked in his slight gut which she had remarked unkindly about, thinking that at forty-five, he wasn't doing so bad—waiting for Doctor Brown to come out.

"Do I really remind you of Homer Simpson?" he asked.

She almost laughed, but kept herself in check. *I'm supposed to be mad*, she reminded herself, but letting a smile appear on her lips while he was in back. *Son-of-a-bitch*, she cursed him.

They had received a letter from someone who worked on the staff of the Florence County Hospital about three months ago, regarding illegal organ donations from inmates. When they investigated, thinking it a hoax at first, they found some very fishy coincidences. Without alarming any of the doctors they hacked, legally by a court order, into the files and found that inmates were dying on the date of a surgery that had been scheduled three months before. They saw fifteen such incidents over the past six years, and one unknown operation scheduled an hour after a state execution. Doctor Brown was the surgeon in all instances, and when they checked his bank accounts, and records, they verified the bureau's suspicions. When they tapped his phones, home and office and cellular, they found the prison connection. A lowly lieutenant named Paul Franco.

She believed Franco was the mastermind.

If Brown would rat on Franco, and the others involved, then the case would be a cinch. That's why they were here at midnight, waiting for Brown to appear, to keep the sting out of sight of any of the town's citizens, who would spread a rumor that would surely get back to Franco, or the department of corrections, and the FBI's advantage would be blown.

"Do you really believe I raped you?" Agent Striker asked with a sincerity she'd never heard in his voice.

"Dammit, Bob, you don't just press your lips against mine, force your tongue down my throat, then jam your fingers in me and say it's not forced—jeezus, Bob, don't you see? Can't you understand that I'm a hundred pounds lighter than you, I was a little drunk, and worse, I was wearing a fucking skirt! And you wonder why I always wear pants to work. Well, now you know, so tell everyone I'm not a bull-dyke."

There was a long silence.

"We all thought you were too pretty to be a bull-dyke, by the way." He paused for a long moment. "I'm sorry, Dawn. I never meant to do something like that, I swear, but why didn't you report it if you felt that way?"

"Oh no, don't try to play stupid. You know damn well why! I didn't stop you from jamming your tongue down my throat, or your fingers in my pussy. You know the questions and the answers. You've seen it a hundred times or more I'll bet—the girl takes off her clothes, and she and a boy fool around, his tool gets hard and she gets scared and says, 'Well, wait a second, Johnny,' but it's too late because he's not Johnny anymore, he's his own penis, and what penis wants penis gets, and afterwards she feels dirty and soiled and begins to feel that she provoked the rape, and believes that that's what the police will think—and they will—so she doesn't report it." She took a deep breath and exhaled loudly. "I'm no different. I didn't try to stop you because I couldn't. I was threatened, trapped under you. Didn't you feel how dry I was?'

"No. Honestly I wasn't thinking about that—I apologize for my actions. I'll never do it again, and I promise not to say anything that would jeopardize your promotion."

"What? What promotion?" she asked.

A dark sedan pulled into the hospital parking lot.

"Car?"

"Yeah, dark sedan," she answered.

"Probably our backup. Good, we can get this done tonight."

"Yeah, and?" she asked.

There was no mention of her getting a promotion, and usually the whole office knew who was getting one.

"I can't say, special agent—"

"Special Agent? You're shitting me?" She knew it was nearly a double jump from her current rank.

"It's not a sure thing—but it is—if you get my drift."

A weight-lifter in a three-piece suit tapped on her window, breaking her out of a new-car-buying reverie. She rolled down the window.

The twenty-two-year-old smiled at her. "Where's the primary?"

"The what?" Agent Striker called from the back of the van. "Does he mean the good doctor?"

Agent Carrol ignored her superior's sarcasm, feeling sorry for the rookie. "Agent Roberts?" He nodded that he was and she continued, "You have a description of him. His shift is over in about twenty minutes, and his cars right over there. Park next to it, and make sure he doesn't get in. That's it." She tried to make it clear.

"Should we take him down soft, or hard?" Agent Roberts asked.

She heard Striker laughing in the back and couldn't suppress a slight smile, and saw that Agent Roberts heard as well, and was trying to look behind the black curtain.

"There should be no take down at all, Agent Roberts, and make sure the others know as well. We want to cuff him, put him in a car, and head back to Phoenix without anybody seeing us. Understand?" she asked.

"Clear. No take-down." He turned and walked back to the car, where two other agents were waiting.

She was thinking to herself that he had a cute butt, when she heard the sirens and an alarm from way off. It seemed to be coming from the prison—

"Oh shit!" Special Agent Striker cursed. He was listening to radio traffic in the area, and heard what it was. "Come on, we gotta get outta here or we're blown." He was moving around in the back.

A MEMORY OF FOREVER

"I think it's a little too late for that, Bob," she said. Squad cars and Arizona Department of Corrections vehicles were flying down the long main road that cut through town, sirens blaring and lights flashing. "Here comes the calvary," she whispered as the long parade of cars and trucks were only a block away.

Agent Striker popped his head out from behind the black curtain and groaned loudly. "Ahh shit! We're fucking blown sky high!" He looked towards the hospital entrance and saw the doctor coming out. "Maybe I can make it," he said and squeezed past the captain's chairs and opened the passenger door.

"What're you doing?" she asked as he slammed the door, and was already walking towards the doctor, who was standing in the parking lot watching the light show.

She started to get out as Agent Striker was within fifteen yards of the doctor, and the ADOC cars were pulling into the lot, one by one, lighting everything up.

"Freeze!" Bob Striker said to the doctor, who gave him a look of confusion.

Two guards, just out of the ADOC training academy, jumped out of the new state sedan, pulling .357 revolvers. The power of holding a gun on somebody was infectious. They pointed the gun at the man who was confronting the doctor. He could be the escaped convict, their guided logic excused them from putting their guns away. Through the windshield, as she came around the front of the van, she saw the impossible happen. Agent Striker was shouting at the doctor, trying to be heard over the still blaring sirens. He was reaching for his identification when someone fired a shot, and she watched as Agent Striker flew to his right and slumped on the black asphalt. He looked back at her, a black liquid leaking from his body onto the ground, "*PUT YOUR GODDAMN GUN DOWN NOW! F-B-I!*" She had pulled the velcro strap so the words FEDERAL AGENT were clear to anyone in front or back or her. If the shooter so much as pointed his gun towards her, she would blow his ass away, she vowed. "*FEDERAL AGENT! GUN DOWN NOW! NOW!*" Both of the wannabe police officers realized their screw-up, realized that the power they had over other human beings didn't carry over to the streets. Both of them put their guns on the hood of the car.

"Get down, fingers interlaced behind your head!" She approached wondering where the hell the other three agents were. Finally they came over and assisted. "You in the back, come out, hands up." She was treating this as if they had murdered him—

"Agent Carroll?" Lieutenant Franco smiled. A chill ran up her spine. *What were the odds*, she asked herself not realizing the implications of him knowing her name.

They had never met before, but both knew each other very well.

The city was asleep, except for the occasional Phoenix Police Department squad car that patrolled the dark streets like a mechanical jaguar searching for food in this suburban jungle of concrete, steel and plastics. A desert breeze blew through the city streets, a dry fine grit in the air, filtered through the structures and parked cars.

He was hunkered down behind the huge air-conditioning unit on top of a roof of a mini-mall. He'd heard the eye-in-the-sky, or a police helicopter, a few minutes earlier. He knew they had heat detectors and infrared scanning, so he was staying out of sight, moving around the unit. His bare feet were raw and tender from the small rocks that acted as some sort of cover on top of the tar roof.

Dutch hoped the burglary technique worked. His neighbor had bragged about plenty of burglaries, and the knowledge was picked up by anybody within hearing. Dutch had heard, but never thought he'd be doing it. He put his back to the circular vent and pushed. The screws were supposed to rip right out, but it took some muscling before they wrenched free of the wood and tar roof. The aluminum vent made a loud noise as it rolled away. He cringed until it stopped, leaving him in a loaded silence of apprehension and expectancy.

He was supposed to have a flashlight, he remembered George saying, but he was also supposed to be wearing clothes. He dropped down, half in and half out of the three-foot space, which was the attic of the clothing store.

"I'm a burglar now too," he said cynically, then went all the way in. It was pitch-black, except for little pinheads of light coming up through the drop ceiling. "Ow! Son-of-a-ow!" He grabbed a hold of a support beam and lifted his foot. It felt like he'd stepped on the tip of a nail or screw or something bit him. "Ow-AHHHH!" Something was attacking his other ankle. The pain was so great that he let go of the support beam, accidentally moved his foot from the hanging frame, then fell through the ceiling.

He was in the air longer than he expected to be, and all the while he was falling, something was biting him. It was like a dream, that sensation of falling endlessly, but having a terror that you know is true. There is a bottom, and the horror of impact...

"Umph!-son-of a bitch!" Cardboard boxes fell around him. He was on a pile of them in the back of the store. There was just barely enough light to see, and what he saw drove him over the edge; Ten or more, different sizes and colors, scorpions all moving very fast, on him, on the boxes around him. He felt one clinging to the hospital gown by his right arm. One was dangerously close to his crotch. He was up and started to dance away, falling over boxes, and stripping off the gown. He swiped at ghosts and feelings, and his legs burned where the little monsters had bit him. He couldn't stop moving for ten minutes, even then he felt their tiny feet skittering on his flesh, giving him the chills and drawing his eye, then his hand.

"Little bastards!" he cursed them.

He walked over to the other side of the storage room and started opening boxes of clothes. He found jeans, slacks, dress shirts. He looked for shoes, and finally found some. He got his sizes, every so often checking the floor and the area where he landed, and started putting on some clothes, and stuffing some in a gray duffel bag he'd found in one of the boxes. *That is okay though,* he thought, *because no luggage means no waiting around in the high security airports.*

"Jackpot!" he said, finding some boxes with expensive sneakers inside. He put two pair in the duffel bag.

After he was dressed in gray-colored slacks, a light-blue dress shirt, with a suit coat over that, and a nice pair of leather loafers on his feet, he walked towards the front of the store. He saw a light coming out from beneath a door. He wasn't sure if someone were inside or not, but it raised the hairs on his arm as he listened. They would have long since called the cops, if there was someone in the office. He sweated the entire time he waited, then decided to go for it. He set the duffel bag on the cement floor and gave the door a kick. It was not meant to hold up under an attack, only to provide a little privacy, and flew open—

Beeeoooouuuu! BEEEOOOOUUUU! *BEEEOOOOUUUUU*! The siren deafened him instantly, so loud that it hurt his ears. The small one desk and chair office was empty. He looked on the desk and saw a small yellow pouch with dollar bills sticking out of its opening. He snatched it up, turned and grabbed the duffel bag, and ran to the back door. He hit it harder than he'd hit the office door and was stopped cold. Like flesh running into steel. His foot hurt. He pushed on it, but knew it wouldn't give. It was key locked from both sides.

"Shit-shit-shit!" he cursed, the alarm blaring. He could sense people coming out of their houses, police cars turning and heading towards the mini-mall.

BEEEOOOOUUUU-BEEEOOOOUUUU-BEEEOOOOUUUU!

He went back to the office, but continued past it, into the storefront itself. It was brighter than he expected, and he felt an instant sense of exposure, like a doe walking out from a stand of trees into an open field (a bow hunter camouflaged and waiting). He ran bent over to the glass front of the store, stuffing the yellow pouch into the duffel as he went. Then a pair of headlamps shone on the window front, and passed by.

He slid and bumped up against the window front, right below a large painted "25% OFF SALE" sign, and saw the car fully. A Phoenix Police cruiser was stopped for a light at the intersection. Dutch watched the car, unable to hear anything but the loud siren. That was what his world consisted of—

BEEEOOOOUUUU—BEEEOOOOUUUU-BEEEOOOOUUUU!

—and the damn cop sitting in his car, the light having turned green ten seconds earlier. Dutch didn't breathe, as he willed for a miracle to happen—

The officer thought about turning off his A/C and rolling down his window, until he heard dispatch. "All points bulletin on escaped inmate, Dutch Giovanni, white male, approximately six feet two inches tall, two hundred pounds, hazel eyes, sandy blond hair." He depressed the accelerator, fully intending on being at one of the three routes from Florence to Phoenix.

Dutch watched the cruiser's tires spin, and then the car was gone. He picked up a steel pole off of a clothing rack and smashed the smallest window he could find. *I caused enough damage already*, he told himself. He crawled carefully through the hole, then stood up, feet crunching on the glass.

He breathed in the fresh night air that infused him with sudden energy, and started walking towards a twenty-four-hour liquor store across the street, barely able to hear the siren outside of the store. He tried to recall something sweeter in the air, but couldn't.

He could not remember her name, though he knew he would know her by sight, the thought invaded his escape plans.

"Can I get a cab at the AM/PM liquor store on Baseline and Fortieth Street?" he told the cab company.

5

GENOA, ITALY
PRESENT DAY

EVERYBODY GREETED HER as she rolled down the winding sidewalks. Today her flaxen hair was in a ponytail, which would keep it out of her way when she was painting. She had a smile on her strong, but somehow delicate Roman face, which came down through the upper-level gene pool. The cornflower hair and perfect skin shouted for all to look and stare. Her sky-blue eyes coming at you like the summer sky falling down upon you. If she could stand, she would be five feet five inches, and symmetrical. But she could not stand up, not for nearly a decade, since the accident.

It felt good to be out in the sun, rolling and moving about her small town. Often she saw women her age heavy with child, and turned away due to the pain. A soft penetrating burn in her heart, which traveled in a hot flood to a space behind her eyes. She didn't want that to happen today. People always reacted funny when they saw someone in a wheelchair crying.

She saw Claudia in the small tourist shop, alone, waiting for customers. There weren't that many tourists coming to Genoa lately, most of them going to Venice, Florence, Rome, or other more known places. But Claudia had kept her shop going.

Claudia waved to her as she passed by the glass storefront and she took her hand off a wheel and waved a gloved hello to the forty-year-old proprietor, who reminded Serena of an elder Aphrodite.

"*Buona sera, Serena! Come va?*" Marco called from the fish shop across the street. He wiped his hands on an already bloody apron and waved to her. He always had a big smile for her.

"*Abbastanza bene, e tu?*" she called back. In middle school she'd had a big crush on him. Now they were just friends. In fact, she was best friends with every boy in town, but none went beyond the inference of "just friends." Seeing Marco ten years later, potbellied, and not as handsome as he once was, lent to her thankfulness that a crush didn't amount to anything but that. Still, she would have given anything just to be touched, or held, by someone who was not her "friend." She gave him a smile.

She avoided the cracks in the road by keeping her wheel on the cement gutters, as she passed by the fish market, and headed to her favorite spot. All around her things were calm, familiar. Nothing had really changed from when she was a walking, talking and laughing little girl to now. The technological influence didn't influence the base structure of Genoa, which was and would always be a coastal fishing town. She didn't like the cobblestone roads as much as she used to, but they were pleasing to the eye, and lent an air to the old city. Nothing changed, except the sea.

That's where she was heading, a backpack full of paints and brushes, and a couple canvases, ready for her to use. It had at first been her hobby, painting and sketching, but it had turned into a very fruitful and pleasing career. She loved to sit atop her cliff, alone, painting and dreaming and painting her dreams, letting her visions and memories, which had grown stronger of late, become reality upon the canvas. It was the creation from sight, from memory, that grabbed her most of all. That sense of seeing, making the intangible tangible. Making the wind become substantial, captured in-gust, the white mists blowing off of the white caps. Plucking a diving sea gull from the air and freezing it for all time. Sometimes she would face inland and paint the docks, the harbor, the marina, the peddlers and buyers haggling over a price. She'd even painted everyone she knew in town.

Often she watched young couples, painted them, and sat for hours staring at her picture. The man's face always drew her eye, because it came from somewhere deep inside of her, and rarely looked like the subject she was painting. Only a familiar shape that someone could look at and say "that's him," but she knew better. It was *him*. Her dream lover. It was his eyes, hazel and perfectly shaped, staring back at her.

She knew the face well. On the day of her sixth date, with a boy named Stefano di Giafarrini, she had seen the face across the street. A flash of recognition, enough to draw her stare, to draw her soul, shake her from the moment that was and would be, like a vacuum sucking in thick steam, her momentum carrying her into the street and her date not warning her. The light had long since turned green, and she was sure there had been no traffic coming down the hill, just a fraction of a second before, her foot coming down, then the other, and she saw him. Her lover, captured in the glare of a glass front of Genoa's only pharmacy, staring back at her and she was blessed with never hearing, seeing, or feeling a thing as the delivery truck smashed into her eighteen-year-old body, her last thoughts were of his profile, the smile, the way the mustache rode his upper lip, the long lashes—so wanting to see his eyes—her heart fluttering in her throat—

Tires barked on cobblestone. Stefano staring, speechless, near to cowardly. The driver saw the young woman too late. It seemed she were staring into the drugstore's plate glass window, but as he was applying the brakes he could see nothing there of interest. He was thankful that she had not looked into his eyes as he ran her down. He heard the thump, but she didn't fly. His tire rode up the right leg, and her body slammed the road as the truck drove over her. He was grateful there were no thuds under the carriage, although he still didn't think she could have lived. His ten-wheel delivery truck versus her frail body did not give too much hope for her survival. Finally the truck stopped, and he swore he would kill the brake mechanics as he jumped down from the cab and ran around the truck. Tears were already in his eyes when he saw her lifeless body. Her stomach on the ground, something pink below her head, eyes open and so beautiful.

The doctors had said that it was the junk-filled purse that had ultimately saved her life, and the delivery truck driver who had given her CPR, and forced air into her collapsed lungs. Her head had slammed down with such force that all sixteen of her sketch pencils were shattered, but her skull wasn't fractured. As she came out of the coma, in Rome's finest neuro-treatment center, she caught a glimpse of *his* profile again, and then there were lights and pain, her father sitting by the bedside, tears in his eyes, smile on his wrinkled face. He ran down and bought her a pair of sunglasses, until she could get used to the light, from which she wanted to depart, to return to her dream world of a past she was just beginning to realize. Then she noticed that there was no feeling in her legs, from her thighs down, and started to cry.

Sitting atop the cliff, a hundred feet above a rocky shoreline, she remembered her father bringing in a romance novel, like an omen of her future. Although she had her facial beauty and what people called "her unique eyes," her ability to express herself, to dance, to move about, was forever gone. Even her ability to dress up was limited. Everything had a limit and a cost. The city felt sorry for her, a pity that at first was acceptable, but later was unbearable. It seared her heart to see her friends find boyfriends and marry, when she had, at one time, been the most beautiful girl in Genoa. Now, as if punishment for her beauty, she was the cripple.

At home there were now ramps, which guests would comment about until they saw her. The inevitable routine of depression and self-pity set in, especially when Stefano had come to the hospital, passion replaced by uncertainty. He had been the one, her ravisher, her first love. The relationship petered out in the weeks following her waking from a coma, and she found out that he'd found another girl. She was thankful for the in-hospital studies, so she wouldn't have to roll through the school hallways before her friends, even though all of Genoa knew what had happened.

The brake shop and the delivery truck company paid for all the medical treatments, mostly due to the public outcry, which was nation wide. It was either they do that or take their business out of Italy.

She had agreed to an interview with the local newspaper, which also went national, and everyone found out that she enjoyed painting and drawing. Soon her mail box was full of supplies, and there were offers to buy certain paintings, and even a few orders for her to appear at art galleries with her paintings.

She floated in the memories of her childhood, and the days after the accident, trying to place a sailboat in the Tyrrhenian Sea, under stormy gray clouds of ages past. It was looking more like a blotch of paint, than the distant boat it was supposed to be—

A shape in the sky drew her stare, and her heartbeat began to pick up. The smell of the sea, once distant and cleansed, now surrounded her and suffocated her other senses. She could feel that disquieting yet warming presence, like when she was getting dressed for her first date. The blur in the sky was crossing her path, heading east, like the many airliners heading for Rome. Her brush dropped to the ground, instantly dirtied and ruined, sand clinging to the oil paint, and she had the sensation of being pulled towards the edge, towards the cold sea crashing upon the rocks below. Fear gripping her chest, not because of the fall, but because she might somehow survive it, and—

"No! Not again!" she ordered herself, placing fingers at her temples to drive away the nightmare. "Deep breaths, deep breaths," she told herself, obeying.

After a moment she opened her eyes and looked around. She was done painting today, she knew, then started cleaning her brushes and packing her supplies away. *Figaro*, her artistic manager, *will have to wait for his paintings*, she told herself, folding up the tripod that steadied her canvases. But the fright had not left her completely, and she was even more fearful of the night to come, and what would come with the night.

"Stop it, Serena!" She bit her tongue to keep from crying.

Dreams and teeth and blood and—

"Stop it!"

6

A Verse from Swan's Song

THE DREAMS BEGAN when she was fourteen, the same night she started her period. Her mother told her she was just becoming a woman, and told her how to keep healthy and from ruining clothes, but not how to stop the nightmares.

It had been a fun time, filled with great expectations, and anticipations, and boys. Her mother would call the parents of certain boys who met her standards, and invite them to supper, purely for the reason of seeing how Serena got along with the boy, although this aspect was closely chaperoned.

Many a boy's hand she had had to jab with a fork under the table.

But it was the night after her first supper when she had had one of the most terrifying dreams—

She was in the middle of a town plaza. A town she didn't know, but felt familiar with for some reason. Smoke and ash lingered in the air, bodies laying about as if they'd been killed instantly on the spot they'd seconds before been standing, walking, or laying. She started walking, unable to stop the unconscious action. Things became clear to her. She was no longer in the twenty-first century, but a time far lost and far gone.

The ground beneath her began to shake. She could smell the scent of rotten eggs rising from beneath her, and then the bricks underfoot started to liquify, sucking her bare feet into a quicksand like substance. She started to run, like a cartoon character running through molasses, legs pumping but her body barely moving.

A shadow down the alley to her right. It grabbed her attention, then was gone, but she looked for it, kept her sense open to its evil presence. Then a cage fell from the roof of an adobe building, and a man reached out his hands, but would not look directly at her. He seemed to be looking for something, but she didn't care because she was going down into the muck with the rest of the dead bodies, and then she was holding his hand, a spark of energy traveling between their hearts, causing her senses to come alive, her strength to double, in a way that was marvelous and exciting. Smoke poured over her and her caged companion, thick and hot, wetting her lungs with each breath, while below, the quicksand turned to a frothy black water. She could taste, touch, smell, hear, see, and intuit everything around her, so long as she held his outstretched hand. For a moment she was scared of nothing, until she sensed something stalking her. *Look at me*, she willed the man in the cage. His forehead was shiny with sweat, but he didn't seem to struggle, as if his muscles were frozen and locked, but still under immense strain.

He was only an arm's length away, but his profile seemed distant, as if she were looking down a telescope backwards. *Why is he behind bars?* she asked. He only stared off, looking at a large mountain in the distance. She knew it was Mt. Vesuvius because she'd seen it many times in pictures and history books. Something was tugging at her thoughts. She realized, finally, that he was starting to turn, as if he were a statue slowly coming to life. Slow motion. Below her the water began to churn, the black water bubbling white and pinkish red, a weight tugging her down below the waterline, his fingers tightened around her wrist and pulled her head out of the water. She sucked in a breath, but couldn't. She felt her chest being crushed, and saw a shadow beneath her, all around her, and then she saw its black eye because it shone back at her like sun on a slice of lava rock. *Why wasn't his cage sinking?* her mind was asking in the panic, feeling comfort in the fact that the cage wasn't sinking and maybe she would make it, and then she went under again and felt his hand slip off of her wrist, and water filled her lungs and she began to scream bubbles into blackness.

A month after her first really bad nightmare, she had another. It went like that, in cycles, one really bad one a month and a few small ones clinging to its nightmarish plotline. But the day she turned sixteen, she had a nightmare so real and vivid that she'd had to reevaluate her sanity, and the world around her.

The day had been sunny, and she and Marco were in the garden, talking, getting ready to kiss. All the other kids had left the party, which her mother had organized. She could hear her mother washing dishes by the windows, which looked out upon the garden. They were sitting behind thick gardenia bushes, on a stone bench. Neither had spoken, each waiting for the other, bees making more noise than them.

"Should I leave, Serena? You look awfully tired and I wouldn't want to take advantage of a beautiful, but tired, princess," Marco whispered in her ear.

She smiled back, her ear hot, and her face flush. "And how do you know it is not I who is taking advantage of you?" Her look was triumphant, and he moved in closer to capture her. She remembered her mother advising her not to get too close to this boy, because his father had been sent to prison for molesting a young girl. This did bother her more than she let it show to her mother.

She saw the stars above, bright and twinkling. His hand fell on her knee, and his lips on her ear, and his tongue tickling her earlobe. She giggled. No one had ever tongue'd her ear before—

"Serena! Serena?" Her mother called through the kitchen window.

"If you're in the garden, you can see it's way past time." She heard Marco groan inwardly.

He stood up, gave her a light peck on the lips, then walked out of the garden and onto the driveway. "Ciao, Serena." He waved, then was gone.

"Mama! You knew I just went out in the garden five minutes ago," Serena said a little bit angrily, which caused her mother to give her a look of reproval.

"Is he gone?" her mother asked.

"Yes," she said, then stomped off to her bedroom.

A half hour later her mother came into the bedroom and started to scream. Serena was jerking and seizing on the bed, eyes rolled back, the entire bed was wet—

—She was helping some men, because she had been drafted to help the death squads by some man in Roman soldiers garments. He had a sword and lorded over the others, and over her.

He and three other men were going from house to house, finding the dead, and burning down the house with the bodies in it. It was all so illogical, she had voiced to him.

"It's all going to burn anyways," she told him. She saw the sweat on his face, streaking the mud and ash. There seemed to be a fever burning in his eyes, in his soul. She had seen it many times in the past two months. It was the sign of the plague that had been killing people lately, even most of her own family.

She saw dried blood on his sword, and on his scabbard, and knew she must escape. She knew the stories and rumors about some of the

Roman soldiers, and how they raped and brutalized women. She also knew that if he should catch her, he would slay her without a second thought. *Or worse*, she thought to herself.

"I know this family," he shouted, ignoring her. "They are many." He seemed to be having difficulty breathing, with all the smoke and fine ash in the air.

They approached a stone house, with pink marble steps leading up to a double door entrance. It was the home of wealth, she knew, because of the brass knocker and family insignia. *They must own cattle*, she guessed, because most families didn't have insignias unless they needed one. She could see a dead man, a sword in his hand, sitting under a window. She knew him. He was the family's manservant.

One of the helpers fell to the ground outside the house. The soldier prodded him with the sword.

"Get up, citizen!" He kicked the scrawny man, who was blackbearded and shriveled. The fallen man didn't move, and the soldier ran his sword through the man's lung. The man twitched and moaned as the soldier twisted the blade, then finally sliced through the man's heart.

"Oh Lord!" the man's servant whistled a hoarse scream, tears flowing freely down his dirty cheeks. "He was my master for many, many years." His sorrow turned to anger and hate and—

The Roman knew that the man was building up his courage, and was waiting, when the man charged at him, fists balled. He cut him down with one slashing stroke, the head flying, the body falling.

It looked so easy, she thought, watching the demented soldier wipe his sword on the tunic of the headless man, then put it back in the scabbard. Then he scanned the faces of any other would be problems, like a lion surveys his pride. With that look he dared them not to obey instantly.

"How goes thee?" she asked the soldier, trying to sooth the man's dementia.

"Why doth thee care?" he asked, as the three of them walked into the family room. Then he stopped and smiled at her.

She knew the look, and regretted her kindness, praying that she would find an opening to escape.

Marble pillars supported a heavy wooden roof, under which they saw the majority of the bodies. All of the bodies were taken to the master bedroom, which was made entirely of wood. The smoke was getting too thick for breathing, but she had a veil over her mouth and nose, which filtered out much of the ash and foul air. Both of the men would break out in coughing fits. She felt sorry for her cohort, who was about her age, and very boyish. He reminded her of a younger version of her husband—

"Get to work, woman! I have seen worse than this!" His coarse laugh turned to a hacking cough that brought him to his knees. When she came near to help him, just because he was a human being, he drew his sword. Finally he stood up and motioned for her and the boy to carry the last three bodies into the bedroom.

She was watching her helper from the doorway. He was placing wood and furniture near the bodies. Some of the bodies were fresh, and some were two and three weeks old, bellies full of gases and festering odors that caught in the back of her throat, making her throw up what little was in her stomach. The soldier shoved her roughly into the room.

"Help him!" he ordered, following her into the spacious bedroom.

The soldier poked a couple bodies, as if making sure they were dead. When he poked the sharp tip of his sword through the overripe belly of a dead woman, it nearly exploded, the contents flew out with the putrified contents, landing on her enslaved cohort. She dry-heaved, not able to scream, as the soldier laughed at the young man, who was white beneath the dirt and grime, gagging, trying to throw off the muck, which seemed to be alive and pickled at the same moment. Then a heavy smoke filled the room and both men were coughing and she was running away from those fevered green eyes, and broken-toothed smile.

She could hear them both coughing and the soldier cursing, as she jumped down the steps of the house and ran down the road. She knew inherently that she was far from her own home. She looked up and around and saw the angry mountain spewing orange plumes into the air. It wouldn't be long, she knew. There were shadows all around her in the smoky air. People running for their lives.

She turned, and started running down a wider road that led down to the bay, hearing footsteps behind her, and a foul stench creeping through her veil. There was a rumble from below, and then an explosion that made the earth shake. She knew it would be soon. She heard someone calling her name—"Swanlake! Swanlake!"—and she called back, turning and running towards the voice—

A shape flew through the window, just off to her right, and crumbled on the road in front of her. Someone had thrown a woman in the street. Naked. Bleeding. Dead.

The soldier jumped out of the window and she ran into him full force. He fell over and his sword clattered on the cobblestones. She tripped and fell herself, but fear made her leap instantly to her feet. Lust made him get to his feet as well. Part of his face seemed to be paralyzed, and when he caught hold of her tunic and turned her around, only one side of his face smiled victoriously. She saw past this physical deformity, into the true depths of the soldier's fever pitched dementia, and then he ripped her clothing off in one swift motion that left her standing before him naked. She kicked at him and struck his face. Her nails raked across his angry red flesh. Blood sprayed from the vein at his temple, wetting her face, but still he held tight to her forearm, smiling the broken-toothed, and now crooked smile that chilled her to the bone.

A backhand. Everything changed. Her whole head spun, and she fell without knowing she fell. When she shook off the blow ten seconds later, she looked around. His two thick calves were before her, and she was on her back. Above her she could see his diseased club, hard and thick, puss oozing out of the sores along its length, an open sore on the head, and beyond that was the soldier's face. One side of his face smiled at her, the glow in his eyes having a clear purpose now.

He had her ankles and dragged her to him, her buttocks scraping on the rocks and grit, as she reached behind her and searched for a hold of some sort. She kicked, but he was too strong, and then her fingers found, and locked onto, the hilt of his sword and she swung it with all the strength she could muster. It sliced off his right ear and the dull blade tore off part of his cheek. At last the blade sunk into the soldier's right shoulder with a loud crack, not unlike a walnut being stepped on. The arm still hung there, but she knew he could not use it. He smiled at her still, only its delivery was much more hideous and sanguine, and she could see the bleeding gums, which supported so many broken teeth, like a fresh skeleton was half of his face. She felt him come down on her, blood flowing from his mangle face onto her stomach, her breast, and finally her face as she tried to free the sword from his shoulder.

She felt his disease touch her and she screamed and fought against it, but lust was his master. Its foulness and evil enveloped her and she wanted to puke, was heaving, hanging onto the hilt and in her panic to get his thing away from her, she pulled sword full out, lifted it above her head, and brought it down upon his head. Once. Twice. Three times. She screamed as he still tried to penetrate her body, then at last he slumped. She screamed in anger and heaved his corpse off of her and ran. She held tight to the sword, and ignored the pain in her gut. She felt soiled to the very core of her being, and wanted to get home. She had the feeling, a sinking sensation that the soldier was not dead, and when she turned back, she swore he was rising, and she ran faster. *No way he can catch her*, she told herself, *and he doesn't know where I live either.*

She stopped, naked and trembling, at the entrance to the house. She hoped her husband wasn't there, for he could not see her in this state. It would drive him mad to know such a thing and not be able to do anything about it. She looked into the windows of their house and then went inside when she felt it was empty.

Their home was quite large for a couple as young as they were, but Julius made enough money, and her father owned this property, so that they were well able to afford it. She walked through the entry room, where she had once treated guests to wine and crackers and cheeses, and walked down the hallway to the bathing area. She found one jug of water and poured it into the washing basin. She used half of the jug to clean up and wipe off the dried blood and soot, then quickly got dressed. She tried to ignore the ache in her womb.

"Swanlake? Swanlake?" she heard.

"Julius? Julius!" She cleaned up the dirty rags and placed them in the dirty clothes basket.

She ran across the kitchen area and into his arms. He held her and whispered her name over and over. She could see his tears of relief and happiness, and she, too, began to cry. He felt so good against her body. Even now, after she had been soiled, he brought about a desire in her that was hard put to rest. Even among the dead and decay and coming doom, he made her feel safe. She felt his kisses, accepted them and responded with passion, longed for more—

"AAAGHHHH!" She felt his body stiffen, and caught a whiff of putrid stench, and she opened her eyes and lost her breath—

She wanted to scream as her lover fell limp in her arms, and the soldier, eyes gleaming out from a red pulp, stared back at her. He licked the blood off of his dagger, then smiled at her, and then she began to scream and scream and scream—

Her wheelchair was especially made. After she found out she was going to be stuck in a chair for the rest of her life, she decided that it may as well be something a bit more comfortable than the standard issue. Her father, as usual, anticipated this and took her to a local bike shop. There was a brand-new wheelchair sitting with the bikes. She had hugged him, then got off of the big wheelchair into the much more comfortable racing-type chair. The wheels were a little smaller, and had two grip wheels. One for speed, the other for the many hills in Genoa. The front wheels were slightly bigger than others, because of the cobblestone roads. It was a blessing.

She was thinking this as she came down the road, back towards the busy fish market. She guessed it was near to noon, or past. Marco waved to her as she passed his shop again. She wondered if she had ever thanked her mother for stopping her that night, and for making sure she never continued dating Marco. She waved back and gave him a smile. His apron was nearly red, and she saw now the effects of too much alcohol and stress. The town grapevine had Marco beating his wife on more than one occasion, and that it was he who broke his daughter's arm, not the *fall in the tub* he'd told Doctor Donatello. She never asked him about these things when they did share lunch. It was none of her business.

"Back early today?" Claudia said, stepping out of her shop.

"Sea gulls are trying to add to my painting," she lied.

Serena reached behind her into a little pouch and brought out a bottle of water, took a drink, and waited for Claudia to speak.

"You know, my brother Mario is visiting from America—if you want to go out next week, I'd appreciate it. Plus I am bringing my boyfriend—we could double date?" Claudia saw Serena start to make up excuses not to go. "Stop feeling sorry for yourself, Serena, you are the prettiest girl in Genoa, might always be, even in that damn wheelchair." Claudia looked down at Serena. "Think about it, okay."

"Okay."

"Is there something wrong, Serena?" Claudia asked, concerned for her young friend.

"No, just a little melancholy setting in or I'm getting sick." Serena smiled at the older woman, who always reminded her of a grandma, even though she knew Claudia was only forty-something.

"Well, you go have some ice cream and you think about coming with me, and don't you worry, Mario's my youngest brother." She smiled and patted Serena on the shoulder before walking back into her shop. The small bell tingled.

Serena put her water bottle back into its pouch and started rolling up the road, which was all up hill from here to her home.

At the bottom of the hill she caught a ride up to her house on the back bumper of a car, which went slow just for her. Before she wheeled down the driveway, she looked out over the city of Genoa. The view was rolling green hills, dotted with homes and white buildings and the church at the eastern edge of town. She followed the trees down to the wharf, and marina. Far off she could see the mirror image of her own favorite cliffs, except these were further away. The sights drew her heart and soul, made her want to take out her paints or charcoals and put the images to paper.

She looked at her home. Her parents were lucky to have it. They weren't rich, just upper middle class. The home had been inherited from her uncle, who was also an artist, but who never married or had children. He died in a boating accident off the shores of France. The house was left to her father, much to the chagrin of many family members, who, in time, conceded and accepted the fact. It was a modest home with five bedrooms and two bathrooms, two large dining areas and a living room. Once she started making more money than she knew what to do with, she was given permission from her father to add a small studio and a dry storage room for her finished canvases, under the house.

A MEMORY OF FOREVER

She coasted down the driveway, looked out through a small space between the trees, then rolled up the ramp. The door was open, and the smell of freshly baked bread lingered in the air. She saw the suitcase, and knew that her father was going away on his biweekly business trip. She didn't know what he did for a living, except that he was a powerful business man. Candles were lit around the house, and she knew she would soon hear her mother humming.

At the entrance to the kitchen she stopped. Her mother was humming "Granada" and kneading pasta dough, instead of using the machine she'd bought her for Christmas. Serena watched her mother for a while. She was a shapely woman, going on fifty next spring. Her hair had a gray tint to it, but it was still a golden blonde, and she wore it well off her shoulders. She was not very tall, but she had a presence that could draw the attention of everyone in a room. Finally she turned and smiled at Serena.

"My favorite daughter!" She rushed over and kissed Serena on the forehead.

"I'm your only daughter, unless you've been hiding a sister from me?" Serena joked.

"My lovely artist, how you kid. Would you like to help me roll out the pasta?"

She loved the way her mother's Italian flowed like a song, as if she were constantly singing in a low and soothing voice, always sure of her words and phrases.

"Mama—do you think I'm pretty still? Don't lie to me, I know my legs are flabby, and—"

"Shhh, Serena—don't speak of the bad. You have a beautiful face, eyes that were given by God himself, and you have a wonderful spirit. Any man who would pass you by is *stupido!*" Her mother soothed.

"But I'll be thirty soon, and not one man, Mama. I'm still a virgin—"

"Oh, my baby." Her mother held her for a moment. They had gone through this many times before.

"I'm sorry, Mama, it's just that I feel lonely and I've been asked to go out on a date with Claudia and it's been so long. I'm not sure I'll be—you know—accepted, or good enough. No man has paid me any attention except as a friend."

"Some things are meant to be, or not meant to be. You must have patience, remember I didn't meet your father until I was twenty-one years old, and back then that was an old maid." Her mother kissed her on the forehead again. "Stop thinking and go with your heart. God will deliver a miracle. Now help me finish. Your father is leaving for Rome tonight, and we want to send him off satisfied so he'll return to us." Serena smiled and wiped away her self-pity, and a couple tears.

She was starting to feel good, when the hairs on the nape of her neck stood on end, and outside the window she saw the clouds, a ray of sunshine. *This is starting to happen too often*, she told herself, wheeling up to the kneading board beside her mother, not able to shake the ominous feeling that something bad, or good, was about to happen.

7

FLORENCE COUNTY HOSPITAL

LIEUTENANT FRANCO LEERED at Agent Carroll from behind. *She is a fine piece of ass, for sure,* he told himself, then chuckled. His belly wobbled like an evil old St. Nick. He had the pictures to prove it.

"Something funny about a federal agent dying, Lieutenant?" she demanded. "Don't you have a convict to catch?"

He was sitting on a hospital chair, as she paced the floor, but now she focused all of her pain and worry and hatred at him. Franco checked down the hallway behind, saw nobody there, and smiled back at the female agent.

"Listen, I don't pretend to like you feds anymore than I like convicts, what with you all butting your heads in where they don't belong, but that don't mean I'm not sorry for your partner—if he would've identified himself as an agent, this wouldn't have—"

"You fat prick!" she interrupted. "That prison guard should never have had a gun. He'd only been working three days as a guard, and his prior experience was as a gas station attendant!" she said. Her anger was rising, and she tried to control herself. She would shoot the glorified prison guard if he kept up his sarcastic attitude and indifference. Even though he had committed some pretty horrible crimes, he was still supposed to be a cop, or at least on the side of good, but he acted as if he were a hard core criminal. Maybe he was.

"I realize you're distraught over the loss of your partner, and your lover, but—"

"What?" she blurted, her face turning bright red. The hairs on the nape of her neck stood on end, and she got a chill. It came from his eyes, evil dark-green eyes, staring at her knowingly. *He knows. Somehow he knows*, she thought, for the first time scared of her future.

"I think you know, Agent Carroll, so let's not bullshit ourselves on that matter, okay, or you can read all about it." A 5x7 appeared in his hand. "I especially liked this one—don't you? Dawn?"

Her heart stopped. She couldn't breathe for fear that this moment would somehow divulge itself to everyone around, explode into print, and be known by the world. She became aware of someone down the hall, the doctors in their offices, nurses walking by, cockroaches crawling around the hospital cafeteria, the beating of the fat pricks heart, and her own. As she stared at herself, teeth gritted as if in pain or pleasure, sitting on Bob Striker's lap, she remembered. At that point she had been raw as he drove in and out of her, his fingers had just found one of her nipples, and his other arm was snaked behind her and that hand was gripping her shoulder, being used to bring her down in a pile-driving action that had at first been so violent that her teeth had been clacking until she adjusted. *It does not look like I was raped*, she thought, not really remembering up until now that she had, in fact, gotten on top of him after he had entered her.

"You prick," she hissed, reaching for the picture.

"Ah-ha, Agent Carrol. This is for my photo album." He put the picture back into his ADOC jacket's inner pocket. "Let's say you and me strike a bargain, Agent Carroll? I mean, you wouldn't want Washington, *Inside Edition*, *Hard Copy*, or the talk show circuit to get these pictures. I mean, what would the taxpayers think about two FBI Agents fucking their brains out in an unmarked? Catch my drift, Agent Carroll?" He stood up, the chair creaking, and offered her his hand. She only stared at the beefy paw. He laughed and walked away.

She stood there, stunned, and grieving the loss of her own integrity, for she knew there was no choice.

"Agent Carroll?" a doctor in bloody scrubs started. "I'm afraid I have bad news—"

He caught the first flight out of Sky Harbor Airport. His blond hair was now black, but still past shoulder length and in a fashionable ponytail. He was dressed like a man going on a business trip to Los Angeles. It had not been his choice, but it was the first flight out.

He landed at LAX and checked out the prices for flights to Europe. Spain was the cheapest. He only had five thousand from the store's pouch. Even still he needed a passport, visa, and some sort of identification, and thought he might know where to get one—

—at 3 in the morning he was sitting in a lonely twenty-four-hour tea shop in Chinatown, scanning newspaper ads which promised fake IDs, resumes, college transcripts, and whatever else, except passports and visas. He put the paper down, sipped his tea, and looked at the young Chinese man sitting behind the counter. This was why he'd come here.

"You know where a guy can get a passport?" Dutch asked point-blank. *What the hell*, he figured, *there's nothing to lose.*

The man, about twenty and as thin as a rail, with a slight acne problem, looked up and squinted.

Foon Luc had thought this man was way out of place when he walked into the Chinatown All Day Night Tea Shop, but now his mental gears shifted. Maybe he could conduct some real business instead of sitting here all night while everybody else was sleeping.

"Yeah, from court building downtown." A not yet mature shark smile, eagerness to continue this check and cross-check game.

"No, I mean a fake passport that'll get past security?"

"You cop?" he asked quickly, looking—scanning the streets through the windows.

"Nope." Dutch smiled, knowing he was about to start the real game.

"How much you afford?" Foon Luc asked.

Dutch stood up and walked over to the counter, not feeling right talking loudly back and forth across the serving area. He figured out the price of the flight , and about how much it would take to before offering a price. " I can afford about three bills for passport, ID, and some fake credit cards," he lied. He could afford about two thousand, but this was how it worked.

Foon Luc laughed. "No, no—you get saran wrap with picture for that—you need five hundred for passport, eight hundred for good ID with credit cards."

It was his turn to laugh, as if the prices were absurd. He could see the college student-looking man trying to figure him out.

"Do I look rich to you? How about eight hundred for all three?" Dutch asked, sipping his hot tea.

A few cars passed by outside, and they waited until the cars were completely out of hearing before resuming negotiations.

"One thousand—take or leave." Foon Luc made his final offer.

"Deal." Dutch gave the man his hand, and Foon Luc stared at it for a moment before reaching and tentatively shaking hands.

"Deal." Foon Luc smiled. "How fast you need?"

"Yesterday." Dutch smiled.

Foon Luc was about to protest and reopen the bargaining, but they had already shook on it. He knew something of American customs, so he nodded, impressed by this big man's bargaining skills and upset with his own stupidity.

Ten minutes later, they were in a small room on the second floor of a dilapidated apartment building. People were asleep on the floor, on couches, and in dark corners. It was packed with bodies, young and old. An old woman, face filled with wrinkles, was in a kitchen stirring something in a ten-gallon pot that was perched precariously on an old stove.

"Want some breakfast?" Foon Luc asked.

"Nah, I'm cool man." Dutch smelled dish soap and a plain pasta smell. His stomach grumbled, but he wasn't going to take the chance.

Foon Luc kicked a body out of a doorway, and opened the door to a small, well-lit room. Dutch stared down at the little girl he'd booted, and she smiled up at him as he stepped over her small body, and went into the room. He watched as Foon kicked an old man on the couch, and the man woke with a start, then saw the tall white man and smiled and rubbed his hands as if in preparation.

Dutch saw that there were two large boxes filled with passports, plastic cards, and other miscellaneous items needed in creating fake IDs and credit cards. He listened to the quick instructions that Foon was giving the old man in Chinese, wondering how they understood each other. The old man went over to a desk in the middle of the room and turned on a small plastic lamp, then cracked his knuckles and smiled at Dutch.

"First you get picture," Foon told Dutch.

Dutch noticed that each wall was a different color; Light blue, off-white, tan, and straight white. The old man came over and gently pushed Dutch back against the off-white wall, stepped back and raised a camera. A flash. Done. The old man turned and spoke to Foon for a moment.

"He say you want government ID?" Foon translated.

"Why not? Cost anymore?" Dutch watched Foon think about it and shake his head, then the old man was maneuvering him to stand in front of the tan wall, then the blue. All the while the old man was smiling happily.

"What's he so happy about?" Dutch asked Foon.

"Deeyeeay!" the old man said happily. He went and sat behind the desk and began working, bringing out blank passports and stamping pads and other such paraphernalia.

"He say you DEA Agent." Foon twirled his finger around his ear, giving Dutch the worldwide signal of someone being crazy.

The old man looked up and asked Foon something.

"Where you go?" Foon asked Dutch, but saw the guarded look on his client's face. "Take it easy, I just ask because I have family and contacts some places. You know. Maybe you go there and I give you something to deliver? No?" He spoke in Chinese to the man, who looked up, smile gone, and then tossed away the passport he'd been working on muttering in Chinese.

"Maybe Spain—"

"I know Madrid—have family there," he exclaimed. "How 'bout Paris?"

"I might get there too," Dutch answered cautiously, going with the flow. He didn't plan on staying in either of those cities, because he had a specific destination in mind, just not the name. Not yet.

'I give you bargain. One thousand dollar American you take gifts to Madrid, maybe Paris, all legit. Fool proof." Foon Luc had just remembered something his uncle had told him a few days ago. Maybe he could turn this into a bigger deal and gain respect at the same time.

"What gifts? Drugs?" Dutch asked.

"No-no-no. No drugs." Foon Luc laughed as if he would never suggest such a thing. "Just gifts I swear...NO DRUGS!"

"Throw in extra credit cards and another passport and you got a deal." Dutch offered.

"Deal!" This time Foon Luc put out his hand, and Dutch looked at it, then tentatively shook it, all the while wondering if he was being played the sucker.

Dutch felt that something was up, that he was being played. He would find out when he got his hands on the suitcase, because he didn't need to get stopped by some drug-sniffing dog, or busted at customs, and then all hell would break loose.

Foon spoke to the old man, who grunted, then tore up the stuff he was working on.

"What's he doing? Hey?" Dutch started to move forward, but Foon's hand stopped him.

"Never make it past gate with that junk. Relax. Take a nap and I go take care of some things," Foon offered, leading Dutch to the couch. "Relax. You friend now, no worry."

Dutch sat down, still confused, but willing to go along a while longer because he had no other choice. He watched Foon leave the room, then the old man who was digging deep into the boxes and bringing out what was probably the "good stuff." The old man was writing, or drawing on the passports, talking to himself, and constantly rechecking his work with a magnifying glass. All this got boring and Dutch leaned his head back and his eyelids began to droop, the exertion of the past six hours coming upon him heavily—

—someone was pulling him away from her—

"—wake up! Hey, come on." Foon shook his new friend, who would earn him five thousand dollars if he made it. "You ready to go."

A MEMORY OF FOREVER

Dutch blinked, then saw Foon staring down at him with a big grin that offered yellowing teeth. But behind Foon stood two solemn men dressed in black suits. One had a large Gucci suitcase, the other a serious look.

He wiped the sleep out of his eyes and stood up. Surprisingly, both of the Eurasian men were about his height, only slightly shorter. They eyed him cautiously, unsure if he was friend or foe, and this made him uneasy. When he reached for his duffel bag, the man holding the suitcase started to reach inside his jacket.

"Relax," Foon told the man.

The old man appeared and walked up to Dutch and handed him a Gucci billfold, which was fat, thick, and used-looking. He smiled at Dutch and spoke to him in Chinese. Then he handed him a used-looking passport.

"You keep money, credit cards separate from passport. Never have both passports together at same time. Remember who you are," Foon translated.

The old man bowed and left the room.

Dutch stuck the billfold in his inner coat pocket, and his passport in the other inner pocket.

"Come—you flight leave in thirty minutes." Foon smiled at Dutch and motioned for him to go back out the way they'd came in, then spoke to the two men, who followed.

Outside it was still dark, but getting light with the coming dawn. A Chinese cabby was waiting, and both of the men in black got into it. Dutch turned and shook Foon's hand.

"They go with you to airport, see you off—Good luck, Dutch."

Dutch froze, hearing his name and knowing the implication, and suddenly looking around for the police.

The guard not carrying the suitcase was in the back seat, and he tugged on Dutch's cuff. The Chinese cabby protested about how early it was until the Triad member up front gave him a look. Finally Dutch got into the back seat. Foon smiled and waved and then disappeared into the darkness of an alleyway that led back to the tea shop.

Dutch looked at the man beside him, who looked to be the leader of the two, if there was one. "Am I on TV yet?"

"In a half hour you'll be all over the TV on the five o'clock news. Maybe national—maybe not. We know because you're all over the police network and the internets and government computers. They say you were involved in the killing of an FBI agent?" The man smiled at him. "You're one dangerous man."

"I didn't kill no FBI agent." Dutch couldn't believe it, but then again, he could, because that was exactly the type of propaganda to turn every police agency against him, and the public as well.

"Could be inter-related on computer. Sometimes when things happen at same time, they get mixed up."

"What's my chances?" Dutch asked.

"Good, if plane leaves before five." He laughed. "Here, you might need this too." He handed Dutch a black mole and a dark mustache.

"Came prepared, did you?" He got no response, and all these sudden gifts were like weights around his neck, a carrot on a stick.

"Lick and stick, here." The man took the mole, licked it, and stuck it on Dutch's chin. He chuckled. "Perfect. Do the mustache."

Dutch did as he was told, and let the man adjust it to the right position.

"Nobody ever figure out who you really are. Here, first class ticket, and phone number for when you arrive. Do not use airport phone, no matter what happens." The man handed Dutch a slip of paper.

"Why?"

"They're all bugged and listened to—now remember not to drink hot beverages or sweat too much. Glue lasts twenty-four hours, give or take. You receive money when you arrive in Madrid. Okay."

"That's all cool—but what am I taking?" Dutch looked at the suitcase which the man up front had between his legs.

The man next to him looked at the cabby. Dutch had seen the gesture many times in prison, and knew that it wasn't cool to talk. He still wasn't sure about going through with it because it was all too good to be true, and happening so fast, that it seemed as if fate had put him on the fast track to good fortune. *It's about time*, he thought, as they pulled into the airport unloading zone.

As they reached the ticket counter, Dutch saw a young Chinese woman dressed in an airline uniform. She took the large suitcase, tagged it, and then a luggage handler appeared from behind the wall and grabbed his suitcase, and then it was gone.

Oh shit, he thought. He felt a hand on his bicep, and a voice in his ear. "It's not a bomb, relax, you're a friend."

The man looked him in the eye, and Dutch felt that he was sincere. He hoped.

8

BARAJAS AIRPORT MADRID, SPAIN

THE B-707 DESCENDED to the blinking tarmac, the city crowded, and all around the rectangular patch of darkness. A pretty stewardess nudged Dutch awake, and he came groggily to, then noticed the smell. It was like he were landing in a new world, a place of different origins, of an older—more trodden and used—soil.

The door opened for 1st class passengers only, and Dutch was let off of the plane, the stewardesses smiling and polite.

The air itself was muggy, even at 2 in the morning, and there was, in addition to the baser scents, a hint of rain in the air. He walked to the baggage catch and grabbed the suitcase.

"Damn!" a surprised hiss; It was heavier than it looked. This worried him (two Spanish police officers walking by).

At the terminal, where he'd disembarked, the other coach fliers were beginning their stampede to the customs counter, a mere thirty feet ahead of where Dutch now stood. The two officers had stopped a few feet from a small waiting area.

He heard them speaking Spanish, talking about him.

He carried the large, heavier than should be, suitcase towards the customs area, the voice in his head screaming that he'd better find a place and check the contents, before trying to get past customs. He felt lightheaded and dizzy suddenly, and found a bench, deciding to at least have one small look. The other passengers were still way down the terminal.

There was a large piece of yellow tape over the seam, marked U.S. Customs, as if to stop would-be thieves. He sat down at a bench and was about to open the suitcase when he saw them—

—Cameras following him from behind two-way mirrors. "Shit," he muttered. He could feel them turning to follow him as he stood up, stretched, then picked up the suitcase and went to the counters. Beyond the counter was a short foyer area and then, surprisingly, the city of Madrid. He looked at the sign; Customs: All Bags Inspected, it read in English and a dozen other languages. He and seven other people in first class were the first people off the plane, and now stood in line, at an empty customs counter.

He learned something he didn't know about first class; it wasn't just better seats, or food, or friendlier service, or bigger seats, or prettier stewardesses, it was also a better way of life, not to mention that you had a choice of movies.

A door opened and a customs official in a very colorful uniform targeted Dutch with a smile. "Over here, Señor," he told Dutch.

Dutch lifted the heavy suitcase onto the thigh-high counter, and set his duffel bag down.

"Passport and ID please. Do you have anything to declare? Money, fruits, vegetables? Why are you visiting Spain? What is your occupation and current employment?" The customs officials didn't slow for answers.

Dutch was feeling lightheaded and started to sweat. Something inside was urging him to break for the doors, where only two police officers stood, unarmed. *It has to be something I ate*, he figured, trying to remember what he had on the plane.

"Sir? Are you ill?" The official stared at him.

"I think I ate something—"

"No problem, if you'll show me your passport and another form of identification, I'll speed you through this—you don't have much luggage," the official requested politely, starting to feel a fever coming on himself. The official looked up at a camera and made a face.

Dutch handed the man his passport, but not before he caught the look. He tried to take out his identification, but gave up and handed the official his entire billfold. The official stamped the passport twice with practiced quickness, then gave it back, at the same time unzipping the billfold and flicking through the credit cards to the ID.

"Excuse me, sir? You are Drug Enforcement Agent?" the official asked, this time with respect, then looked up when he got no answer.

Dutch was looking at his own identifications. There was a picture of his fictional family, a wife and two kids. He had glanced over them on the plane. He was, according to the identification, a DEA Agent, lived in LA, and had a wife and kids.

"Yes," he heard himself say. His breath seemed hot, and his stomach seemed to pitch and roll. He could feel beads of sweat rolling down his spine, his legs, and forming like thunder clouds upon his brow.

"Good, that makes my job much easier—are you sure you're feeling well?" the man asked, this time genuinely concerned. He handed back the billfold.

He was having a hard time focusing, and took a deep breath in the hopes of shaking the fuzziness. The smell around him sickened him, and he could taste the bile rising up from his stomach, but most perturbing was the mole walking slowly down his chin. It slid on a shiny surface, and felt much like a large bumble bee walking on tender skin. Dutch could feel the customs agent watching it—

"You're free to go, sir," the official said too soon.

—slide down his face, and he quickly picked up his two pieces of luggage. As he bent over, the mole fell onto the white counter, sweat dripping like rain drops around the black blob.

Grab the bag and go outside, he willed himself, turning and walking quickly towards the doors and fresh air. *That's all I need*, he told himself, moving faster and faster. The two cops were talking and not paying him any attention as he stepped through the automatic sliding glass doors. He took a deep breath of Spanish air.

A whistle blew loudly behind him, and he started running towards a cab parked across the street, out of the long line of parked cabs that would have a hard time making a getaway.

The fifty-one-year-old cabby had been driving tourists all his life, all over Europe. It was his family trade, and how they earned a good living back in Corsica, which was his home. The family of gypsy thieves had recognized this hustle when the first car was built, and had ever since owned the International Cab Company, though you wouldn't find that name on any cab they drove. Tonight he wasn't too happy with his chances of picking up even a straight fare. The union cabs had him blocked out, even at this time of the morning. He was just closing his eyes, when he felt his cab rock and the rear door opened and a American tourist jumped in. He could spot the nationality of almost any tourist, and judge their affluence as well. The latter was the most important of the two, for this assessment determined which hotel the cabby took the client to, or which spot—

"*Drive!*" Dutch shouted, throwing over a hundred-dollar bill, and slamming the door shut.

"No problem—you need hotel or someplace to stay—"

"Just drive off!" he shouted, spotting the customs official and the two cops talking to someone who was pointing towards the cab he was in.

The cabby got the point and drove off quickly. He made a few slashing turns and went down some dark streets he knew well, all the while watching the man behind him, who was nervous and sweating. There was something about him that made the cabby cautious, and skeptical about taking him down—

"Listen, I need to use a phone. Can you help?" Dutch was still checking the rear window, not seeing anything but the dark square and expecting that to be filled with red-blue-white lights.

The cabby stopped the car on an inclined road, in what looked like an alley, but with shops and dark storefronts. The cabby honked his horn twice.

"Why we stopping?" Dutch asked.

"You need phone? Use phone in my family shop." The cabby got out and helped Dutch with the heavy suitcase.

Dutch wasn't too sure about this, but he had to get some help, and his only *friends* were at the other end of this phone number.

He could see slats, and squares of light, which came from under small doors and small windows that lined the dark alleyway. The buildings were two- and three-story slivers, mostly constructed of brick or stone, and the silhouette they cast against the not so dark sky, was angled, or crooked, winding up, or down the street. The street he stood on was cobblestone, similar to the bricks at the Indianapolis Motor Speedway. The taxicab was facing up the inclined road, which went up and to the left, dragging the buildings with it, while the declining road went down and to the right. They were parked at the middle of a S-curve. He noticed the smells, much different from any scents in an American alley; fresh breads to flowers, and other kitchen spices. A warm bubble of cinnamon roll scented air surrounded him, so thick he could nearly taste them on his tongue, and then it was gone. He could sense no discernible sounds—

"Hey, American? You need phone or what?" The cabby was standing by the door to a wine shop.

Dutch looked at the wiry man, who was perfectly tanned, and went from one foot to the other, all the while holding the heavy suitcase with ease. There was an eagerness in the cabby's smile that he hadn't noticed before, a sinister, used car salesman-about-to-sell-you-a-lemon-for-twice-the-price-look. He'd seen the look before, saw it on the face of the three men who stabbed the snitch on the weight pile, saw it on the lawyer who sold him out at the trial in that kangaroo court. However, with all this intuitive evidence, he could not see anything wrong, except for the fact that he had the suitcase, which was important to his future.

After a moment he walked over, and the cabby smiled and opened the door.

"I'll take that," Dutch said, taking the suitcase, which the cabby reluctantly gave up.

He walked into a dark wine storage room, and saw that this was the back of a wine shop. There were rows of wine racks, and an open doorway which led to a stairway—

—the door slammed shut behind him, and the lights came on and three men with clubs of some sort came out from behind the wine racks. He felt the hairs prickle at the nape of his neck, and he set the suitcase down against the door behind him.

He smiled his own smile at the three would-be robbers.

They seemed frightened and confused by his lack of fear, which was unlike most of the tourists they'd confronted. In fact, not one had ever given them a reason to use the clubs. Most handed over their travelers checks and money and jewelry and expensive tennis shoes and that was that. The two twins were only eighteen, and this was their fourth time. They had rotten pieces of tree limbs, which they'd never had to use. The older of the three was in his thirties, had a black mustache, and a scar running up the left side of his face where a bull's horn gouged him badly.

"Give suitcase and traveler's checks, no you get hurt," the older one said in broken English. He had the rolling pin.

Dutch grabbed a wine bottle off the rack nearest him, and smashed it against the brick door frame. He felt wine splash against his dress slacks, and he remembered how thin the material was, but it felt good.

"Let's rock and roll then," Dutch challenged in prison slang Spanish. He hoped the hot flash and dizziness would go away.

The three backed up a little as Dutch brandished the jagged glass at them. He would use it if it came down to him or them, but he had a feeling they didn't want to tangle with him. He saw it in their eyes, a fear of actual combat, of facing the beast they had by their own actions unleashed. He thought about all the people these hustlers had robbed, maybe even hurt, or at least ruined their vacation or honeymoon, and it made him angry. He growled, looking mainly at the older one.

The lights in the stairwell flicked on and a woman appeared at the bottom of the steps. She was heavyset, very large headed, and was wearing a baby blue nightgown that went to the floor. She looked at her three sons, then at Dutch. She let her gaze rest upon him for a moment, then became infuriated with her boys. She started speaking so fast that nobody knew what she was saying, and Dutch was no longer the true threat to their well-being. She landed two powerful blows on the twins, and a few more as they ran by and up the stairs, and then she turned her attention to the elder son. He tried to talk his way out of it, and dropped the rolling pin, all while backing up towards Dutch, who lowered his makeshift weapon. The older son reached out and flicked a secret lever that unlocked the door, and was gone.

Dutch watched the woman, who looked at him and the wine spilled on the floor, then went and picked up the wall phone. He turned and reached down and found his suitcase gone. He snatched up the duffel bag and bolted out of the shop, then stopped. The cab was gone. Dutch looked down the road and saw the man who stole his suitcase, trying to run down the alley. He chased after him for a block, when a pair of headlamps appeared.

The man stopped, and was framed by the lights. *Maybe this will be my day, after all,* Dutch told himself, as the car doors opened. He could see the silhouettes of two men standing up behind the car doors. The Spaniard's body suddenly jerked, lifted, then fell backwards onto the cobblestone. There hadn't been a sound. As Dutch approached he saw the holes in the Spaniard's shirt, and blood running down his scarred cheek. *Poor bastard,* he thought.

"Sorry we're late, Dutch, we lost you when you ran from the customs." It was a casual tone, as if the man had not just killed another man.

"Grab the suitcase, Mister Pee wants to see you, and you'll need to see a doctor immediately." A different voice.

Dutch started to grab the suitcase, then puked all over the dead man. He tried to lift it, and then he heard rapid fire Chinese and a man was picking him up and then he lost consciousness.

"Ahh, he's coming too," Mister Pee said quietly. "A brave man." The last was said for himself to hear. He had much respect for Dutch Giovanni, who had beaten the odds, and then some, to get his expensive package out of America and into Europe.

Dutch found himself in a silk robe, and nothing else, under a thick cool quilt, in a soft bed. There was a cup of juice on a bed tray, and a cup of coffee. He opted for the juice first. As he sat up in the large bed, he found himself in an even larger room. There was a Chinese woman standing next to him, whom he hadn't noticed upon opening his eyes. She climbed onto the bed, wearing only a kimono, and watched him with doeful eyes. After he finished, she took the glass and set it on the bed tray, then took the bed tray and herself out of the room. Then he saw the camera, in the far corner.

Ping Li, the smaller of the two men that had lost and found Dutch, came into the room and looked at Dutch.

"Are you well enough to walk?" he asked, then added, "the doctor say you are fine, only a little sick. Mister Pee would like to see you now, if you can walk."

The last was more of an order than a request, but Dutch did feel much better than he had. "What doctor?" he asked, throwing off the covers and slowly putting his legs over the edge. The bed was very low, his head very high. *Whoa*, he told himself, feeling a little light-headed.

"Mister Pee will explain these things to you," Ping Li answered evasively, coming over to assist Dutch if need be.

He let the man lead the way through the expansive, and doubly expensive, house. The interior was richly decorated in a cross cultural revolution of Spanish antiquities and Chinese artifacts. He noticed more than one Picasso, and a Van Gogh, and wondered if they were real, because he was sure he'd read in some catalogue that these specific paintings were in museums. There were statues filling one room they passed through, and then they reached a pair of ten-foot high oak doors that were ornately carved. They swung open quietly of their own volition, as his escort neared them. Beyond the doors was an expansive glass room, with a surreal sunset sky in the background, and plants hanging all about. A slight man in a red robe seemed to come out of the sunset towards him.

"Ahh, Mister Dutch Giovanni." Sling Po Pee, supreme leader of the entire American west coast and European Tongs, put out his hand. A smoking cigar was in his other hand.

Dutch knew this man was powerful, not by his dress or fat cigar or shoes or glasses, but by the man's confidence, and by the cold, yet determined look in the man's eye, no matter that Dutch was a foot and a half taller. After shaking hands, the man led Dutch, by the arm, over to a glass table which was near the edge of the room. The purple sunset seemed to throw rainbows of refracted light through the prismed table legs.

"Call me Dutch, Mister—Pee, is it?" Dutch offered, sitting down in the glass chair. Dutch checked to see if it was some form of clear plastic.

A MEMORY OF FOREVER

"Yes, my friends call me Mister Pee. What a lovely sunset," he offered. "Coffee, tea, you must be hungry after the long flight?"

"Some coffee would be nice." Dutch watched the sunset. It had been a while since he'd seen an unimpeded sunset, but even still, he didn't remember one as beautiful as this. A purple and red mixture, with a distant layer of clouds cutting through the scene, giving it the essence of natures perfect imperfection, for what would a sunset be without a few perfectly hung clouds. A servant came into the glass room through a different door, which was in the wall that the double oak doors were in.

Dutch watched as the man set down a tray with pastries and rolls and coffee and juice, bowed, then left them. All this was done without a sound. Dutch noted this last because *it must be hard not to make a sound on the white marble floor*, he surmised.

"This is a lovely room," Dutch said, pouring coffee into a mug. He couldn't resist the temptation and grabbed a roll as well. Just two days ago he would be lucky to get a piece of toasted three-day-old white bread and two-day-old coffee. People always thought prisoners got good food, and had it made, but that was all propaganda for the politicians, who promised more time, lengthier sentences, and tougher time. If you had family who could send you enough money each week, then maybe you could eat decently, but that wasn't the case with most convicts. Dutch was no exception. The roll tasted sweet, and he had finished it quicker than he thought was polite. "Sorry, I'm starved for some reason," he apologized.

"I would be also, if I hadn't eaten in a day and a half," Mister Pee said with an understanding smile.

"A day and a half?" Dutch asked, incredulously.

"Actually, it's closer to two days, Dutch. You were near the suitcase a little longer than we anticipated you'd be."

It registered with Dutch slowly but surely, but before he could get angry or ask another question, Mister Pee interrupted.

"Would you like to see what's inside the suitcase?" Pee offered. "Come."

Dutch followed the small man down a very tight stairway, which was not well lighted, and had no rails. It was more like a square tunnel going from one door to another. Mister Pee placed his hand against a piece of glass, and there was a flash of light, then the door slid open with a whoosh of air. *Not unlike an old Star Trek whoosh, when the doors opened or closed*, he thought. They entered a room that was lined with stainless steel panels. The two men who had picked him up were operating a pair of robotic arms, via a control panel, that were behind a thick lead-lined glass panel. Dutch saw his suitcase, and the robotic arms opening it, and spreading it wide, to reveal three grapefruit-sized orbs. They were very polished.

"Oh shit." Dutch knew, and felt tricked and used.

Mister Pee gripped his bicep, not unfriendly, but to bring more emphasis to what he was about to say.

"Weapons grade plutonium, specifically designed and molded." The robotic arms carefully grabbed the silver balls and set them into another, steel and lead-lined, suitcase. One ball nearly fell, and Pee rapid-fired a stream of Chinese at the larger man. "Don't worry; I don't believe in terror, not when I can sell—each ball for three million dollars to a more stable buyer.

"Who, Egypt?" Dutch knew he'd spoken a little too sarcastically to his benefactor.

"Would you believe, France?" He looked at Dutch.

Dutch believed him. "So he wasn't lying after all?"

"You must be speaking of Foon Luc. No, he wasn't lying, except I have other, much safer plans, than having you take further risks to your health. Plus, you are one hot property right now." He spoke to his men, then put his arm through Dutch's. "Come, let's discuss these matters over dinner."

Pee looked at Dutch, who looked at the nucleus of the nuclear bomb, and understood the young man's feelings and thoughts. He knew what he would be thinking. Back when he was a kid, being much smaller than the other boys, he'd been tricked into doing things that he might not have done had he known the dangers, or consequences. But he did them, and sometimes, with extreme cold bloodedness to get his point across and earn respect.

At thirty-four, he had enough respect and power to become the leader of the Hip Sin, San Francisco's largest Chinese Tong. Once established, he started his own investment scheme, by putting U.S. Citizens of Chinese descent through college, with specific curriculums that were geared towards the future; computer sciences, physics, chemistry, biological, genetics, other advancing areas of science.

Now, at age fifty-five, he controlled the entire West Coast and European operations, with law-abiding Tong members deeply entrenched in U.S. government research, thanks mainly to the liberals and equal rights fanatics, which he supported with vast amounts of money. When the American government started talking about dismantling nuclear weapons, his many insiders began planning the fake destruction and storage of weapons grade plutonium.

He left the heroin trade, something he felt was dirty business, to his Asian Triad brothers.

Dutch could sense a deeper understanding in Mister Pee, sitting across the table from him, scooping noodles into his mouth with a pair of adeptly wielded chopsticks. He saw a softening in the man's eyes, almost paternal, and knew that he was being taken care of. He enjoyed the conversation, learning that he was known worldwide, and that they had leads that he had indeed jumped continents. They had pictures of him with his black hair, but those were taken when he'd gotten off the plane in Los Angeles. They must have had cameras everywhere. *Big brother is always watching*, he told himself. The egg rolls and chicken fry were excellent, the best Chinese food he'd ever had in his life, and he put it up there on his lists of best foods to eat for future reference. The rice wine was also as good, and crept up on him.

Pee laughed when Dutch slurred. "It creeps up on you, eh? Old family recipe."

Once finished, two delicate Chinese women walked into the room and cleared away the dishes, then stood patiently by the door. One wore a red silk kimono, which matched Mister Pee's, and the other a blue kimono to match Dutch's robe.

"Tomorrow I have arrangement's for your safe getaway. I have friends that will take care of you from here to your new life, although I shall miss your company." He stood, and the women in red came over to him, and they both walked through a door.

Dutch knew that the lady in blue was waiting for him, but his head was filled with questions and more questions. He had truly reaped what he had sewn, for he had gone to Chinatown specifically for the exact outcome that he was now experiencing, only this was a steroidal version of what could happen when you dealt with the Chinese Triads. Now he was on a roller coaster ride to who knew where.

He felt a soft hand, surprisingly warm, on the taut muscles of his neck. Fingers cut into his traps, and dug into the tension, and then stopped, for this was all she could do from there. He turned and she smiled with pouty lips, her almond-shaped eyes, a button nose, even with her heart-shaped face. Then, he felt her hand on his own, and he was following her into a different bedroom than he'd woke up in.

9

GENOA

HER FINGERS DUG into the pillow as she screamed aloud in frustration. Clothes were strewn about everywhere, yet nothing to wear to a blind date. All she had was jeans and shirts, and half of them were dotted with paint or stained by turpentine or cleaning fluids. She heard the wood floor creak outside her door—

"Come in, Mama," she called, pushing herself into a sitting position.

After a few seconds the knob turned, and her mother peeked her head in. She was used to her daughter's insecurities, and knew exactly how she was feeling right now. As soon as she saw the clothes, she knew the problem. "Oh, baby, why the tears? I thought you'd be overjoyed at going out on this date?"

She hugged her daughter tightly and rocked her gently. She always enjoyed her daughter, even at these times when Serena was afraid and insecure. She knew, after raising an outgoing child who loved to try new things and experiment and explore, that it was her disability that brought out this vulnerability. She was glad, at selfish moments, that she had someone at home to take care of when her husband went on his "business trips," although she prayed each day for her daughter's legs to be given back to her.

"I'm acting like a baby, I know, but I don't have anything to wear out on a date, and I saw a picture of Mario—he's quite handsome."

Her mother laughed kindly and stood. "Come, I have some things that would be perfect. If you keep this up, I'll have to take you shopping in Rome, or Florence."

Serena rolled off the bed and into her wheelchair, in a practiced motion, not unlike a gymnasts dismount from a pommel horse. For her it was like walking, these movements and upper body positions, which she had to use in order to have the leverage to move her useless lower half.

Once in a while her foot would move, or her leg would twitch, without conscious aforethought, or by any other means, accept by her leg musculature having contracted. This was happening more often than she wanted to admit to herself, or to anyone else. The fact that it might be happening confirmed what the doctor had said about the nerves and connections in her spinal cord regrowing and reconnecting because of her youth at the time of the accident. She didn't dare let her hopes escalate to a surety, from which she could fall into that state of depression, which lies dormant in everyone, at the base of Mount Hope.

"Ohh—this would be perfect." Her mother showed her a dress, but she shook her head.

"No dresses." She remembered more than one boy trying to ride her thigh with a hand before the accident, and with her not able to feel her thighs, she was uncertain about wearing dresses to occasions that could offer up opportunities. *What are you afraid of?* she told herself. *Might as well get some*, the voice continued.

A MEMORY OF FOREVER

Waiters were flying by with huge three-foot round trays packed with pasta and seafood dishes, which were the staple dishes if you came to Luigi's on any given night, except on Wednesday's steak night. The attraction, besides the excellent food, was the flying waiters with the huge trays, and the fact that if a waiter dropped one on a customer, that table didn't have to pay. There were twenty or so tables, all covered in a traditional red-and-white-checkered table clothes. It was, by far, the best restaurant in Genoa, but it was so discreet that there were hardly ever any tourists there.

Tonight was no disappointment. She felt she could have eaten another plateful of spaghetti, which she and Mario had agreed to order and share. After a few bites, they found fun in giving the other a forkful of spaghetti, and using the thick garlic bread like sponges to wipe off the thick red sauce from each other's chin and cheek. She was usually shy and unsure, but she found herself brought out by Mario's careless and carefree attitude, and she sensed Claudia watching their playful antics, but she *was* having too much fun to care. There was a very handsome man, with dark eyes and bushy brows and full lips and strong Italian features, a little thinner than she liked but she would forgive, paying attention to her. It felt great.

He had commented on her black leather skirt, which she checked much too often, just in case. She felt that her legs were too flabby and thin, even though she worked them each day; part of her ritual. Her white blouse with puffed shoulders, long sleeves, and silver cuff buttons in the shapes of butterflies, went perfectly with the black leather. She had put on little makeup, because her mother always told her she didn't need it. It all seemed to be working in her favor, and Mario had smiled genuinely upon seeing her.

"My sister says you are a famous painter?" Claudia's boyfriend asked her as they waited for the strawberry cheesecake.

"I'm only famous because of these." Serena pointed to her legs.

"Don't let her self-effacing manner fool you. Her paintings cost a small fortune," Claudia said, to Serena's embarrassment.

"It takes a lot of money to keep this heap moving," Serena said in the way of an excuse for her high-priced paintings.

"But how long have you been painting?" This time it was Mario who asked the question.

She stared into his black eyes, which were bright and intensely captivating. Finally she answered. "I guess it's been nearly ten years, maybe more."

"Well you must be very good then," Mario whispered, only for her ears to hear.

"What types of pictures do you paint—what inspires you?" Armand asked her.

Serena hoped that her friend would save her, but she was as interested in the answer as Armand, and now Mario, was. She had been asked this question many times, and each time she'd been saved by one thing or another. How could she explain her inspiration to people who knew her only as a handicapped painter, whose *normal* life had been exorcised by a bad-brake-having delivery truck, like a Catholic priest ridding a body of demons. Could they understand her visions or second sight, the world she saw when she truly dug into her reserves and creativity and imagination, that world where she felt her true love existed, where the sky was slightly brighter, the moon much bigger in the night.

She felt a hand cover her own, then a squeeze. "You don't have to if you don't want to," Claudia said understandingly.

She smiled at Claudia, then said, "It's hard to explain my inspiration, except that they come from another person inside, and another world, where things are different."

"Maybe I should take a look at one of your paintings," Armand joked.

"They're very good," Claudia assured.

The waiter came quickly from the double steel doors that led to the loading area, fire blazing from the top of their strawberry cheesecake, flames seemingly licking the ceiling as he came towards the table. Serena was thankful for the distraction.

She usually didn't let people push her wheelchair, but she had relented under Mario's persistence, and her own reluctance at putting on her old black gloves. He was now pushing her up the road to her house. The sun's light was fading from the sky, and the night sounds were coming to life around them. In the background they could hear the waves crashing against the rocks, but mostly they could hear the sounds of other families sitting down to dinner, or getting up from, rebounding through the forest around them, as if loud ghosts were at play within.

"It's lovely here," Mario said in the passing darkness.

"Yes," she answered wistfully.

"Is this your home?" They were rolling towards a driveway that went down and stopped in front of a lighted patio.

The house was semi-perched on a hill facing the Tyrrhenian Sea. The roof was a red Spanish clay, which stood out next to the green cypress trees, and oaks, which grew tall around the home. A row of six-foot high cypress bushes aligned the driveway, and provided privacy from the two-lane road, so one could only see the house if they stopped at the entrance to the driveway.

"My mother's up," Serena said. She looked through a small tubular hole in the bushes. It was a spot where even as a child she could check to see whether her mother of father were home, or if anyone were in her parents' bedroom.

"How do you know?" Mario asked.

"Look through here." She pointed to the hole, and then felt his face come down to her level. His profile was handsome, and his complexion was clear. She would love it if he would turn and kiss her in this intimate darkness. His earlobes were small, and perfect for her lips. He smiled, then started to turn, and her heart began to thump, her thin blouse suddenly feeling too thick for the heat coming off of her body. She felt hot, even on this cool night.

"You have the loveliest blue eyes I have ever seen," he said, his lips mere inches from her own.

"Are you going to kiss me? I haven't kissed a man in a very, very long time—" she started, but her words were smothered under his lips, his masculine touch searing her neck and ear, her chest and lungs. The woman in her demanded more, as his fingers lingered over her pulse, teasing her jugular, as if they could enter her bloodstream and charge and electrify her senses, toy with her secret places from beneath her skin and nerves and womanly microsensors.

Two headlight beams shown upon them, and then a car stopped next to them. Her father got out of the cab, pulled out his luggage, and paid the cab driver, all the while pretending not to see his daughter and the strange man.

"Serena," her father finally greeted, then he cast a look at Mario.

"Good evening—" Mario said. He put out his hand and her father gripped it with his own. "Nice to meet you." But this was ignored.

They stood like this for a moment, and she started to worry, for she'd never seen her father grip a man's hand like he was doing now. The embarrassment from being caught kissing was now turning to anxiety and apprehension.

"Be true to my daughter, for she is as special as the last second of sunlight, and as beautiful as each morning's rising sun, which promises a new day of life unexpected," she heard her father say.

He let go of Mario's hand, smiled at her, then walked down the driveway. Her mother ran out of the house and greeted him with a passionate kiss and hug, before they disappeared inside the house.

"You have nice parents," Mario told her.

"Yes, I know." She smiled and patted his hand, hoping he would start kissing her again.

He pushed her to the front door instead.

"I had a great time, Serena," he said, then bent down and kissed her softly, but nothing close to what she needed to douse the fires burning inside of her body.

"Me too," she said after he stood back up. "Maybe we could do this another time?"

"Sure." He smiled back at her, but checked the windows to see if her parents were watching, then said, "Ciao," and walked up the driveway.

Serena rolled over to the side of the house, where there was a view of the sea, lit by the moonlight. The view struck her profoundly, and she felt a chill, and something else.

The front door opened a minute later, and Serena's mother walked onto the patio, knowing that her daughter would need comforting. A cool breeze ruffled her cotton nightgown, and blew strands of her mussed hair behind her. The night was cool. She saw Serena's moonlit silhouette, near the side of the house, facing away, towards the sea.

"Serena?" she called, then smiled to herself and walked over to the view point. The smile on her lips faded as she neared her daughter and found her wet and stinking of the docks. Then she saw Serena's eyes. Her mouth opened wider than it had in forty-nine years and a scream of terror issued forth, every cell of her body releasing its oxygen content in the scream, as she viewed her daughter's cataract-colored eyes—

"Julius, come for me," she heard her daughter say as she was backing away.

"What in Heaven's name?" Serena's father said, as he bumped into his retreating wife.

10

THE CHASE BEGINS

DAWN CURSED HIM, and her own stupidity, for the first time in her life committing murder seemed a viable option to solve her problem. Break the law she swore to uphold. It would definitely be premeditated. Maybe over in Europe, if the pictures were, in fact, Dutch Giovanni. *I can't get caught,* she told herself.

A car swerved out in front of hers.

"Another prick, I'll bet," she hissed to herself.

The Phoenix Chief of their division had suggested—*more like order,* she thought—that she team up with Lieutenant Franco, and somehow she knew that Franco had planned it. But before she was going to pick Franco up, she had gone to Agent Striker's apartment. What she was looking for; A .32 semi-automatic, made completely of carbon fiber and plastic compounds, that would pass through any airport metal detector. *My plan versus the fat pricks,* she told herself, feeling her confidence rise, and the holster making her inner thigh itch.

She swung the car into the prison parking lot, nearly running into a few guards. *It must be change of shift*, she thought, because there were too many guards milling about and doing nothing. They were all carrying weapons, from shotguns to HK-5L7s, with a few M-16s and Mini-14s thrown in for good measure. She swore she could even see a few MP-5s, which were strictly special operations weapons. Not even she was allowed access to some of the weapons that these prison guards had.

"Jeez, an army of untrained macho idiots," she whispered to herself.

The hundred-plus guards were waiting for orders after having been issued weapons and ammunition from the prison armory.

They were launching a full scale search of the town. Any off-duty guard not scheduled to work the swing-shift (1 p.m. to 9 p.m.) had been ordered to report to the Central Unit parking lot. Not that they needed to be ordered to dress in camouflage clothes and bulletproof vests, and tote semiautomatic and full-auto weapons. Some even perpetrated a higher fraud by wearing the all-black uniforms of the SWAT and ESU type units. Even on this 110-degree day. Later, these beer-drinking brawlers would be bossing their own neighbors around, trying to go through people's houses, all in the name of catching a convict, like some totalitarian army with no constitutional guidance, like they did to the prisoners, behind the walls, out of sight of the public. A few men and women would be injured, but it would be acceptable in the course of their search for Dutch Giovanni, who was being charged fifteen thousand dollars (if they ever caught him) for today's search.

The attitude of the masses was a worker-bee mentality, while the administration, knowing what a boring job being a guard was, tried to keep the state prison employees and inmates in constant conflict. This created an army-enemy complex, the guards being the army, the inmates locked behind bars being the enemy. When one has an enemy, then one has a goal that is not so menial as just "guarding" another human being until his sentence expires. The punishment, according to the law, was that loss of freedom. The prison system, by their own accord, have started to arbitrarily punish men and subject them to torturous psychological games and physical punishment, far beyond any measure called for. They had unleashed an army of men with overinflated egos, in the name of keeping criminals at bay, whose mass has now grown to monstrous proportions, bulging with too many budgets, and too much power, with lies and corruption pooling beneath it all.

She didn't feel comfortable enough to get out of her car because she had drawn a few suspicious looks from the predominately male group of guards, who acted as if they were law enforcement. She stepped out into the heat, and the loud talk and laughter of too much testosterone in the air. Her training consisted of dealing with the psychological mentality of a hostile crowd, and she felt she might need it today, as five or more men walked towards her, hands on their weapons, as if—

"Federal agent!" she spoke loud enough for anyone within fifty feet to hear. She had her badge in her hand, silver shield in view. She wasn't taking any chances, not in this prison town. It was like dealing with a bunch of territorial idiots who were suffering from the Zimbardo effect, and liked it. Even still a potbellied man, with two bars on his collar, decided to check her out.

"Ma' am—"

"Agent Carroll," she told him.

"Agent Carroll. Nice name, ma' am—uh—what brings you to Central Unit? Oh, excuse me, I'm Captain Koontz, OICOfficer in—"

"I know, officer in charge." She smiled sarcastically, but it didn't seem to get past his smile.

The captain put out his hand.

Well, maybe they're not all that bad, she thought, reaching out and shaking his hand, then nearly losing a ring, trying to get it back. *Maybe they are.*

"You sure are pretty for an agent. Could I see yer badge again, ma'am." He feigned suspicion.

"Do you know where Lieutenant Franco is?" She saw worry lines appear at the corners of his eyes.

"What do you need him for?" he asked, a bit defensively.

"Did you hear me, Captain Koontz? I'm an F-B-I agent looking for Lieutenant Franco, regarding a criminal investigation, and an international fugitive search warrant for one Dutch Giovanni," she said slowly and firmly.

"Oh that, yeah, we're gonna do our own search. That's why the troops are together. We're gonna sweep the town, make sure it's clear, you know, plus it'll be good training for some of the new officers. Got lots of newbees coming in—"

"Listen," she cut him off, "do you know where the lieutenant's at, or not?"

"I just might," he teased.

"Jeez, never mind." She shut her car door. "I'll find him myself."

"I don't think so, ma'am, and I'd like to see—"

"Or what? You gonna have your army of overarmed wannabe cops strip search me?" She couldn't believe this was happening. No wonder why no recording devices were allowed behind the walls, by inmates or guards or visitors. NO RECORDING DEVICES, a sign read, along with many other warnings.

"Actually," he looked her up and down, "I'll do that myself."

"Captain. Agent Carroll." Lieutenant Franco stood behind Dawn. "Do you two know each other?"

She saw the captain visibly pale. "Lieutenant." It was a greeting of sorts, thrown out like a fishing line to see if it would be accepted or rejected.

"How's your wife, Captain?" Franco smiled a shark's smile.

The man turned and walked back into the throng of activity without another word.

She saw that Franco was smiling triumphantly, even though the man who had just walked away, dejected and conquered, was supposed to be his superior officer. *I will be glad to leave this backwards prison world, which,* she thought, *belonged in some pseudo Lord of the Flies novel. Men do change when given absolute power,* she thought, before turning her full attention to Franco.

"So, we're bound for Europe," he said nonchalantly.

"How'd you know? Never mind, I don't want to know." She got back in her car and started it before rolling down the window. "You packed?"

"Follow me. My stuff's at the house." He pointed to a yellow house just beyond the prison gates.

"Figures," she thought aloud. On her way in she had wondered who would be stupid enough to live one hundred yards from the prison walls.

She was parked and waiting when Franco came out of the house, which, she had to admit, was a nice home. A woman pushed the screen door open, walked down the steps, and when Franco came out, she gave him a tender kiss. Dawn watched the woman's lips, and knew that she had told Franco that she loved him.

"Every dog has his day," she whispered to herself, her stomach churning.

Franco's previous wife, and mother of his twenty-year-old son, had died in a fatality car crash just ten miles from where she was parked right now. It was a suspicious crash; the brakes having went out and another car having been involved. The bureau, after quietly looking into the files, had found a forensic examination document regarding a dent in the victim's car, and paint chips from another vehicle. There was no follow up. In fact, the case was shoved under the rug, and handled as an accident. Franco had friends everywhere.

"Ready to go?" Franco said as he got into the car.

The shocks and springs adjusted noticeably. "Japanese cars," Franco mumbled, but wore a smile.

He seems too damn happy, or up to no good, she thought to herself, pulling onto the two-lane road. Her inner thigh holster, where the .32 was, began to bother her. She wriggled, hoping that would alleviate the itch-like irritation, and felt his eyes come to bear on her.

"Something wrong, Agent Carroll?"

Someone was shaking him gently, a soft whisper in his ear, and the fresh smell of cinnamon in the air. He could feel her in his arms, his true love. Swan, yes, that was her name. Then a gentle rocking again, and a soft whisper—

"Are you awake?" The young Chinese girl smiled down at him.

—and then the dream was fully gone. He smiled back at the naked girl, wondering if he had even slept with her. She was quite beautiful, but he remembered falling asleep when she was giving him a back rub.

A man with a small black bag walked into the room, and the woman quickly put on her kimono, and glided off of the bed.

This was all confusing for Dutch, who had barely come fully awake, and was still suffering from the effects of the pleasant dream. The man came right up to the bed, and smiled at him, while reaching and checking his pulse.

"How are you feeling?" the Chinese doctor asked.

"A little dry mouth, some dizziness yesterday, but otherwise I feel good," Dutch said.

"That is residual effects of the radiation," he said. "I think the medication and rest was all you needed. You should suffer no long-term effects."

"I guess I'll have to take your word for it." Dutch looked at the thin Chinese man, who seemed to shift under his gaze.

"You get dressed. Mister Pee is waiting for you in the dining room." The man got up and left the room without further courtesy.

"Breakfast." He threw back the covers and forgot his nakedness.

The woman smiled at him and started to approach him in anticipation of pleasuring him, which she had started to do while he was asleep, but did not.

The door opened just as she came over to the bed. Once again she turned, grudgingly, and walked back into the bathroom. Mister Pee, and Ping Li smiled brightly, upon seeing his excitement.

"I see my ladies have been satisfactory." Mister Pee smiled, and tightened the knots of his red robe, looking at Dutch's nakedness. Ping Li said something in Chinese to Mister Pee, and Pee smiled and nodded in agreement. "He says you may have ruined her." The two men laughed.

Dutch was used to being naked in the presence of men, but not to being sized and measured and complimented. He stood up and searched for the robe.

"You know where my duffel bag is?"

Mister Pee looked questioningly at Ping Li, who was already moving towards a closet. He opened a closet door. One of two.

Dutch took the hint and walked over to the closet, which seemed too large for his few clothes, that were hanging neatly on thick wooden hangers. He grabbed a pair of slacks and a dress shirt and quickly stepped into them. He saw the girl peeking out from the bathroom.

A MEMORY OF FOREVER

At the table they were left alone after the servants brought their breakfast, which consisted of cinnamon rolls, fruits, milk, juice, and fresh ground coffee.

A kimono-wearing servant brought him a pair of house slippers and Mister Pee took him on a tour of Hacienda del Gravado. As they walked along a glass-enclosed walkway, which went around the back of the house, giving a pleasant view of the entire grape orchard, Mister Pee explained and apologized. The servants followed far behind, but as they rounded the corner, which led to the large glass room he'd been in earlier, he could see them trailing like the light trails of a comet. All the extravagance and multitude of things to view, including the massive magnitude of the exterior, gave him a headache. He was used to the prison cell, the Spartan simplicity of living, watching his back, and writing a few letters, or—at least trying—writing a novel. He had no need to worry about food, or housing, only the necessities, in an extended actuality of Walden, except in a desert prison.

After they were once again back at the glass table, inside of the huge—and it was bigger than the house he grew up in—patio, the servants brought more coffee and pastries, although he was sure that his stomach was quite full from the breakfast of moments ago. It had *only* taken them an hour to walk through most of the rooms, as Mister Pee explained in a museum guide's animation what each piece was, and the hundred-yard walk around the rear of the house.

They sat for a moment before Mister Pee spoke, and this silence made Dutch feel as if he were about to be bestowed with something important, or worthy of a king…or emperor in this case.

"I have decided to call my good friend into this matter, and I have made arrangements for your new identity, and a half million-dollar bank account." Mister Pee was watching the orchard people walk down the rows of vines.

Dutch was thinking *A HALF MILLION DOLLARS!*

"Will that be enough…to right these wrongs done to you?" It was not, yet it was, a question.

"That's more than enough, when you may well have just killed me," Dutch spoke in a flowing Italian.

"Ahh," Pee smiled, "that is perfect, Mister Lorenzetti." He took out a Gucci billfold, and pushed it over to Dutch.

These guys are Gucci crazy, Dutch thought, still a bit thrown off at hearing himself speak another language aloud. Before it was just a guess that he might be able to understand Italian, but he never thought he could speak it.

Even then Dutch was thinking in Italian.

"I live in Naples?" He was thankful for his English.

"Yes, you own a small bakery and have been traveling for the past ten years."

"The guy in the picture has short hair?" *The guy in the picture is me*, he thought, then reached up.

"I have taken liberties, for your own safety."

His hair was gone, nearly all of it except for about an inch.

"I always wanted a crew cut," Dutch said with a smile. *Fuck it*, he told himself, *the hair will grow back*.

11

...WILD RIDE

FABIO LORENZETTI. The more he said it to himself the more he liked the name. He was also dressed the part of a wealthy, self-sufficient, Italian businessman; new suit, tie, shoes, and the Gucci billfold.

Mister Pee told him that someone would meet him at an airport in Marseille, and would take him the rest of the way. No names were given, but it would be clear who was who, he told Dutch. It was like a spy game, and this was a comfort, because he knew they could just off him at any moment, save themselves a half million dollars, and at the same time, be rid of a potential witness. He had been subtle in his wariness, taking what they gave him, but not showing that he was in survival mode. He had learned this trick in prison, where a showing of wariness or fear was like a beacon attracting the predators. If he were in Mister Pee's shoes, he would have thought about this option.

The windows were so tinted that he could hardly see Madrid, nor the outskirts, as they drove to a small private airport. The dark-blue

Mercedes was sturdy, and powerful beneath them, which made Dutch feel comfortable. Often he was envisioning himself with *her*, living together in a small comfortable home with not too many distractions to lead them away from their love for each other. He was daydreaming of a few children when the car stopped.

When he got out, he saw a short asphalt runway, and two planes. The badly-in-need-of-painting terminal was a rickety structure that looked as if it would fall over if there was a strong gale. The smell of airplane fuel and oil was heavy in the air.

"This is my airport," Mister Pee said, as they walked towards the double door entrance.

Inside the main area of the one room terminal was a dusty desk, and even dustier chairs. Some things were on the ground, and a bathroom door was off its hinges, leaning against the door frame at an off angle. Something skittered around inside the women's bathroom, but Mister Pee didn't even glance, heading for the double doors that opened onto the runway instead.

"Good, they're ready." Mister Pee rubbed his hands, watching a large American with long dirty hair putting away the fuel hose.

The man turned and saw them. He smiled a big smile, a limp cigar jammed past a mustache, which lifted then fell. "Ready to go, Mister Pee," the pilot said in a deep crackling voice, not unlike the drunk captain of the fishing boat Orca in JAWS.

"Thanks for your help, Mister Pee." Dutch put out his hand, which Pee took firmly in his own.

"Here is a card, if you ever run into trouble." Pee handed Dutch a card. "You have any trouble getting where you're supposed to, give the number call, however, things should go smooth, or I'll hear about it. I admire you, Mister Lorenzetti. Be safe." He bowed and walked away.

"Wow man! He must like the hell outta ya!" The pilot nearly shouted in Dutch's ear. "I ain't never heard him say not so much as by your leave." The last was said in sarcasm. "Hell, the pay's good! That all the luggage you have? Come on, plane's ready to go!" He started to pat Dutch on the back, then saw the oil and grease on his hands and stopped in midair.

The pilot led him to the rusty twin-engined beast. It looked like a smaller version of an old DC-3. The pilot walked up into the open door and went inside. Dutch threw up his duffel bag and then climbed the three steps to the cabin.

"Hey, shut that door, will ya!"

Dutch turned and shut the door. He was surprised by the new leather interior, which betrayed the rust bucket exterior. The engines roared to life, and maintained a throaty growl. Once accustomed to the shaking and vibrations he took a longer look around. The cockpit was exposed to the twelve passenger seats, which made for a very informal setting. There was a bar, a computer, and a small table. First class—

"Name's Manuel Noriega, why don't you stow that carry on and come on up!" he shouted.

"Yeah right," Dutch said to himself, then threw the duffel under a seat, and walked up front. "Names Du—Fabio, nice to meet ya."

"Yeah right," the pilot said aloud, then showed Dutch some very white teeth, and taxied the airplane onto the runway.

"How long will it take to reach Marseille's?" Dutch shouted above the roar of the engines, now understanding why the pilot shouted.

The pilot turned to him as the plane was speeding down the runway, and Dutch was suddenly sorry he even asked.

"I fly fast, man! Should only take a few hours at most—you'll have to excuse me for a moment!" A smile.

Dutch saw the quickly approaching vineyard, and then the bottom fell out and the plane was seemingly going straight up, the pilot yeehawing happily. Only now did he noticed that the sky was partly cloudy, with patches of blue, as they rocketed up towards that alluvion of earth's light-blue floating sea. Then they were righted and level just above the clouds.

"Yeehaw," Dutch said quietly, his stomach slightly queasy.

"*Holy shit, man!*" Dutch yelled, eyes wide, every muscle bracing against the impact of the ground, though they were still a few thousand feet above the Mediterranean Sea. He'd only just drifted into a nap.

"Okay, we might be having some trouble," the pilot finally admitted. "Didn't mean to wake you."

The plane's number two engine had just quit, and the heavy plane had rolled to the left, then the right, and then started to dive. Dutch was watching the gauges, listening to a low-toned alarm, but otherwise he thought it was eerily quiet.

"Restart the engines? Maybe you don't have the fuel."

"It won't just restart!" the sweaty pilot interrupted, as if he were a teacher in a fifth grade classroom.

"Oh shit indeed," the pilot admitted, his bugged-out eyes seeing the Med below.

Dutch wanted to strangle the pompous ass, but he was too busy looking at the gauges and switches and meters and dials. *Both engines just don't quit at the same time without there being some sort of human screw-up involved*, he told himself, then saw a switch on the panel; Reserve tanks — Main tanks. He switched it from the main tanks to the reserve tanks, because a voice inside him said that this was the problem. He'd tried to kickstart a bike for a half an hour one day, when he was about thirteen, until finally his uncle came out, laughed, turned the fuel flow dial under the gas tank, put his foot on the kickstart and put his weight on it, and the bike instantly reen-nee-neeeed to life. Maybe the principle would parallel, and the engines would suddenly roar to life, and if not, he'd at least die seeing the pilot sweat.

Engine one fired, then engine two, and Manuel Noriega strained against the diving plane, pulling the bar back into his crotch, the sea coming up fast, individual white caps now clearly discernable on the navy-blue-green canvas.

"Help! Me! Pull! The! Wheel! Fabio!" The Pilot strained, and Dutch grabbed the wheel in front of him and pulled it towards him with all his strength.

The elevators and ailerons were alive in his hands, fighting against him, trying to keep the plane pointed towards the sea, and inevitable death. A full day could have passed in the fifteen seconds before the plane finally sighed, and dug into the air, and leveled off. The dials stopped their click-clacking, and spinning, and the low-toned I-told-you-so alarms quieted. Ten meters below a cold sea still waited patiently to claim them.

A MEMORY OF FOREVER

"Whooooweeeee!" the pilot shouted, looking over at Dutch, who was looking in front of the plane, face pale.

A huge tanker zoomed in at them, in slow motion, and the plane shot up into the air at a forty-five-degree angle to avoid the hull. He could see the oil workers on the deck shaking their fists or waving. He could see the six-inch bolts that kept the hulls steel skin attached to the frame, and the thick cable, which ran around the edge of the entire aquamarine-colored deck. It was half a football field wide, and at least three long.

The engines over-revved as the plane once again leveled off. Manuel, sweating, smiled at him, but then looked out front again.

"Pretty close, man," Dutch joked.

"Fuck you—but I like you anyways," the pilot said quietly.

The plane taxied dangerously, but he could handle anything now. Dutch stepped out and his vision was drawn to a man standing next to a tint-windowed black Mercedes. The man was Italian, barrel-chested, around fifty, with a full head of pepper-gray hair and a solid jaw. Dutch could see that the man's nose had been broken a few times, as he neared.

"Nice flight, Mister Lorenzetti?" Señor Giuseppe asked.

Dutch was about to tell the tale when the pilot jumped in.

"A great flight, Señor. Take care, Fabio—I'll be your wingman anytime." Then he shut the door and the plane began to taxi back onto the runway of the private landing strip.

"Quite a character, that man," Señor Giuseppe commented, then turned his gaze on Dutch. There were dark, intelligent eyes behind the clear gold rimmed glasses. "I was asked to drive you to your new home, and teach you basic *Italiano*. My name is Señor Giuseppe."

Dutch shook the man's hand, then picked up his duffel and checked to be sure he had his Gucci billfold, and the necklace, which he'd superstitiously held between his fingers as the plane had been descending.

During the scenic drive, on a swerving and curving road that was crookedly parallel to the coastline, Señor Giuseppe instructed Dutch in basic Italian, and the ways of Italians, and about where he was going. He noted the oddly old world pronunciations that the American made, and even some words that he himself had forgotten existed. Then Dutch asked a complicated question in Italian without blinking, and he stopped the car—

"You bullshitting me or what?" He asked, seriously.

Dutch knew this man would be a tough man to defeat in a one on one fight, and that he was a very serious man. Señor Giuseppe thought about his explanation, then drove off, mulling it over, as Dutch looked at the passing vistas.

The exhibition along the road to Monaco was distracting, and inviting. At some spots one could look from the road to the sea for as far as the eye can see. At other areas there were thick stands of cypress, juniper, oak, elm, pine, evergreen, acacia, apple, cherry, peach, plum, maple, and even a beech tree. Once, when they were driving very close to the coastline, he swore that he saw a couple palm trees.

Many of the hills and low mountains were massive granite and lime stone formations, which were thrust out of the earth's crust, and over the centuries had collected little splotches and caches of greenery. Castles and cattle joined natures cacophonous symphony of growth, as if the fifteenth century had never left France. The smells varied from wet grasses, to sweet cherry tree blossoms, to alfalfa and straw, to damp moss, to the fresh sea untainted by man's mechanical menagerie of ships, cars, and cranes. Dutch's unexposed senses could not discern some of the scents. The sunshine was only rarely blocked out by drifts of clouds, which differed from the America version of a cloud. These seemed lower and lighter, as if they would dissolve at any moment into that light blue canvas above. They passed small tractors pulling heavy loads on tipsy-looking wagons, even a couple of horse-drawn wagons that looked a century old, save for the rubber tires. After many curves on the rocky face of a jutting mountain, going up and up, back and forth, and back and forth once more, he saw the Principato di Monaco, and its port, La Condamine, filled with activity.

Señor Giuseppe drove slower than was necessary, so his passenger could see the port and the city from this high road. The port, he saw, was dotted with many cruiseliners, while, in the marina, there were many large white yachts of the rich and famous—and sometimes infamous—he knew.

As far inland as one could go before reaching the tops of hills, or mountains, there were hives of buildings on the Northeastern face of the concave curve of the mountain. Castles and palaces could be seen, and then the road turned inland and went steeply downward.

They stopped at a two man road block, which passed for customs. Señor Giuseppe did all the talking and smiling and nodding. His own passport was looked at, stamped, and passed back. They were told where to get a visa if they planned on staying in Monaco, or gamble in the casinos.

The plan was to make Genoa by nightfall, and hand his package over to a cousin from Naples, who knew nothing of what was really going on. His other plan had not panned out. He was suspicious of someone in the famiglia trying to gain power, which meant they'd have to take him out, but to his delight it did not work.

He had told his son his exact traveling plans, because it was he who Señor Giuseppe suspected, after much thought and inner turmoil. He'd had his best man follow him to the French border, and then waved off the protection. If they were planning a hit, it would have been somewhere in Italy, just in case, where officials could still be bought and local police swayed. This was also why he would be handing Dutch over in Genoa, instead of taking him all the way to his house in Rome. Just in case. He could not afford, and nor would it be honorable, for him to not return this favor to Mister Pee.

Señor Giuseppe also knew that Monaco was not the place to be wanted by the law, even if you owned the biggest yacht in the marina, or had the biggest car in town. The police officers in the province were polite, but very bored, and tended to be zealous in their endeavor to catch a criminal. How he knew this was because he had been chased by them, under a different name and face, twenty years ago. It was a young Chinese Tong member who saved his ass, and they had a friendly arrangement ever since, even though he was a member of the Italian mafia, "Cosa Nostra," or "Our Thing." His family name went all the way back to the Sicilian Vespors who revolted against the French Angevina, in 1282, when the French ruled Sicily. He'd earned his respect like most others do, against the advice of his father, and to the approval of his grandfather. This family name was well known in Monaco, at least to the elder French law enforcement officials.

Señor Giuseppe spent twenty years earning his respect, until finally he was appointed underboss of the second biggest family in all of Italia. His "family business" could be anything from delivering a legitimate package of goods to murder to driving an escaped convict cross-country to a new life.

Señor knew that Fabio Lorenzetti was the American who had escaped from prison, and had possibly killed an FBI Agent and somebody else, in the doing. He understood Pee's secrecy, however, he was too old to jump into something that could turn into an international scandal without checking it out. Due to the fact that Mister Pee had expressed a near emphatic promise of safe passage for this man, he was doing it himself. If someone else had done it, and screwed up, it would be an embarrassment to the entire famiglia Castiglione. But he also found himself enjoying Dutch's company, and quiet confident manner, though, Señor Giuseppe was still unnerved by the spooky genius Dutch had at learning the Italian language.

Dutch didn't say anything as they drove through Monaco's crowded streets, even though he wanted to get out and play, live a little, get rid of the anxiety and cabin fever that had grown during his stay in a cell, for twenty-two hours a day seven days a week for over seven years. Women, in string bikinis—that wouldn't be allowed on an American Beach, unless declared a nude beach—walked, no, strolled by like champion bred quarter horses. He started to roll down the tinted window to get a better look, when he felt an arm on his own.

"Tourists—American tourists." Señor Giuseppe kept his hand on Dutch's arm, but the window was already moving up.

"Right, they could recognize me," Dutch said in Italian. He felt Señor Giuseppe's hand lift off of his arm.

Even still, his eyes searched out the faces and expressions of the women, hoping to see her, the one who would make him throw caution to the wind, jump out, and chase after her. She would recognize him, he knew, and she would run to him and jump into his arms and he would swing her light body around and around and kiss her over and over—

"Mister Lorenzetti?" Señor Giuseppe got his attention. The car had stopped.

Dutch saw two police men looking in through the windshield at them. It was the only glass on the Mercedes that wasn't tinted.

"Don't say anything—do you have cigarettes?" Señor Giuseppe asked.

"Yeah," Dutch answered.

"Have two packs ready."

"Good afternoon, officers," Señor Giuseppe said in fluent French. "Do you know the easiest route to the Italian border?"

Dutch lit a cigarette of his own, which caught the attention of the one officer who was leaning down, looking through Señor Giuseppe's open window. He smiled a confident smile and took a drag, remembering to look confident, though he didn't need to try. He offered the officer a cigarette, with a simple gesture.

"Let me have two packs of cigarettes for these kind police officers," Señor Giuseppe said.

After giving instructions, which Señor Giuseppe feigned needing, the officers smiled and walked away. Dutch saw them lighting American Marlboros, and patting each other on the back, through the rear window.

"Suckers," Dutch said under his breath. He didn't like cops, American or French or Zimbabwe. The two cops who had testified at his trial had flat out lied, and the jury believed them, simply because of the badge and the uniform. Even when evidence pointed the other way, the jury had looked past it, as if the facts were like a thin fog that would dissipate at some later hour. Those two cops had a purpose as well; to put a twenty-year-old in prison. Dutch would have received probation, or county time, for the true crimes, which were simply being stupid and drunk. This prejudice went beyond the two street cops, into the prison, where the same badge-wearing affliction ran rampant. The Zimbardo effect was like the splitting mass of an atom, that throws off enormous amounts of energy, infecting everything around with a cold and hot fire, leaving invisible and visible scars, which will last so long as a man lives. Ninety-five percent of the guards were suffering from this psychological syndrome, and the Arizona Department of Corrections meant to keep it that way. That's why he hated them.

Señor Giuseppe put the car in gear and pulled away from the curb, continuing the fifteen mile per hour cruise through Monaco's winding, and tourist-filled streets, which he knew well.

"I knew the one officer—He arrested my son two years ago."

"How many bills you slip him?" Dutch queried.

Señor Giuseppe smiled mischievously. "Only a couple."

"Pretty slick, Señor Giuseppe. I don't think that other cop saw a thing."

"I try to keep in practice by slipping my grandchildren and nephews money under their parents' noses." Señor Giuseppe laughed.

"Wish you were around my house when I was a kid." There was a flash of sadness. He'd never had the chance to see his own grandparents, and the only moment he had was the ring, which was on the necklace around his neck. Dutch's grandmother had given it to his father, who gave it to his mother, whose finger he took it off after the accident.

They drove in silence for a while, Señor Giuseppe watchful, Dutch surveying the new sights, the things and beings one loses track of while in cement boxes and behind bars.

"Beautiful," a whisper; the sun made its final bow to night.

"How long were you inside?" Señor Giuseppe queried, after the sun dropped below the horizon, splashes of purple and blue and yellow above.

"About ten years. I didn't even do the crime." Bitterly.

"I did five years in a Sicilian jail, before my family got me out with a little push—"

"What? A bribe?" Dutch was curious.

Señor Giuseppe looked him in the eye to bring the point home. Then he spoke. "My family hung the judge outside of his courthouse on the flag pole—his own son was the one who had committed the crime I was locked up for." He paused, flicking the headlights on. "I know the bitterness you have, but you'll have to get rid of it or it'll give you ulcers. Believe me, I know—"

They were rounding a bend, leaving the city, going up towards the Italian border. The customs road block came into view, then the road dipped. It looked like there were too many cops at the check point, and he interrupted Señor Giuseppe to voice his opinion.

"Get in the backseat," he said in a voice that left no room for argument. "And don't speak—"

"English," Dutch finished, then jumped into the backseat.

"Keep your passport—I have one that Mister Pee provided, just in case they were writing names down." The heavy car began to slow at the lighted checkpoint.

"Seems like a lot of cops." Dutch commented again.

"Yeah." Señor Giuseppe's gut was churning. Something wasn't right here, and he swore he recognized two of the officers by the small guard shack.

He stopped the car, and the customs official tapped on the window.

"Please, step out of the car, sir."

Dutch had a sense of *deja vu*, and prepared for the worst.

12

She was with him, could still smell him if she closed her eyes long enough, and willed his face to appear, even in the cold environment of this room.

Alfredo Donatello's office near the Artist's Plaza was small and spartan. The walls were a light avocado green and were bare except for two certificates, one from Roma Medical College, and another from a Swiss School, each dated in the 1950s. The wooden floor was polished and dark. An examination table off to the right, if one were to walk in through the only door, while to the left was a large desk, with two chairs in front of it. Outside the door was a small waiting room, and one nurse, where Serena' s parents were at now. He had been their family doctor for over forty years.

"Can you tell me what you go through when you have a seizure, Serena?" he asked. He could find nothing, physiologically, wrong with her, except that the lower reflex test caused her right leg to jump, and her toes to curl. However, when he asked her if she could move her toes, she could not. He didn't want to give her any false hopes, but he was sending her to the specialist in Rome. The only other odd thing was her clothes and hair, which smelled of the sea, as if she'd just taken a night swim. But she could not possibly swim.

"I feel as though I am somebody else, in some other time—I can't explain it any better than that, Doctor Donatello. I'm sorry." *And I don't even want to admit that much*, she thought.

"It's quite alright, Serena. Have you thought about going back to Rome to examine your spine and legs?" he asked. "Have you been experiencing sporadic movement of your lower extremities—legs and feet?"

"Yes, but not that often." A sparkle of hope was creeping into her voice, and she fought hard to keep it from her heart.

"Well, your nerves may have healed, or are almost healed? It's not impossible, though improbable. I'm not a specialist, so don't get your hopes up." He laughed kindly. "But I see that I have already given you some hope—listen, I am going home this weekend, if you'd like, I will personally make sure that my friend takes a good look at you and tells you what your chances are." He smiled, then came around the desk to the chair she was sitting in. He held the wheelchair so she could slide into it. "I shall escort you myself to be sure."

Her foot moved, and she checked to see if he saw it.

"Did you—" she started.

"I sure did." He smiled and pushed the hair out of her face. *She is so very lovely*, he thought, then walked to the door.

Her mother was in her father's arms, and he was comforting her. She was wearing a heavy long coat over her nightgown. They weren't as scared as they'd been when they found her. She didn't like the way her mother was staring at her, wide-eyed, shying away from her when she rolled near to them. *What can I do about it?*

"I'll meet you at home, Papa," she said in passing. He started to say something, then thought better of it, and smiled at his daughter.

It was very dark outside in the small square, which most people who lived in Genoa, called the Artist's Plaza. There was nothing really significantly beautiful about the brick plaza, except that many people walked through it on their way to the markets, and were, therefore, likely to have their faces put on some artist's sketchpad.

A MEMORY OF FOREVER

The facades of every building facing the square were red brick, and when she had begun to sketch people's faces, she found that the pedestrian faces stood out from this dark red backdrop. She had drawn and sketched a hundred portraits and a thousand faces, when she was young, but always found her gaze drawn to the skies, buildings, or something other than a human being. Even now, as she wheeled her chair over the bumpy stone, she was looking at the night sky, which was alive with stars and planets and unknown twinkles that some astronomers tried to categorize.

She wondered if her lover was staring at the same sky at this very moment, then rolled home.

He had a way of soothing her, and loving her, and holding her head close so she could smell the man beneath the tunic and awful ink smells he sometimes carried home. His hands, strong like her own father's were, touching her everywhere, finding the real woman beneath the clothes, bringing her violently to life, like a chasm of hidden pleasures splitting, the senses imploding inside of her every fiber, filling her head, with scents and sights and stars. Millions of stars. She could taste him, even after she was jolted out of his arms and back into this world without him—

"Serena?" Her father's worried voice was loud.

"I'm fine, Papa," she called sleepily from her bed. She heard the floorboards creak. "Come in, Papa."

"Serena?" he said cautiously, stepping into her room. She turned her lovely gaze upon him, and it hurt his heart not to know if she would ever be whole again. His little baby, always happy and smiling as a child, so tragically cut off in her prime. He knew he was wrong to be even the slightest bit glad about it, but deep inside, where his instincts were bared to only him, in the secret recess that no one but God would ever see, he had at one time been relieved that he would not have to give his baby girl away to another man. He felt guilty for feeling this way sometimes, though he would accept it if some good man came along and married her. For him it would be a sad and happy day.

She saw a flash of sadness in his eyes that always melted her heart and made her want to hug him around his thick neck, like she used to when she was a little girl. He was always so kind to her, had never raised a hand or voice in anger, even when she did something bad, or disobeyed. He had always sat her down and explained to her about what she had done, why it was wrong, and what happens if you continue to behave in that manner. She and her mother were never in need of anything, although she didn't quite know what he did for a living. Not exactly.

"Papa?" she asked, pushing herself up against the wall so she could sit and talk.

"Serena," he faltered, "your mother, well she wants you to see the priest after you come back from Rome." He had not personally seen the "white eyes" that his wife had told him about, but he knew his wife did not make things up so lightly, or exaggerate like many women did, although it was difficult to believe that these sky-blue eyes looking back at him could ever become a "milky white."

"Why?" Serena was truly confused. "I go to church almost every Sunday."

"Your mother believes that you had demon eyes, that they turned white!" It sounded absolutely ridiculous said aloud.

She'd watched *The Exorcist*, with Linda Blair, a month ago with her mother, on a dark Friday night when her father had been away on business. It was their usual Friday night ritual, ever since she'd come home from the hospital. The movie had scared them both, and after it was over, they had gone around checking doors and turning lights on, looking in closets, and ended up scaring themselves. They were thankful when he returned, she remembered with a smile.

Serena tried to roll her eyes back and brought her hands up and made her fingers into claws. "Where is she at?" she said in a rough throaty voice, which nearly made her cough. "I am—" She couldn't keep it up, because her father had scooted off the bed and was buying into the act. She started laughing.

Then he smiled and attacked her with tickle fingers until she was out of breath. When she begged him to stop, he did. He pushed her golden hair out of her face, and kissed her on the forehead.

"I'll talk to her, but you think about doing it for her sake." He stood up to leave, then turned. "Serena—" he paused. "I'm sorry I interrupted you last night, for what I said."

He started to leave. "Papa—those were the most beautiful words I've ever heard you speak."

He smiled, then left the room.

She looked up at the stars painted on her ceiling, and the excitement and hope of finding out if she would walk again kept her up for many hours, until finally he came to her, and took her away.

The train ride was always a nerve-racking experience for her, even when she was with someone. Nobody came out and said rude things to her, but she felt it in their stares. As if her chair were taking up too much room on the crowded car. Doctor Donatello was having a time with two of her finished oil paintings.

They were older paintings, which she hoped Figaro couldn't tell were old. She'd done them last year, but she was sure that he wouldn't be able to tell, not that she was being deceptive. She had at least thirty paintings in the dry storage, and she never made agreements to give away "new" paintings, or "just done" paintings. Not often, but sometimes, she would sit on her spot above the sea, rapt in revery, amidst the pines and oaks and junipers behind her and the sea before her, the sea gulls squawking and diving, the waves booming against the rock formations, unaware of time being consumed by the great time piece above. This was not time subtracted from her life, but the realization of what the Orientals meant by contemplation and the forsaking of work. In this time she grew, but her paintings did not get done. *Thank God I have a back supply*, she told herself more than once.

Doctor Donatello had sat next to her, and questioned her further about the seizures. This was what he had decided they were. She was reluctant to reveal too much for fear of him thinking her mentally unstable, or worse, possessed by a demon. She smiled at this thought.

Prior to leaving, she had spoken to her mother and told her that she would see the priest, but by then her mother had calmed down, and Serena was sure that her father had spoken to her. Her mother believed it must have been a trick of light, or the full moon, but when she went to hug her mother, there was still some trepidation in her eyes. It bothered Serena that her mother would think her possessed, but she admitted to herself long ago that she experienced strange happenings, like the water, or the realistic visions and experiences.

She didn't want to think of those things now, as the train pulled into the station, which was smack in the middle of Rome's business district. She prayed that Figaro was at the station, like he'd said he'd be. The passengers all came to life, as if they'd just experienced a thrilling ride and were now safely land bound having escaped death. Most were polite enough to let her off first, but she heard the grumbles of the impatient and rude.

"Hey! Watch it!" Doctor Donatello told one young man who'd nearly knocked the paintings out of his hand.

"Serena! Serena!" she heard.

At age thirty-five, he was probably the third best art dealer in Rome, and openly gay, to the disapproval of many Italian art dealers and members of Italy's art world clique, many of whom were under the thumb of the Catholic church. Some thought he was a heroin user, or had AIDS, because he never went out in public without a long-sleeved shirt and he was so slim. These facts wouldn't be such a big deal if he'd only wear a business suit, Serena had suggested many times. Plus his size. He was at least six-foot-five, and everyone around was five-foot-nine. His superior attitude and perfect Van Dyke beard didn't help, only added to his announcement to them all that he was different from the rest of the world. He was. That was why she had chosen him, out of the many applicants who had made promises, and guaranteed massive amounts of money that she didn't need.

He took her hand and kissed it, as he always did when he saw her. "Ah, Serena, Serena," he greeted casually. "You look marvelous." His black Ray Bans did not reveal his eyes, but he was in a good mood.

"Thank you," she said over the hum of conversation. "For showing up."

"Oh, my heart! My heart!" He feigned a casual death. His green shirt and black pants stood out amongst the more conservative Romans. "I thought I was forgiven? Oh Lord!" He saw the paintings being roughly handled, and rushed to take them out of the doctor's hands.

"You must be Serena's art friend," Doctor Donatello said, almost in disgust, seeing the colors of his walls on a pair of men's pants.

Figaro checked the paintings. "Thank God you prepared them for a sea cruise," he said to Serena, before acknowledging the doctor's presence.

"Play nice, Figaro, this is my doctor." Serena couldn't keep from smiling though.

"Fine. Nice to meet you, Doc." Then just as quickly, he dismissed him and turned to her. "I'll meet you at the gallery, say sixish?"

"Fine, Fig, I'll be there."

"See you then, Doctor." Then he was plowing through the crowds, defending the canvases with his body.

"You have strange friends, Serena," Doctor Donatello said.

"You have to know him," she said, then patted the doctor's hand.

As they went up the hospital elevator she couldn't help but feel a giddy excitement, and a flash of hope, which spread through her whole body, *even*, she thought, *to my legs and feet*.

She waited almost a half hour after the specialist examined her, before he finally returned with the x-rays. She was still laying on the examination table.

"Well," Doctor Angelo started. "I can see several minor changes in your lower spine, but not enough to say that you could get up and walk away tomorrow. The reflex text I gave you, and the pain test, were negative."

"What about the sporadic sensations?" Doctor Donatello asked.

Doctor Angelo put his knuckles together. "Pretend my knuckles are the ends of electric wires, or your spinal discs. Not connected, but still held together by muscles, and still close enough to pass current every so often. This is what you're experiencing—your nerve ganglia is lining up every so often, and you're having sporadic connections, which cause movement. In many cases this lasts a patient's entire life." He smiled consolingly, and put his hands down.

"So what do you think, Michael?" Donatello plied his friend.

"Prognosis wise?" Doctor Angelo gave his friend a look, wishing he didn't have to answer the question in front of the patient, in front of another doctor, although Donatello was a good friend.

"I can't say whether or not she'll ever walk again. Nothing reconnected soundly enough for her to even exercise her muscles, although I must say her legs are in better shape than most paralytic patients. I'm sorry, but it's really a toss up, although I'll be prescribing some nerve growth enhancers, which may speed regrowth, or do nothing at all. The drugs are experimental, but I wouldn't prescribe them to you if they weren't safe. Okay?"

"Thank you, Doctor." She tried to smile.

Doctor Donatello patted her on the shoulders and looked down at her. "You need help getting dressed?"

"No, thank you," she said, keeping the pain out of her face, and the tears from her eyes.

After they left the examination room, she couldn't fight the tears off, and sobbed into her hands. She knew better than to get her hopes up, another voice asked, with her legs and feet moving every day now for the last six months. Doctor Donatello had seen them move, certifying that their movements were not just her hallucinations.

Tears stopped instantly as the familiar disorientation smacked into her body with such a new force, she could have swore she was someone else for a moment. Her first thought was to hurry and get dressed, because she didn't want to trance-out while she was in this hospital gown, or naked. Her head spinning, she suppressed a gag, cold sea water spraying out of her nostrils, and suddenly she felt the pressure of four-fathom deep water on every molecule of her skin. *Nooo*, her mind screamed. Not here, or they'll put me in a psych ward—

—and then it was gone, and she was still dry, and she quickly pulled her pants up her legs, thanking God in a silent prayer. Her left leg jerked, she could feel the cool loose denim against her tingling skin, coming up over her feet, calves and thighs. *Little tingles, lovely tingles, exquisite tingles*, she thought. It felt so good she forgot about the nearness of that inner feeling. The toe where the doctor had stuck a needle in hurt like hell. It was right on the left foot, her big toe, where he'd touched bone. It gave her the chills just thinking about it. She stayed forward, not wanting to move and lose the feeling. She put her other foot in the pant-leg opening, but she didn't feel it. It didn't matter to her at all, she would hobble on one leg if she could. To be upright amongst the people. To feel her leg muscles pull against her when she did her daily exercises. *Oh yes*, she thought, running her hand down the inside of her pant-leg, from her Achilles' tendon along her slim calve muscle to the tender area behind her knee to her thigh. She moaned at the sensation of fingernails on flesh, lightly scratching.

"Serena?" Doctor Donatello came into the examination room and saw her in the position she was in. He thought she was crying because of the bad news, but then he saw her smiling, until she realized he was watching. *Odd*, he thought.

"Oh." She didn't want to, but she sat up and pulled her pants all the way on. "I was just thinking." She hated lying.

"I have an emergency at my house, Serena, will you be okay?"

Serena thought that he looked too serious, and worried. "Is your family okay?"

"No, nothing like that, but someone is injured and I need to be there when the patient arrives. I have to leave now. Will you be okay?" he asked again.

"I'll be fine, Doctor Donatello. Don't worry about me." She smiled at him. She was feeling happy about everything, and if he was close enough, she would give him a big kiss, she would give a big baboon a big kiss, she was so excited. She could still feel the tingles in her left leg.

"Here, let me get your shoes." He bent down and put on her right loafer, then her left. He swore that she was holding her left leg steady for him...*no, not possible*, he thought. He shook his head and stood up, many other things racing through his mind.

"Thanks."

"You have my address if something comes up, or my number. Just come over if your friend doesn't show up. Okay. I don't want your father hearing that I neglected to look after his lovely daughter." He smiled, then left the room quickly. She heard him say something to Doctor Angelo, then he was gone.

As she rolled out of the elevator and down the hall towards the automatic doors, she could feel her leg falling asleep, tingling. She flexed and squeezed her thigh muscles, and wriggled. She returned smiles, which had erupted in response to her own merriment. The doors slid open and she passed through, into Rome, longing to jump up from her wheelchair and hobble to the edge of the sidewalk and put her arm out to hail a cab, instead waving from her seat.

The heat and exhaust fumes and noise of the city didn't bother her. She wanted to shout, to dance, to scream in hysterical happiness, even as the burning sensations in her leg increased, and she wriggled and wriggled and wriggled, until a cab pulled to the curb, because inside she knew things were changing, becoming, discovering, like a stream knows its river brother during the rains.

"Ciao—buona sera!" she said to the cabby. He smiled back as she gave him the address to Figaro's gallery. Her watch told her that she'd be about a half hour early, but that would be fine. She could sit and watch people and dream….

13

OBSTACLES

THE BULLETS SMACKED into the front windshield from all angles. Bubbles appeared in the glass, and with each appearance came the instantaneous popping sound. The heavy Mercedes rocked back and forth with the impacts, but nothing penetrated the interior.

Señor Giuseppe was down in the front seat, but Dutch couldn't see whether he was hit, or not, and wasn't all that confident that bullets wouldn't start flying. He had his head below the back rest of the front seat, but knew they'd both die if he didn't do something fast. *What*, he was trying to figure out. He didn't even know what had happened, except that one minute Señor Giuseppe was starting to open the door, and the next, he was flying backwards, and then the shooting started. The bullets slammed the driver's side door shut, and the glass came alive all around him.

He growled, jumped over the front seat, and slammed the car in gear. The motor was thankfully still running. He was sitting on Señor

Giuseppe's shins and stomping on the accelerator. He hoped the man was okay, in the back of his mind, as he heard shouts and warnings. He felt, then saw, a body roll over the front windshield, and thump-thump on the roof. "How'd'ya like me now, suckers!" he shouted. A loud snap as the heavy car snapped the wood barrier, like a large branch cracking under the weight of too much snow.

He fought for control, his head against the windshield, looking for the road. The gunfire stopped, but he kept his foot heavy on the gas pedal, thankful for the semi-straight road, at least not a winding one.

Señor Giuseppe moaned, and Dutch realized he was still sitting on his legs.

He didn't have time to stop and look, because there was still a good chance that they were being followed, and he couldn't see.

He wondered when the sirens and helicopters would swoop down and then the chase would begin until he either crashed and burned , or ran out of gas, or until a police ambush could be set up. Then a barrage of bullets. *At least that's how it's done in America*, he thought, trying to figure out his next move. He looked back through the rear window and found it hardly even scratched.

Nothing. An empty road.

He slowed and saw a dirt road that led up into a wooded area. He drove up the dirt road for five minutes, then parked underneath a huge oak tree, sure that the car couldn't be seen under the expansive canopy of leaves. A little smoke came from the radiator, and there were holes all around the hood and doors, but no bullet had done the damage it was meant to do. He left the dirt road about ten meters back, and there were rows of aligning oleanders, which hid the car from view. *We should be safe*, he hoped, then got out of the car.

There was a bullet entrance wound in the thick muscle of Señor Giuseppe's chest. Dutch knew this meant it was either a lung wound, or a shoulder wound, the difference between life and death. He needed water.

"Oh yes," Dutch said to himself as he gazed at the contents of the spacious trunk. "You gotta be kidding me?" He picked up an HK-SL7 submachine gun with silencer. One 9mm Ruger with silencer. A sawed-off shotgun, and one Remington Model 600 sniper's rifle with a long silencer. A couple of U.S. Army M-61 Fragmentation grenades and two Laws rockets. Dutch checked the magazine on the HK, and the Ruger. He put the 9mm in his waistband, at the small of his back.

He spread out a blanket under the tree, then went back for Señor Giuseppe. He took the first-aid kit and the three-gallon clear plastic jug of water from the trunk and brought them over to where he'd laid the injured man.

Dutch cut away the jacket and shirt so he could look at the damage. He didn't think it was a lung shot, or there'd be foam coming from Señor Giuseppe's mouth. He found the exit wound up behind the ear, at the end of an angry red welt that went up the man's thick neck.

"Good thing you work out," he said to himself as he wiped the blood off of the neck.

The bullet had entered the right pectoral muscle at an upward angle, hit the breast plate, went upwards into the thick neck muscles, and exited just behind the left ear. That was probably why Señor Giuseppe was knocked unconscious. He brought out a small medical book, and thumbed to the index for bullet wounds. He found three pages, and turned to them. The book was in Italian. He had no trouble.

"Clean wounds. If patient is shot near head or spine, do not move, and seek medical attention. That really helps out." He tossed the book back in the box and brought out some gauze and a bag of saline, then cleaned and bandaged the wounds. There was no really heavy bleeding.

After he was done, he waved the ammonia vial under Señor Giuseppe's nose. The eyes fluttered, the mouth opened, and Dutch felt an extremely strong hand gripping his ankle.

"Hey, Señor Giuseppe?" Dutch spoke calmly, trying to bring this stranger back into the conscious world.

"What's going on?" Señor Giuseppe asked, eyes still closed.

"You took a hit."

Dutch watched the older man's face turn red. The man was angry, and started cursing in old Sicilian. Señor Giuseppe started to get up, then moaned and fell back. He put a hand to his ear and moaned in pain. Dutch smiled and shook a few extra-strength pain killers into his hand, and poured some water into a bean-shaped irrigation dish.

"Here, take these." Dutch gave him the two pills and poured the water down his throat.

"Grazie, grazie."

"I was gonna tell you that you got shot in the chest, but the bullet came out of your head."

Señor Giuseppe understood now, but he was still mad as hell. The last thing he remembered was the muzzle flash and the instant sensation of sleep. He looked over at the car and smiled, which brought pain.

"I told my number one that it would save my ass one day." He laughed, even though it hurt to do so. "Come on, my friend, help me to stand."

Dutch stood up and reached down and they clasped hands. Dutch leaned back and pulled, then caught Señor Giuseppe, who wobbled a bit, then steadied. Dutch walked him to the dented hood. They both stared at the car, as if an old ship that had gotten them through a hundred-year storm.

"Good thing you proofed that glass," Dutch said.

He patted Dutch on the back. There was a bond now, which Dutch knew sprouted from the aftermath of battle, when you found who would, and who wouldn't, put his ass on the line for you.

"I'll frame the windshield in my hacienda." Señor Giuseppe walked towards the trunk, keeping a steadying hand on the car. Dutch followed and watched him bring out the silver suitcase, which Dutch had not bothered to check out. "Ever see one of these?" He popped the latches with his thumbs. Inside was a complex satellite communication relay phone. Señor Giuseppe turned to Dutch and smiled.

"He who dies with the most toys wins?" Dutch queried jokingly.

A half hour later they heard the whine of a Jet Ranger helicopter.

She felt like upchucking the entire shitty airline dinner. It kept coming up and going down, each time filling her nostrils with the acidic scent, and a worse aftertaste, like her esophagus was one of those teeter-totter wave makers people keep on their desks to help relaxation. The fat prick seated next to her was sleeping like a baby, and to top it off, the bowl of chili he'd ate at the Sky Harbor airport was now making a second appearance in the form of gaseous bursts.

"Oh my gawwwd!" She stood up. "I can't take this any longer." She walked down the aisle towards the rear of the 747, where the closest bathrooms were. Maybe she'd get lucky and find an empty seat she could plop into. No such luck. The plane was packed.

She sat down on the toilet seat, thankful she was wearing nylons, but still keeping her knees away from the grimy vinyl walls. A moment passed before the handle rattled as someone turned it from the other side. She'd forgotten to lock the door. She started to reach for the lock, but the door was jerked open.

"Hey, honey, thought you were gonna try and jump off the plane," Franco said with a knowing smile. "Well, your panties are still on, your skirts up, so I gotta ask—what are you doing?"

"Fuck off!" But he started to squeeze into the small bathroom.

"Excuse me, sir? There's a special bathroom for larger people, sir?" A feminine voice said from behind Franco.

"Try this again and I'll shoot your balls off," she hissed into his ear as she squeezed past him.

"I can handle that," he said to her back.

Bitch is a cool customer, he thought to himself, sitting down on the toilet seat to relieve himself. There would be a time when she would be vulnerable and he would pluck her cherries one by one, and eat them too. He started to fantasize about her, but then he heard Dutch Giovanni's laughter in his head. He had been humiliated by the convict, and would make sure to exact a certain payment, for him, and for ADOC. That child-molestor doctor would get some payment too, as soon as Franco was through using him.

He couldn't believe that the director had tried to sweat him over forgetting to assign an extra guard detail. It was a mix-up. A lack of communication, but still the administration was blaming him. It came back to Giovanni, who was the catalyst of his troubles. He'd bring back the prisoner, minus one liver, if he had to cut it out himself. So long as the FBI was on his side, he would be okay.

"Please fasten your seatbelts. The no-smoking sign is now on. Put your seats in the upright position. Thank you. Welcome to Spain."

"Shit!" Franco muttered.

She walked with one purpose in mind; to make the fat prick sweat. At the customs counters she flashed her badge at an official.

It was the same one Dutch had fooled within the last seventy-two hours. He looked at it closely, and noticed a large man with a ruddy complexion come up behind her.

"I'm Agent Carroll, and this is F-B-I Consultant Franco. I'm sure the bureau called, didn't they?"

He eyed them both suspiciously, then gestured for both of them to follow him.

"Agent Carroll." Interpol Agent Caroulez had been an agent for one year, and had been assigned to Madrid. This was one of the first times he'd had the opportunity to deal with American law enforcement officials. *If that's who they are*, he told himself.

"I'm Agent Carroll, and this is Lieutenant Franco, my consultant in this case. Is there a problem?" she asked, looking at the dark sunglasses.

"No problem. May I see your weapons and identification please, as well as your passports?" He turned to the customs official. "Please retrieve their luggage."

She handed over her two guns, one standard issue, the other a personal backup, which Franco had forced her to bring for him. He set them on a small counter against the wall, which was more like a shelf. The room was like an elongated closet, with a door at the other end. It was painted light-blue, and there was nothing but a few shelves with stamp pads and notepads on them. She saw a few pens and pencils, but that was about it. The floor was a synthetic short-hair rug, a reddish orange color.

Agent Caroulez smiled and took out a notepad and pen, then looked at the make and model and serial numbers of her guns, then jotted them down. "We have to log your guns into the records, just in case…You understand?"

When he was done, he handed them back, then took their passports and stamped them each twice. "Do you have any weapons, sir?"

"He's just a consultant," Dawn made clear.

"Okay. We have everything arranged for you, and due to the homicides, I will be accompanying you. Once you get to the hotel and clean up, we'll have dinner and I'll tell you about the new development in this case. You'll be very surprised." He smiled and handed them back their passports.

Franco could tell that this stuffy Spanish bastard was hiding something they needed, and this added to the fact that he didn't like him to begin with. The man was too skinny and his suit too loose, plus he looked too fragile to be of any use, except from behind a desk or on his knees. The slick-backed black hair was just like the wetbacks back in prison, and that was another point against him. Plus the fact that he hid his eyes behind dark sunglasses. He didn't want him accompanying him and Dawn anywhere, Interpol or not, he was screwing up his plans.

And he had plans....

14

No Place like Rome

THE HELICOPTER LANDED in a small grassy field. The four bodyguards in the helicopter were the first off, then Dutch jumped down. An ambulance was parked close by, and there were two more bodyguards with powerful looking machine guns in their hands as they surveyed the farmlands to the south, north, east and west.

Before the helicopter had arrived, Señor Giuseppe had told him what was going on. More precisely, what he knew had happened, and who had done it, and why. It didn't come out straight away, but Dutch figured out that Señor Giuseppe was a caporegime in the mafia.

He then explained his reasons for exhorting Dutch himself. He couldn't help but have sympathy for this aging man, who had been betrayed and nearly killed, by his only son.

It was one thing to want power, and another thing to seize power by murdering your own flesh and blood. This was a severe violation of the code that Dutch knew could not go unanswered. In prison a similar code would have demanded he act with quick brutality, or be thought weak, and therefore, prey for the predators.

Señor Giuseppe, once helped off of the helicopter, was now in a short argument about riding in the ambulance. His voice could be heard even over the whine of the helicopter as it took off. Dutch watched them all, staying close to Señor Giuseppe, but distant from everyone else. Each bodyguard had a black suit on. The two men near the ambulance were still rubber-necking, machine guns at the ready.

They had all looked at him curiously, until —Señor Giuseppe explained his part in saving his life. Some shook his hand, but Dutch suspected that any one of them could be a Judas. He had kept the 9mm tucked in the small of his back for that reason. His Gucci billfold was in his inner coat pocket, and the duffel at his feet.

Finally an agreement was made that the ambulance would drive in front of the black Mercedes, like a decoy, and the men would follow in the other cars, but not until the EMT driving the ambulance looked at the wounds and gave in. Many of the soldiers wanted to ride in the black Mercedes, to protect him with their own lives. Señor Giuseppe chose his two most trusted soldiers, and Dutch, and the rest would ride in the two other cars.

Promises of vengeance and blood was on the lips of every one of Señor Giuseppe's soldiers, but when Dutch commented on this, he received only a knowing look, as if they were in the presence of the enemy at that moment, right there in the Mercedes.

At the gallery she found herself amongst the rabble and rubble of another artist's preshow props. She didn't see Figaro, but she knew he was somewhere in the gallery or he wouldn't have left the door open. She was content to sit behind the large glass pane and watch the cars and people passing by.

She found herself pulled to this activity, searching out the faces of passing pedestrians, and the drivers in their cars. The sun's last rays shone on the opposite side of the street, bidding all a warm farewell. She felt the pull grow stronger, an unknown, yet identifiable being calling her from a shorter distance than ever before, somewhere out there. A buzzing in her head as she scanned each face, now with a fervor, a worry that she could miss *his* passing, like an asteroid passing through the earth's gravitational field only to be slung farther away as a consequence—

"Lord, help me, I'm going crazy," she whispered to herself. "Bring him to me," she added.

Her eyes were suddenly drawn to a long black Mercedes, the kind that her father sometimes hired when he took them to Rome, or Florence. Its windows tinted black, like the eyes... Some kinesthesia within her was pulling her, like a whirlpool in the middle of the ocean sucking her into its bottomless funnel. To that other place, that other world of dreams and screams and teeth and the all permeating cold of the sea, where lies that other—

—Every thought, suspicion, muscle cramp, and worry stopped for one purpose; through the tinted windows, across the street, a face behind the window of an art gallery. His fingers, without his conscious control, were searching out the door handle, even as the car rounded the street corner and the gallery's facade was out of sight.

"Stop the car!" he said in perfect Italian. "Stop the car now!"

"You heard what he said—stop the car!" Señor Giuseppe ordered, backing Dutch up. He'd been watching his new friend, and knew that something terribly important was going on. Dutch looked back at him, his eyes almost pleading. "Georgino, go with him and keep him outta trouble, bring him to the doctor's house."

Dutch exited the car before it stopped and was hurrying back up the street. The bodyguards in the second car were watching him, worried, as if he may have done something to their boss and was trying to make a getaway, until Georgino waved them off.

He didn't care about any of this, because in his self, that core of all being, of all longings, and of all needs, there was a piercing scream of destiny demanding he move over these cobblestones, past these pedestrians, to the siren calling his name. He was a tall redwood beginning to fall, unstoppable, fated to land at that space in time, before her, to see the color of her eyes. The gold chain, broken as he yanked it from his neck, was in his hand. The ring free, ready. It was an unconscious physical action. He could smell her again, feel the silken strands of flaxen hair, the sunbaked heat of her flesh as they lay on their secret beach—

—she could feel his muscular fingers teasing the soft skin below her breasts, while she giggled and wriggled, arching her neck to make sure nobody was spying on them from the bushes behind them. The sand was warm and white, and soft beneath her, and above her, lips, wet and urgent and teasing, in the perplexing but joyous sensation of her strong-willed mind yielding willingly to the cries and demands of her body.

The daydream lifted, like a low cloud evaporating in the morning sunlight, and she saw him standing outside the door. Staring back at her was her dream, and as if her mind had strobed, he was gone, the throbbing of her heart in her throat, tears welling, the gallery door opening and he was crossing the threshold, and there was nothing physical separating them from becoming whole, his eyes never leaving hers, and then her love was bending down and touched her hand and a jolt of electricity shot through her body, lighting it on fire, as he placed a ring on the ring finger of her left hand, where it fit perfectly—

Figaro was walking towards the front when he saw the man enter his gallery. There was also another, much shorter, man with him. But it was the first man who bothered him, because his jacket and shirt were bloody, and there was something he couldn't put a finger on, that worried him. He didn't like any fans approaching his number one artist, especially Serena.

"*Hey! Nobody comes in before the show!*" he shouted. The man didn't seem to hear, or notice him, until he pushed him towards the door, then out the door, and even then, he swore the man didn't know what was happening. "The gallery's closed. No fans unless invited." He didn't have to put up with this crap, and neither did his client, *although the man is kinda handsome*, he thought, then turned back towards Serena.

Georgino backed away from the large man, who towered over him, and was even taller than his Capo's friend. He knew Señor Giuseppe didn't want him to let any attention be brought on them, so he backed down, although he wanted to bring out his knife.

Dutch couldn't hear anything except the sets crashing on the beach, her voice in his ear. Her musky scent was heavy in his nostrils, and the taste of her salt making his mouth water. He reached out. She was gone, as if the riptide had pulled her out from beneath him.

"What's going—where's she at?" Dutch panicked, started for the gallery door, and found it locked. He pounded on the door, but she was gone.

"No, Señor, no!" Georgino saw people looking at them. "We'll come back when it's open—I know the woman.

This caught Dutch's attention, and he snapped his head around to look the shorter man in the eye.

"I know who she is," Georgino said quickly. "I know her father." He had an idea, at least, but was fairly certain she was the one.

Dutch realized that people were indeed looking at him, and the reality of the situation pressed upon him, but not without the effects of being alone without her face, or her pulse in his fingers, like a thousand butterflies suddenly flying away at the same moment, the winds snatching them away in one gust, a flash of color and painful regret of not capturing them on film, on canvas, on anything to preserve such beauty denied him. The saturation of loss depressed his drive and allowed him to be swayed, so long as he knew who she was and where she lived.

One last look told him she was gone.

"What's her name?" Dutch demanded softly before he would budge.

"Serena Repetto—come, we must go before someone calls the police, if they have not already—look at your clothes, Señor—we must go. The doctor's hacienda is close by." He tugged on Dutch's arm.

Dutch looked down at himself for the first time since the Monaco Border incident, and saw that his shirt and jacket were bloody. It looked as if he'd been shot, but he knew it was probably from Señor Giuseppe. Then he allowed the soldier to lead him away.

The aftereffects of his presence left her woozy, a film over the reality around her lingered, and had allowed her to be led away from her strongest desires unknowingly, in the confusion of memory and moment intertwining. Then her tongue was freed and she screamed.

"*FIGAROOO!*" Serena yelled, realizing she was in the kitchen of his small apartment. "Where is he? Figaro!" she demanded.

Figaro came running back into his small kitchen, looking surprised that she wasn't injured or on the floor. When he'd brought her back here, she wouldn't, or couldn't, respond to his questions, as if she were in another world. Now she was staring at him in a way that worried him.

"Where is he at? Where did he go?"

"He left—what're you talking about, Serena? Why are you screaming at me?" he asked sincerely. "I thought he was a robber, or a pesky fan—what was I to do?" His outstretched hands begged forgiveness.

She touched the ring on her left hand, wanting to lash out at him for his unknowing actions, but realized it wasn't his fault. He didn't know what was going on. If she weren't confined to this damn chair, she could've chased him down, held onto him, or at least stopped Figaro. The only thing that kept her from bursting into tears was the fact that she knew what he looked like, and he knew what she looked like, and either he would find her, or she him. Instinctively she felt it, and that gave her cause to truly smile for the first time in nine years.

"If ever you see that man again, Figaro, I want you to hold onto him for dear life and bring him to me. Do you understand?"

He saw the dark clouds in her sky-blue eyes and knew she was serious, that if he didn't agree, he might never see her or her paintings again, except in some other dealer's gallery.

He bent all the way down, so he was on the level with her eyes, which were still looking dangerously uncertain of him. "Ah, Serena, Serena, just tell me what you want and it is my heart's desire. Okay?"

She reached out her hand and took his big one in it, accepting his friendship once again. "One day I shall explain it to you."

"How 'bout we get some pizza and strawberry soda," he offered.

She nodded, feeling a little sad and forlorn, because her love was back in the writhing ocean of society, where the Fates play their cruel games, where he could be drowned or lost once again.

"Alas! Pizza and strawberry soda it is!" He stood up, twirled, and grabbed the phone.

With seagulls squawking in the recess of a memory she knew wasn't made in this lifetime, she prayed that she would find him, but soon.

Very few people knew who he was, or his true name, or even where he lived. That was the way he had started and the way he would end. He lived humbly and would die humbly, and so long as his wife and daughter were taken care of, which he'd made arrangements for, he would go happily into the world hereafter.

Right now, as the Underboss of the famiglia Castiglione, he had a crisis. Had left his home on a weekend, by private helicopter, to deal with this.

As a father he was worried about his daughter. He had made sure, soon after the accident, that the best specialists were flown in to look at Serena's injuries, to see if there was a chance she could walk again. He had cried in private for weeks, while she was in the hospital, until he exacted a more personal revenge. Neither his wife, or Serena, would ever know.

His investigators had found out that the brake shop was scamming customers by replacing the old parts with used parts, instead of new ones. But worse, upon closer examination, the same shop had been responsible for ten other accidents in the past five years, two of which were fatalities. Not to mention the thousands, maybe millions, of dollars they cheated from their own customers. The names of the men who'd worked on the delivery truck's brakes were found out, and the owner turned out to be the head shyster, instructing his employees to paint over and reuse old parts. Their audacity was so great that when the investigator took in a decoy car, with perfect brakes, the mechanic took a caliper and a shoe off the car, cleaned off the grease and dirt with a chemical cleanser, and charged him for brand-new replacements.

One year and two months after the delivery truck had run down his daughter, the brake shop owner's car experienced a brake failure on a winding coastal road between Florence and Genoa. Ironically, reported one newspaper, a highly flammable chemical cleaning fluid was accidently mixed with an acidic fluid common to most mechanic shops, and the brake shop exploded; on the same sunny day. Three brake mechanics received third degree burns over most of their bodies, and the same man who'd put the brakes on the delivery truck was killed in the explosion.

"Señor Repetto? Boss? You okay?"

He looked up at his number one man, shaking off the memories. "What's the news from the doctor?" Señor Repetto asked. "Señor Giuseppe took a bullet in the chest, but Alfredo says he'll live." Anthony Lobotelli watched his friend mull things over, and knew there was much indeed to mull.

Señor Repetto looked at the sturdy fifty-five-year-old man standing in front of his desk. He had called him Lobo since high school, and trusted him with his life, and gambled on that trust and loyalty on more than one occasion. *I may have to do so tonight,* he thought, *because the new generation is anxious to attain power without learning how to control it, or earn it.*

On two separate occasions he and Señor Giuseppe had discussed the matter of his son. Giuseppe knew his son, now thirty-one, was trying to attain a status that he was not only too young for, but that which he had not earned.

"Get the car, Lobo, I want to speak with him, and with Alfredo."

"You should've seen him, Boss!" Georgino was saying with an exaggerated smile, as he finished relaying Dutch's strange encounter. "I think I know the woman too. Guess who, Boss?"

Señor Giuseppe grudgingly indulged his bodyguard, while Doctor Donatello was putting stitches in the neck wound. "Who?"

"Remember Señor Repetto's daughter, the artist—the one who was hurt in the accident, and we got the owner of—"

"Silence!" Señor Giuseppe barked. Nobody was ever to know of that. Not ever. " How much longer, Alfredo?"

He tied the last stitch, then tore off a piece of bandaging tape, and taped a butterfly over it. "There. Finito. I still want you in for a CAT-scan. No buts about it, my friend. I know you well."

He stared at the caporegime, whom he'd served for many, many years, and waited for— the expression not dissimilar to the sight of a ship sinking below the surface, which would tell him that they had a deal, and he would come in for a CAT-scan.

"Okay, okay. Tuesday." Señor Giuseppe shook the doctor's hand. "Would you please excuse me for a moment, Alfredo?" Señor Giuseppe stood up, his bare chest like a thick, hairy tree trunk. He turned his attention to Georgino and waited until the doctor left the room.

Georgino knew that he had been found out. Either someone had intercepted the phone call he made in the doctor's kitchen, or they knew beforehand, which confused him increasingly. Maybe his father's influence would save him. Tears began to roll down Georgino's face, but his hand was fishing for a long, razor-sharp blade, which he kept strapped against the small of his back, in a special sheaf. He was beginning to plead for mercy when he freed the eight-inch long blade.

Dutch, wearing a new pair of jeans and a nice button-up shirt, opened the door. He had the gun in his hand, under the bundle of dirty clothes, as he saw the blade. Instincts took over, like a race car driver swerving to avoid flaming wreckage at two hundred miles per hour, he lifted and fired twice, without hesitation. He hadn't even thought about missing and hitting Señor Giuseppe. Phsst-Phsst, and Georgino fell. A man came in behind Dutch and grabbed him, and started shouting at the other bodyguards to come quick, then Dutch felt many hands on him, holding him.

"Let him go! Let him go!" Señor Giuseppe shouted at his men. "He saved my wretched life again!" There was blood dripping down his face, which made his smile seem clownish. He grabbed the dirty shirt from Dutch's bundle, and wiped his face.

"You're welcome," Dutch said, trying to hide the shock of killing, behind a comedic facade.

Señor Giuseppe smiled wide at Dutch, wiping off the last bits of brain matter from his face, then saw his men with their guns still drawn. "Put your guns down and get this traitor out of here."

He tried not to look down at the man, whose blood was spilling onto the white tiles. *It'll be a bitch to clean,* Dutch thought, his hands starting to shake. He'd never killed a man before.

Señor Giuseppe had to take the 9mm forcibly from Dutch's shaking hand, then toss it to the nearest bodyguard. He then threw down the shirt, and in full view of his soldiers, placed both of his hands on Dutch's cheeks and kissed him full on the lips. The soldiers crossed themselves in stunned silence, because they knew this could only mean one thing; Dutch was being accepted as a fully "made man." My life is yours, my blood is your blood, forever—"

He was not repulsed, as he thought he should have been. Instead he was warmly infused with a sense of being accepted, as being part of a greater whole. He blinked and grinned back at his friend. *My friend,* he thought, then smiled.

"In other words, you owe me." Dutch patted him on the arm. It looked like there were tears in the older man's eyes, and the men were standing solemnly, watching him. "It was nothing. Any one of your men would have done the same thing."

Señor Giuseppe understood that Dutch was being humble, playing off any debts that might be owed him, and he smiled, pushing back his emotions. "Sure thing, Mister Lorenzetti."

They both laughed and the men smiled and looked confused, because it was a rare thing to see their boss laugh.

"Señor Giuseppe?" A servant was calling from the hallway outside of the small room. "Señor Repetto's just pulled into the driveway."

The soldiers made sure the man could not see into the room, as Señor Giuseppe and Dutch squeezed out through the doorway.

"I'll be in the doctor's study." He watched the male servant, who was dressed in a brown suit, walk down the long hallway of the ten-bedroom hacienda, which was as large as his own. He turned back to his men. "Gerardo, Leonardo, Paco, and Telli, you stay and clean this up. I don't want the doctor's household seeing this if possible. The rest, be on guard."

Dutch felt an arm around his waist and he was guided down the hall, then into an expansive room filled with cherry wood bookshelves, which were full of books. Something about the room was familiar, as if he'd seen its make and model before....

15

TOGETHER...

THE SMALL RESTAURANT was filled, as usual, the buzz of small talk loud in the air. If it wasn't for Figaro, they would never have gotten in, but they had, and she was delighted with the excellent food. The perfectly crusted pizza dough melted in her mouth with an explosion of spices, which were baked into the bread itself. The strawberry soda was equally pleasant, tickling her tongue, then tingling her throat.

"Looks like you're enjoying yourself? Feeling better, Serena?" Figaro asked.

There was something else on his mind, she could tell, because of the way he was fidgeting. She smiled. "What do you want, Figaro?"

He put on an expression of extreme pain, his face wrinkling, mouth slightly opened, as if at any moment he would fall over and say, "Ahhh, my heart," but instead settled for "Serena, Serena—"

"No bullshit." That was something she could do without tonight.

"Actually," he started, the game over. "I was going to ask if you didn't mind staying at a hotel tonight? The best of course."

"Why?" she cut in, curiosity pushing her.

"I've got a hot date with a supermodel," he said with suppressed excitement.

For a moment she was saddened at the thought of being alone tonight, but she was glad for him as well. She patted his hand and flashed him a smile. *This might give me a chance to visit Angelina,* she thought to herself.

"I don't mind, I have a place to stay at, and a friend to visit while I'm in Rome...Can you give me a ride?" She was too tired and mentally exhausted. She tried to keep her excitement at seeing her friend fresh, but it grew old when she thought of *him*, and touched the ring on her finger. *Have I ever stopped touching it?* she wondered.

"Of course! Of course!" He was happy about not having to give up his date. It had taken him a while to figure out if Angel Libero was gay. "I would have given up my supermodel if you'd have said so," he told her honestly.

She could see he was happy with the thoughts of his impending encounter. She wondered if she would get lucky, find her lover, toss away all her inhibitions and let man finally make her a woman. She was starting to recall memories, and "other-time" thoughts, and the comfortably invasive presence of *him*—

—and something else altogether chilling, cold, and putrid, waiting there as if to capture her life the moment she grasped for her soulmate. She could sense that evil form, a shapeless, omnipresent corruption, waiting to fall like an invisible blanket, and snuff out dreams, her wishes, her desires, and take her around once more—

Her right leg twitched, and there was a painfully pleasant sensation of her leg waking up after a long sleep. She reached down and rubbed her leg, and nearly moaned with pleasure.

"Something a matter? You look like you just had an orgasm," he teased. "Or is there spinach on my teeth?"

"Nope, you look just fine." She was done eating, and feeling giddy and excited. She felt as if she just might be able to get up and walk.

He laughed at her sudden change of expression. "You gonna hang out in Rome, tomorrow? I'm curious about the paintings, is all—"

She caught her breath, coming back to reality. *He couldn't know, could he?* she wondered. "Is there a problem?"

"No, they just look like something you would've done last year, or the year before—"

"Busted," she confessed. "I've been having some personal problems lately, you know, but I have the paintings outlined, just not painted."

"I know you like to be perfect, so take your time. The world can wait for its star. Are you ready to go?"

"Yes, just let me finish my soda," she said.

Figaro stood up and picked up the bill, and suddenly she was aware of people staring at her, attracted by his height, then by her wheelchair. She flexed her muscles, thinking about standing up and showing them all, then chided herself for the childish notion.

The drive was slow and pleasant, which gave her time to reflect on the day's events, and make some decisions. She thought about going to the police, but thought better of it because he could be wanted or something. Figaro had told her that there was blood on his shirt. She got a private detective's name from Figaro, and decided to call the number from the doctor's house in the morning.

Along the drive she could see the Romans walking along the vistas and lighted malls. There was a small, dimly lit park, where young couples were walking, kissing, or just sitting on the stone benches talking. Every now and then, she could see through a sliver of an alleyway to a small world, where a group of families shared their existence in a cul de sac. Clothes hung on lines strung between buildings, like curtains hiding another world beyond. She knew there were about three million people in Rome, but the city still managed to keep its cultural and historical integrity, not letting the past be suffocated by the wants and whims of a new generation, intent on creating its own history, yet blind to the fact that just being alive was in itself creating a history.

Even still a few people managed to infect the country, to make a history of wars and plights. She knew about the suffocation of ideals and freedoms under the guise of law and justice and democracy. Even in their ally country, America, where supposed human rights and democracy was an example to follow, there were laws and punishments being dealt out and freedoms being taken, all in the name of a "cause" or one person's plight against the individual tragedy. Like laws being made for everyone, because something happened to one person. She knew what it was called, because Italy's own history was dotted with such incidents of mass punishment, and the punishment of one for the deeds of another. Had not all of Europe, and parts of America, burned witches based upon the testimony of the greedy, slandering, and self-empowering corrupt? No wonder the American judicial system and prison systems were bulging, and had become one of the biggest businesses. Anybody could pick on the weak, poor, and infirmed, and so it was easy for the politicians and media moguls to place blame on crime and criminals, for they were almost invariably the poorest men or women in the country. They cried wolf every day, every hour, even over the statistics which showed crime on the same level as it was ten years ago, or less than. She couldn't understand how America, who claimed to be at the forefront of the human rights movement, was also guilty of executing human beings who could possibly be innocent. Even the remotest possibility should cause people to be wary. Human beings were never perfect, therefore the system, which relied upon a human decision-making body could not say to have the surely guilty. Especially in today's world of glory hunting, and political influences.

She didn't like to think about politics or government, because it made her angry that she could do nothing about it. Even now, a few Italian politicians were trying to pass into law an execution statute. This was based upon the actions of a sixty-two-year-old man, who committed a horrible crime. Even still, it was not enough to sway her. She wished she could rise up and enter the world of politics. She knew it was possible, but she wondered if that wasn't how all men, or women, entered the Machiavellian game, only to be twisted and corrupted or spewed out for nonconformity.

"Wow, this is some house," Figaro said.

A MEMORY OF FOREVER

The soft hair on her neck bristled, as the car turned into the driveway, passing the stone front and open gate. Two shiny black Mercedes were parked in the crowded gravel parking area. She swore the cars were like the one she saw. There were two other smaller cars. She swore she recognized the man standing near the closest Mercedes.

"I know that man," she whispered.

"What was that, Serena?" Figaro asked. The tires crunched on gravel as the car slowed to a stop. "I'll have to carry you to the sidewalk," he said. He'd carried her before, so it was no big deal.

"That man, I know him. It's my dad's vice-president, Mister Lobotelli."

"Good, he can carry you and I'll take your chair," Figaro said.

Just then he spotted her, in the front passenger seat, and was about to run and inform his boss, when a tall man smiled widely at him—

"Hello, Mister Lobotelli, could you lend me a hand?" Figaro watched the stocky-looking older man thinking about it.

"It's me, Lobo!" she called through the passenger window with a smile, which he couldn't refuse.

"Ciao, Serena," Lobo greeted seriously. He opened the door as he spoke. "Your father will be pleased to see you. Now come on. Need a lift?" He picked her up easily.

She loved his singsong Italian, so familiar to her own mother's, except distinctly masculine and more serious. She gladly accepted strong arms behind her shoulder and under the crook of her knee, all the while wondering what was happening inside her head.

Her brain was computing the fact that she had left her father at home; there were guards with machine guns at the corners of the property, and by the gate; butterflies were flying in her stomach; and for as long as she knew, Lobotelli had always complimented her in some form or another—it was a game they played—but not today.

It was the gut feeling that most bothered her, made her feel self-conscious, even as she was carried up the steps to the front door, which opened before they reached it—

—and his heart jumped into his throat as he locked eyes with her. He checked her ring finger. Yes, that was his mother's ring. The man was asking him something, and he was not hearing, and then he was bringing her to him and she was in his arms. There was a leap of electricity, as if two electromagnetic forces had joined, the current now flowing around and through both of their circuits. Her face was inches away, as he stood in a doorway that neither was aware of, and her arms were around his neck, their hearts beating to the same beat. Two friends, after such a long separation, together at last. The sounds of the world gone, while another captured all their senses, and opened a floodgate of memories and sensations. He was falling into her eyes, barely able to stand upright, as her skies penetrated his earth, and—

—she couldn't breathe, but it didn't matter because nothing mattered but clinging tightly to his neck, and the feel of his arms hot against her flesh, as if they were both naked. She could smell his breath, and taste his musk on her tongue, making her mouth water. Her body was afire, seeking more kindling, longing to be naked with him, riding him in the kaleidoscope of rainbow colors, while the ceiling spun and vortexed above them, and the world trembling and rumbling as he cracked her open and invaded her barren lands, watering them and fertilizing her soil, but continuing to turn and plow her weeds, making everything anew. She was falling into his eyes, where there was a whole new glorious reality. "Swanlake." It was a whisper, his eyes filling.

"Julius?" *He knows me*, she thought, tears streaming down her ivory pillows. They held each other tighter. Then both wanted more, and—

Señor Repetto had been watching for the past five seconds, and was now starting to come forward, but felt a hand on his forearm. He started to shake it off, but there were a series of troublesome thoughts racing through his mind. *How am I going to explain all of this, and my connection to it.* Señor Giuseppe held him back, but it was Missus Donatello who captured his attention. She crossed herself and kissed her rosary beads.

"Compagno spirituale," she whispered. Soulmates. Then she turned and smiled at him. "Congratulations," she told him. "Your lovely princess has found what few ever find."

That may be so, he thought, *but hadn't this escaped convict just called his daughter by another name? And hadn't she called him by another name,* another voice in his head responded. *How could this be,* he wondered.

"I need another drink—" he said to himself.

Señor Giuseppe smiled, knowing that his friend would not stop the two youngsters, and went to get him a drink. *I need one myself,* he thought.

—their lips met fast, both coming forward to taste what they had so long been deprived of, to breathe in each other at last, and be one united body of flesh and mind. The connection felt so perfect, so right, in the sense that it was exactly what the world destined; for them to be together as one, as if it meant everything in the cosmic definition of all living and breathing beings; what everyone should aspire to be. It was momentous in their thudding hearts, and in their blood, which beat and flowed at the same heightened *pace*. There was nothing and nobody else while they breathed the air of each other's soul.

"Excuse me, folks—you're turning blue," Figaro said lightly. He unfolded the wheelchair and set it down on the small brick porch. "Uhhhummm!" He cleared his throat to get their attention, then looked down at his watch, then back at the kissing couple. *At least the man changed clothes*, Figaro thought, now getting a much better look at him, and approving.

It was Señor Giuseppe who saw the car pass by on the road, then another, and another, as he looked out the living room window while pouring the scotch into the glasses—

"Señor Repetto!" Señor Giuseppe shouted.

A shot rang out, and then the sporadic gunfire burst out into the quiet night.

A piece of oak splintered off the door frame and struck him in the cheek, jolting him and Serena back to reality. His instincts took over and he guarded her with his body, running into the house, and kicked the door shut. He wished he wouldn't have given up the gun. He kept her tight to his body, and called to Missus Donatello. The soldiers were running past him to the front, pistols replaced by serious-looking machine guns and shotguns. He ordered a few of them to the side door and rear hallway, and was surprised when they obeyed without hesitation.

The interior of the hacienda was a maze of hallways and waiting rooms, and he told Missus Donatello to lead him to the back examination room, where there was no windows and only one door in and out. It was also in the rear of the house, and would, therefore, be the most protected from bullets and debris. He only hoped the men had covered the man's body.

A maid and the doctor's daughter ran out and startled him, until he realized who they were. "Follow us!"

Serena saw her friend hesitating. "Angelina, come on!"

He saw the pants leg of the dead man, and hoped the women would handle it with courage. He tightened his hold on Serena and addressed her for the first time in this lifetime, with something more than a one word statement, or question.

"There's a dead body?" He searched her eyes for a sign of fear.

He saw no fear, and felt her hug him back. It was good to hear his normal voice speaking to her, like the sounds of the world must sound to the deaf after years of silence. She turned and looked at the body. It was half wrapped in plastic, face down still.

For some reason it didn't shock her.

He set her down gently on the examination table, and that shocked her. Her arms clung tight, as if she were a child who would not be set down. His lips met hers softly, briefly, and she was lulled into allowing her arms to slip from around his neck, searching his muscles, and—"I've gotta help, Swan." His hands were on her cheeks. He didn't want to leave her, or ever be where she wasn't, where he couldn't just reach out and touch her, or see her, and he vowed that he would make this so once they were out of this little war. But now he had to be a man, the man she loved. He could not act the coward and stand by while he might possibly be able to save lives, and beat back the man who'd tried to kill him and Señor Giuseppe.

She saw the warrior aching for her approval, and knew that if she didn't let him go this one last time, they might all be killed, even though she hadn't the foggiest idea what was going on.

"Go, my love, but come back." She heard her voice say, letting her hand drag along the curve of his rounded jaw. Her mind screaming at this too-soon departure, not wanting to face the possibility of forever without him, without ever having made love with him, or shared a meal and conversation, or felt his children growing inside her belly.

She suppressed her horrors into tears. "Come back, Julius—don't you dare leave me again!" she whispered, inches from his face.

He kissed her hard and passionate and quick, then pulled away. "Thee and me shall forever be," he said, not knowing where the words came from; *me or Julius; me or Dutch?*

His leaving broke her spirit, as if the happenings of the last minutes were flashing by in stills, in jerks and stops, so she was out of context with time, and with her own thoughts. As she looked around at the three women, the dead man, the chair—the pop-pop-popping noises muffled by thick walls in her ears, the smell of rubbing alcohol in her nostrils—she felt an emptiness, like that of a hollow ship ten fathoms below the surface, the implosion imminent.

Dutch saw one of the soldiers in the doorway that adjoined the hall that led to the back door. It was one of the men he'd ordered to guard this area. "I need a gun!" Dutch told the man, who reached into his jacket and pulled out his automatic and threw it to Dutch.

He walked back towards the front of the house, into the battle grounds where the shooting was just beginning to die down, the last soldiers falling back, or collapsing dead into the trenches.

Five minutes had passed since he entered the kitchen, and it was still as quiet as an empty house. He hid behind the cooking island, looking out into the front room. There was at least five couches, and five easy chairs, all Spanish leather.

"Señor Giuseppe? Giuseppe?" Dutch called as he walked, crouching, towards the entryway to the front living room.

A bullet—ricocheting off a pan hanging above his head, which caused a hundred pans and utensils to crash and clamor onto the white clay tile—answered him. He picked up a large pan and threw it into the living room, hoping to bring out the shooter, like a carrot to a mule. He wondered how many of them there were.

16

Lost and Found

AGENT DAWN CARROLL didn't like the helicopters here, any more than she liked the ones back home, but at least the ones back in America had doors. She could barely see, what with her eyes watering like some sort of water dispenser, thankful she had chosen to not wear mascara for once in her life.

"You alright?" She could barely hear the voice over the thwupthwup-thwupping of the blades, ten feet (or less) above her head.

Agent Caroulez was smiling at the female agent. *She has a great body*, he thought, *but God has forgotten to bless her otherwise plain, red buckshot-marked face.* "You alright?" he shouted this time.

"*Just fucking fine!*" she lied openly.

"I apologize, we have a better copter in the shop. We'll be in Rome in five minutes—there's reports of a gunbattle in the city."

"Thought you guys didn't have that problem over here?" Franco shouted triumphantly.

"I'm a Spaniard." Agent Caroulez rebuffed the fat man's attempt to subjugate him, for the tenth time since they'd met. He didn't like this fat prick one bit. He flashed Dawn a smile and turned back around.

She felt a beefy paw on her thigh, like some weighty piece of cooked brisket heating her flesh. She turned slowly towards her consultant-slash-antagonist, looked down at his hand, then back into his eyes. He removed his hand slowly, but immediately. She knew, looking past his thick, hooded lids, into his cold green eyes, that he would pose an even more serious threat to her body once they were alone. She could see, and sense, a fearlessness in his expression, like some form of obsessive-compulsive disorder had clashed with a creeping insanity, and was now in control of his mind and body. He had tried a passive aggressive tactic at the hotel in Spain, like a shark patrolling the depths with an eye to the surface, always ready to strike. Agent Caroulez had accidently foiled the fat prick's plan to catch her in the shower.

After the shower she had taken some time to read over her notes about Dutch Giovanni, which she'd written while on the plane. There was nothing in his file to suggest he was a dangerous man, even though they had him listed as such. That was just police procedure. Police agencies considered this type of propaganda in the best interest of the public, because they'd be more likely to turn in a dangerous man, than a man who might not even be guilty. That was a long shot. She tried recalling the trial summation, which basically put the case into perspective; Dutch Giovanni's word versus two decorated Phoenix Police Officers.

Almost invariably a cop's word is always taken over that of a civilian's, and that was so in Giovanni' s case. There was nothing about his mother dying prior to his being arrested. In fact, it was reported that he had only been in Arizona for less than a month before he was arrested for driving a stolen truck, possessing a weapon, and assaulting the police officers who attempted to arrest him.

Despite the prosecution's assertion that he was some sort of career criminal, Giovanni had no prior record, or history of assaultive behavior. Not that it mattered in Arizona, where if you had an out-of-state license plate, or didn't look "right," you could be pulled over, and once stopped by the police anything can, and might, happen.

The day after she'd reported for duty, at the Phoenix office, there was a big story about police brutality: Officers had used a chemical agent to "restrain" a paraplegic black man, then choked him to death. There were many more incidents involving police brutality: a Tucson police officer had shot and killed a man for throwing rocks at his squad car, a woman was shot and killed for holding and brandishing a knife (wonder where the pepper spray was then?), a fourteen-year-old was shot seventeen times while running away with a toy gun, a sixteen-year-old was shot fifty-six times, in the back and front, for having a pocket knife. And on the list of police involved death went. She learned that the FBI stayed clear of Arizona law enforcement, due to political and economical reasoning.

As for the so-called non-lethal weaponry on the market, it was hardly ever used, if purchased, although the statistics showed an increased use of pepper spray on arrest victims. There was a Civil Rights bill, with laws and statutes, but the federal government didn't like prosecuting "brother" law enforcement agencies, unless it was good for public relations, or had some political motivation behind it.

So long as the police killed minorities or poor people, then it would all be accepted, and the fact that one in twenty, of all Americans, would serve time, was kept quiet, as law makers bred and bred.

The helicopter jolted, started to drop down quicker than she thought safe. To the right she could see a dark blotch of nothingness, which must be the Mediterranean, to the left she saw the lights of Rome, then a building zoomed into her view and they were landing on a lighted landing pad.

Rome was a city that you could get lost in, if you hadn't grown up in it, or at least frequented it often. Not even if you had a map with every little sliver of a road on it.

The sirens were different than that of the American police. Instead of the "you-you-you, we're coming to get you-you-you" sound, it was a "beeyobeeyobeeyo" cry, delivered in a much higher pitch, that rebounded effectively off the stone and brick buildings. There were very few wooden structures, and the tight suburban two lane roads were bumpy, and in some places very slick. From above, the snakelike line of special tactical unit vans, police cars, and other vehicles, looked like a long, lighted sidewinder cutting through the Western most part of the city, slowing, stopping, speeding up, and finally bunching up on a street where there were huge villas and haciendas.

"We're just observing, remember," Agent Caroulez told her when their car finally stopped, and the Italian officer who was driving had exited and ran forward.

In the distance she heard gunfire. A bullet drilled through the windshield and ricocheted around the interior.

"Fuck that!" Franco said. "Gimme my gun!"

Agent Caroulez looked at Franco, then at her, and shrugged.

She reluctantly took out his gun, and handed it to him, relying on his fear of prison or execution to keep him from using it on her.

"Must have come from down the block," Agent Caroulez said, then looked at Dawn.

"No shit, Sherlock!" Franco said.

"Come on, I think it's winding down." Caroulez got out of the car and started weaving through the bunched up police vehicles.

Franco could see where the 'spic was heading; To a big house at the end of the street. There was a long stone wall, then an open rot-iron gate. He wanted none of it. He saw two bodies slumped over the top of the wall, and more on the sidewalk outside. He could care less about getting there in time for a shootout. They could both miss him with that nonsense. He sat half in and out of the car, keeping his left leg out and his right leg in, watching the bitch shake her ass as she followed the skinny Spanish agent. He put the gun in his lap, *just in case*, he thought.

"What a dump," he said to himself, looking at the old Roman style buildings and rubber blackened cobblestones, and smelling the fumes of a nearby sewer line. "I'll take America any day."

He took a bullet three inches above the kneecap, but it struck on the inner side and missed doing serious damage, or breaking bone, however, it was bleeding bad. He took two of them out for that price, but knew that there was one more man in the room, if only the sirens would go away so he could hear.

"Señor Giuseppe," Dutch called, limping behind a couch and finding Señor Repetto. "Señor Repetto?" He shook the man's leg. There was no response, and then he noticed the blood puddle beneath the head.

A bullet tore into the white plaster above his head, showering him with a fine, yet chipped snow. He ducked further behind the old couch, thankful for the Spanish craftsmen who had made such a sturdy, and near bulletproof piece of household furniture.

"Señor Giuseppe's dead!" a voice called.

"The police are here," Dutch taunted the man. "Why don't we call it a truce? You say Señor Giuseppe's dead, then it's over. I'm not against you or for you—how 'bout it?" Dutch bargained in perfect Italian, hoping to irritate whomever it was into one of two actions.

From underneath the coffee table, where he'd crawled, he waited for movement. A man, probably in his early thirties, and balding from stress, came up from a crouch behind the couch and started walking forward and firing a barrage of bullets into the couch behind Dutch.

He squeezed the trigger twice, aiming center mass, and watched the man fall backwards, a stunned look on his face, as if the thought of dying was just now beginning to be considered as a possible outcome for his actions. He couldn't see the man—he had toppled backwards over the couch—but heard a wet cough, and knew the Italian man was done for if help didn't arrive soon.

"Dutch! Dutch!" a muffled voice came from somewhere to his right.

Dutch crawled out from under the table and stood shakily, his head light, and listened.

"Over here!" It was a muffled voice from behind the oak panels at the eastern side of the room, by the shot-up bar. Dutch dragged his leg over to the panel, and put his ear to the wall.

"Push the upper left corner," he heard, and obeyed.

The door opened to reveal Señor Giuseppe and Doctor Donatello, who smiled at him for a moment, but he wasn't seeing things straight, and he couldn't hear. Señor Giuseppe raised a gun and fired past his ear. He turned, mostly with neck and upper body, to see Señor Giuseppe's son fall to the floor.

"And that is that," Señor Giuseppe said, as if wiping his hands clean of the matter.

"Is my wife safe?" the doctor asked.

Dutch could only point towards the rear of the house.

The bullhorns began. The police were coming in.

"Quick, inside!" Señor Giuseppe pushed him into the secret hiding space and shut the door.

The gunfire and noises of battle had never come close to them in the back room. They had listened to the exchange, and a horrendous clamoring of the kitchen being destroyed, but no danger had ever approached their little room. Now it was eerily quiet, except for the muffled sound of a distant loudspeaker. Two servants had joined them, and then Señor Giuseppe and Doctor Donatello had nearly run into the room.

The doctor exchanged a loving look with his wife, but Señor Giuseppe demanded his urgent help without words. They picked up the dead body and quickly took it back out to the war zone, then returned to the room. "This is what happened," Señor Giuseppe began....

17

Dying

He could hear someone scratching and pushing on the panel, but there was nothing he could do about it. The spent gun was on the floor at his feet. His leg was throbbing, and he knew he was drifting in and out of a semiconscious state. He'd tightened a belt above the wound, but that hadn't stopped the bleeding.

When the officer pushed on the upper left portion of the panel, he heard a click, and then the wall seemed to open, and a black-haired man fell towards him and he had just enough time to catch the man's head before it slammed on the hard floor. He saw the wound, but felt for a pulse, then started shouting. They had another live one.

Serena pushed her chair away from the stainless steel table, which held her father's body. The detective had long since left the room, after she'd identified the body. She hadn't been asked to identify the body, but she had wanted to say good-bye one last time, and ended up doing both at the same time. She wanted to see his face, which had smiled and laughed and expressed disappointment and triumph and sadness and love with her. He had taken one bullet in the chest, which had skewered his heart. One bullet and he was gone.

She was not angry with him for hiding his other life, his occupation, which the detective had informed her of. Angelina told her the rest of the story on the way to the hospital.

She reached out and touched his face one last time, her tears falling, but guilt weighing down her conscience, because she knew she should be feeling more sorrow for this momentous loss. But she couldn't. There was a greater loss looming, and that was where her mind kept creeping; *Julius, hang in there.*

"Good-bye, my love, my faithful father." She turned and wheeled out of the room.

The hospital had been on alert ever since the shooting had started, and they were surprised at the amount of injured, compared to the number of the dead. Usually it was fifty-fifty, in other words, they expected one dead for one injured. That wasn't the case here, because either the shooters were good, or just lucky; whichever, there were twelve dead and three injured. One of which was the talk of the hospital, and many news stations; Dutch Giovanni.

> *...the escaped prisoner from America, was somehow involved in the gang land shootout — Unknown sources say that he had even saved the life of the capo-clan of the famiglia Castiglione — Dutch Giovanni is said to be in surgery, where the doctors are attempting to repair a bullet wound to the leg. We will keep you updated on the nights events...In other news...*

"I hope they're not trying to build a sympathy campaign to keep us from taking his ass back," Franco spat, after hearing the translation from an overfriendly Italian police officer.

A MEMORY OF FOREVER

The waiting room was crowded with some of the Donatello family, Agent Carroll and Franco, and many of the relatives of the deceased or injured. It was quiet, except for the news caster talking on the television set. There were sniffles, and sobs, intermittent and short in their delivery. It was a plain white room, large yet intimate, stuffed with chairs and lighted with fluorescent lights in the ceiling.

"Why not? If you get him, you might still have him killed, in fact, I checked his blood type against your own." She waited for a moment to let that fact sink into his thick skull. "I'd say his chances were zero in a hundred at staying alive the rest of his sentence, so long as you're still around." She had indeed done some more research on the phone. She'd even told her boss about the pictures and how they might be used against her. If it wasn't for the FBI's reputation, she'd have put the fat prick in cuffs right now. The doctor had spilled his guts, and confirmed every computer file they'd tapped into and downloaded. It gave her back her spine, and her sense of self-integrity, which she'd lost under his thumb.

"Yeah-yeah-yeah, you just keep your trap shut." He spat back at her, not at all feeling in the mood to put up with her sass. "Keep pushin' it and the *National Inquirer* gets some nudy pictures. Get it," he threatened.

"Send 'em where you want, but feel lucky I don't place you under arrest." She chided herself the moment she said it.

He stared at her for a moment, trying to figure her angle. Then he smiled. "Do you really wanna play this game with me?" He looked around to see if anyone was in earshot. "I mean, you saw what happened to your lover. Bob, was it?"

She started to react, but told herself that she would have his balls soon enough, and smiled back at him. In the corner of her eye she saw a woman in a wheelchair. She was coming towards her and Franco. *She is very beautiful*, Dawn Carroll said to herself, now looking at the woman straight on as she came to a stop in front of her chair.

"Are you Agent Carroll?" Serena asked. "May I speak to you in private?" Her English was nearly perfect, even with the accent.

"Sure," Agent Carroll smiled and stood. "How about the examining room across the hall." It was empty.

Lieutenant Franco stood up and walked over to the bank of phone booths. He picked up the phone, following Agent Carroll and Serena with one eye. He didn't like what she'd said, or how she'd said it, or the fact that Agent Caroulez had demanded his pistol be returned to Agent Carroll once the threat was over. He suspected that Agent Carroll was responsible for that as well. Something fishy was going on.

"Hello, I'd like to make a long distance call to Washington DC— Federal Bureau of Investigations Deputy Director Palmer," Franco told the operator.

"I'm sorry, sir, but he would not accept the phone call," the operator replied after five minutes of waiting.

"What?" he nearly shouted. "Tell him it's Franco, Lieutenant Franco."

"Please hold," the indifferent voice replied.

After three minutes, the voice returned. "He says he doesn't know who you are, and not to call back. Will that be all, sir?"

The ungrateful bastard. I've given the man a second chance at life, and now the backstabber is gonna deny me a return favor. Franco started to sweat. *My safety net has been yanked out from under me, which can only mean one thing.*

"Yes, I'd like to place a call to Florence, Arizona, in the United States, number…"

He was coming out of a colorful dream and into a new kind of white haze. He felt a bed beneath him, then the handcuff pulled tight around his left wrist. His mouth was dry. Through a crack in the curtains behind the bed he saw it was still night, but it felt as if he'd been sleeping for days. He looked down the length of his bed and saw a young Italian police officer.

The toilet flushed loudly, and another officer came out of the rest room.

The fifth floor room was small, meant for only one intensive care patient. The lights were dimmed, but the white walls captured and reflected every stream of light. The bed was lower than the beds in America, at least as far as he could recall.

"Look, Peter, our American gangster is awake!" the officer coming out of the bathroom said to his partner at the door.

"I'm no American gangster!" Dutch said in cracked, but otherwise perfect Italian, which shocked both of the officers. "Can I get something to drink? Go to the bathroom?" Only then did he realize that his understanding of the language had shocked them both.

The officer who'd gone to the restroom kept walking out of the room and into the hallway.

A Chinese doctor came into the room after a moment and took a look at Dutch. "You very famous, you know?" she said in perfect English, while pouring a glass of water. She adjusted his IV line. "You look much better than you did, that's for sure," she said with a smile, then started to hand him the glass, but realized his wrists were cuffed to the rails of the bed. She turned and spoke smartly to the officer by the door, and he came over and uncuffed him.

Something about her is suspicious, or familiar, Dutch thought, unable to pinpoint which, but the water was cool and refreshing. *A funny aftertaste*, he thought to himself, handing her the glass.

"Very good." She took the glass and refilled it. "You have no broken bones, but you had one of your lower arteries severed by the bullet, but I reconnected it, so you live now." She smiled at him.

Suddenly, and quite unlike any other pain he'd experienced in his entire life, his chest felt as if it were going to explode.

His back arched and his eyes fluttered. Dutch swore that he saw the Chinese woman smiling calmly, as if she were a mother quieting a child.

The lights blinked on and of f—on, then off, as a code alarm screamed and faded out at the same moment—

—"Swanlake?" He called out in the blackness. She was here. He knew it, hoped it, begged for it. Somewhere in this despotic dark, he knew she was near, felt her presence. He had heard her voice in the gloom and musty blackness. "Swanlake? Please answer, my love?" He could not feel the sensation of ground on the underside of his feet, and didn't know if he were standing or floating. *Am I breathing?* Julius asked himself, looking around in the darkness. *Am I seeing? Am I dead?* "Swanlake?" he shouted, but could not hear the vibrations of air in his eardrums, in the smothering void of nothingness, and began to panic—

Doctor Woo was sweat-soaked from the effort of trying to save him. She slowly placed a sheet over his face.

"Time?" she asked.

"Ten-twenty-five," a male intern said. He was impressed with the efforts of the forty-year-old Chinese doctor, who had taken over the CPR with a vigor, doing everything within a doctor's power to save the man.

Another nurse handed Doctor Woo a chart, and she signed it quickly and slapped it back into the nurses palm, clearly upset about losing the patient.

Her scream ended and she couldn't breathe anymore, her lungs and heart stopping, as the relaxant flowed through her blood stream. She couldn't see so she shut her eyes and let it take her. She vomited up something hot and acidic, and her gut hurt, with an empty sensation of utter loss. It was the feeling she'd had in the room with her father's dead body, but amplified a hundred thousand times, taking and stopping all her bodily organs, as if death were being invited, willed upon herself, because her heart, her world, was physically breaking apart.

The joy at hearing what the American agent had told her about Dutch, or her Julius, was erased, whipped away in a tide of human error, or fate. The fact that he was not a mass-murderer, or career criminal, had given her a hope for a future together. She would have traveled to America and lived in the prison town, if only to visit every week and write him every day, until she could buy justice and get him out of prison. He was the world, and she would be his moon, but now—

—she could sense the jaws closing, the teeth digging into her hip bones, the base of her spine, tearing her in half with a sickening wet plopping noise, her legs being ripped from the joints, and—

It didn't matter, she thought, slipping into the blackness...

"Julius?" she called out, into the darkness. He was here. She knew it, hoped it, begged for it. Somewhere in this despotic dark, she knew he was near, felt his presence. She had heard his voice in the gloom and musty blackness. "Julius? Please answer, my love?"

"Doctor! Doctor!" Señor Giuseppe was shouting. He saw Serena the moment he got off of the elevator. She was in a room off to the right, the door open, convulsing and jerking. Nobody seemed to care. "Doctor, over here!"

Agent Carroll ran into the room, where she thought she'd left a sleeping Serena in the bed, after the doctor had given her a shot of some sort of relaxant. An Italian doctor followed her into the room, and pushed passed her to examine Serena. Agent Carroll wondered if she would ever be that much in love with a man, to get like this if he died.

"Doctor, do not let this one die!" Señor Giuseppe locked eyes with the man, and they communicated more in the loaded silence that followed.

The doctor rattled off orders and gave Serena another shot, while Señor Giuseppe stepped away from the bed, nearly tripping over Serena's customized wheelchair. He saw that there were three bullet holes in the backrest, and for some reason, they reminded him of Dutch. Tears came to his eyes, and he swore not to let the girl die if at all possible. He did not want to tell Misses Repetto that she'd lost both a husband, and an only child.

He took out his handkerchief and blew his nose, trying to hide his grief from the detectives who'd interrogated him for the last hour, until finally believing the kidnaping story.

As he stepped out of the room, he saw the large man, dressed sloppily, like some used car salesman down on his luck. The big man looked very streetwise, as if he were waiting for something. Señor Giuseppe thought the man very suspicious, because he was following the stretcher that bore his dead friend.

Nobody else saw the chink doctor stick the needle into Inmate Giovanni, nor the look she gave the Chinese orderly, who was now quickly wheeling the body into the elevator. As the door was closing, the female doctor slipped into the carriage. *Something is very fucking fishy about all of that*, Franco thought.

He walked to the other elevator and pushed the down button.

Franco was thinking about what the Pinal County Hospital had told him about Doctor Brown being arrested. It had happened about twelve hours ago. The nurse, a close friend of the family, had told him that there was FBI Agents all around, and they were talking about exhuming bodies from "Boot Hill." Franco knew the graveyard well, because it was where the state buried its indigent or unclaimed men, and one woman. He knew what would happen once they found the bodies without any internal organs, which had been surgically removed and sold.

No way was he going to be arrested when he stepped off the plane, which was what he figured the Feds had in store for him. He only guessed that the reason why they hadn't done it already, was because of the embarrassment it would cause to the bureau. If only they knew.

The door opened and he stepped into the elevator, pressed down, and felt the carriage descending to the morgue. It took a few seconds, then the doors opened quietly, and he was looking down a dimly lit hallway. At the end of the tunnel was a door, with a large pane of smoked glass set into it, behind which there was activity.

He pushed the door open quickly, surprising both the doctor, the orderly, and someone else.

Franco's disbelief turned instantly into a plan to save his ass, then his life.

Serena woke instantly, coughing and choking, fighting for air, and finally being granted a deep breath. She looked around in panic.

He had just been with her, and now he'd been yanked away from her.

She looked around, the movement of her skin causing the sticky pads to pull the flesh of her upper chest. She was in a hospital gown, laying in a hospital bed, in a white hospital room. What was going on, she wondered, spotting her wheelchair against the wall.

"Hey, Serena, Serena?" Figaro said, flowers in his hand. "They said you were too doped up to even talk!" There was a bandage on the side of his head, where he'd cut himself when he jumped into the cement encased flower bed.

"Help me into my chair, Figaro," she asked him. "Something's happening, I feel it. Hurry!" She begged him, but he hadn't moved. "Hurry, Figaro, please."

She moved her left, then her right leg, over the edge of the bed while Figaro looked on, stunned, then came over and helped.

The first breath was agonizingly painful, yet delicious at the same time. He dreaded leaving Swan behind, after just finding her in the darkness, but somehow knew she would search out his beacon and find him again, or he her.

When he could see, he started to panic. The Chinese doctor was smiling down at him, and there were dead bodies to his left and right. Another Asian orderly put the cardiac paddles back onto the charging device, then he, too, smiled down at him.

She was about to speak when the doors burst open, and Franco snarled at the three of them. The doctor and the orderly backed away as the fat lieutenant approached Dutch's body. He picked up Dutch's slack form and slung him like a sack of potatoes.

The orderly rushed at Franco, who snarled and swatted the man down with one clubbed fist. *Just like a riot*, Franco thought to himself as he backed out of the morgue, then ran for the exit.

Doctor Woo picked up the phone and dialed a number. She dreaded informing her superior of her failure, but she had to. The man who'd taken her ward was crazy, and worse, a part of the American police.

A voice asked her a question in Mandarin, which she answered immediately. Then another voice came on the line, the connection clear.

"Is it done?" Mister Pee asked. He wasn't far from the hospital.

"We have a problem," Doctor Woo said humbly, then began to explain.

Franco ran past the security booth, where a man was reading a newspaper, not caring about anything unless it had a motor and wasn't paying the parking toll. Sweat poured down his face as he ran into the dark empty street.

The taxicab nearly hit Franco dead on, tires squealing, front end sliding left and right as the cabby fought for a better grip, then finally stopped a few inches from impact. He had no choice but to accept the fare, half of which was thrown into the backseat.

"Drive!" Franco barked, tossing two one-hundred-dollar bills onto the front seat.

The cabby thought he recognized the unconscious man in the hospital gown. The man's face was familiar, but the short black hair threw him off. *Couldn't be*, he thought to himself, as he drove off.

"Whadaya lookin' at?" Franco barked.

"Nothing, Señor—I need to know where you going?" the cabby asked.

"The coast—you know anyone with a boat for hire?" Franco had an idea.

"Si, Señor, I have a cousin who lives in marina and owns a boat for hire." The cabby smiled humbly.

Dutch was listening to the voice coming from the front seat, the timber and tone very similar to a devil of a cabby he'd ran into just a short time ago. He kept his eyelids down, peering through his lashes, hoping to be able to preserve some element of surprise. As he took all this in, he couldn't help remembering the presence that had been with he and Swan in the dark place, like a father, or the Father, protecting their spiritual form.

"I know you're awake, Giovanni—don't try that shit on me," Franco said in a quiet, but deadly serious voice, which Dutch had heard during shakedowns and night raids.

The cabby recognized the name. The Chinese men who interrogated his cousin had mentioned it, before they killed him. He'd just stepped out of his cab, saw his younger cousin and asked him to watch it, then went and grabbed two cups of coffee from his aunt's café, which was only three blocks away from the wine shop where his other cousins were supposed to be taking care of the American. When he returned, he heard the noise of fist striking flesh, which he knew well, and therefore, caused him to lurk in the shadows, until he could see who was striking what. From the vantage point of a shadowy doorway he watched the two Triad members kill his young cousin. Then he knew his mistake, and when he found another cousin had been killed, in connection with the fare he picked up, and dropped off, he told his family and fled to Italy to work. Now he couldn't believe his luck.

Mister Pee was talking on the phone in the back of a long black limousine, when he saw a big man, with a sack or a body slung over his shoulder, nearly run over by a small taxicab.

He had flown to Italy the moment his people in Monaco called him, and had changed course, from Señor Giuseppe's to the hospital, the moment his sources informed him about the shootout.

Now he was sure that this cab ahead had Dutch, and the big man that Doctor Woo had been telling him about. He was determined to see Dutch in a safe place, even at personal risk. He had his pride and reputation, and most of all, his honor, to protect.

"Follow that cab, Fung Li," he ordered, then dialed a number.

His phone buzzed irritatingly inside of his inner coat pocket, and he knew it could only be his wife, the Boss, or the *consigliere*, who were the only ones to have this number. He dreaded having to deal with business at this time, or some other emergency. He only hoped his wife had not been told about her son, but he knew she would feel it like all mothers do.

He popped open the phone and put it to his ear, and listened for a moment, his jaw-mouth opening, and a sense of hope infusing his body. Señor Giuseppe started walking towards Serena's room, while making frantic gestures to his driver.

"Serena, he's ali—"She wasn't in her bed. "Maybe this isn't the room," he mumbled to himself, and back-stepped out of the room.

He walk/ran to the counter. "Nurse, where's Serena Repetto's room?" He watched her look at the chart, then back up at him.

A MEMORY OF FOREVER

"She's right there, sir." She gave him a questioning look, then came out from behind the counter and walked to the room Señor Giuseppe had just come from. "This is her room. I don't understand, she couldn't have left—not with these injections," she whispered the last while looking down at the medical chart.

"Get the car," he told his driver.

18

ALIVE

ROME WAS NOT BUILT *for the handicapped*, she reminded herself, the wheelchair bouncing and slipping into the ridges of the cobblestones, or cracks in the street.

"How do you know we're going in the right direction?" Figaro asked breathlessly. "I'm not sure I can make it, Serena?"

"Head for the marina—that's where he's at?" she told him, her hands keeping the gown from flying up into her face. There was no place else for them anyways, since Figaro was pushing her, and there were no hand rests.

She saw headlights behind them—

Then she was flying through the air, and she heard Figaro tumbling—shouting after her, the wheels of the car squealing, then the lights were bright in her eyes until a shadow of a man stepped in front of them.

"Miss Repetto," Señor Giuseppe greeted, then bent down and picked her up, while his driver grabbed the wheelchair.

"Will you be alright?" Serena called to Figaro, who was dusting himself off, and still breathing hard.

He looked up and gave her a tired smile, and a more tired wave.

"Drive!" Señor Giuseppe ordered, then turned his gaze to Serena.

"I need to go to the beach, Señor Giuseppe! It's a matter of life or death."

"The beach?" He thought about what Mister Pee had told him. "What do you know, Serena?"

"I don't know anything—I just feel—I know he's alive and going to safety, to the beach." She spoke with such an intensity that her fists were balled, as if ready to fight. "He's in danger, Señor Giuseppe!"

"We have people watching the marina, and Dutch has made powerful friends, who are even now trying to help him." He paused, listening to the powerful hum of the German-built engine, before continuing.

"But how is it you know Dutch?" He patted her leg and saw it move. When she looked away, not wanting to speak to him about it, he spoke softly. "He has saved my life twice today, Serena, and I would not for my own flesh and blood allow him to be harmed. I know you have suffered much today, and I will respect your privacy of course."

She thought about it for a long moment, not knowing if even she knew the how, or the why, or the what, then began to give him an abridged version of what was going on—at least one he could believe.

The cabby got out of the car and opened the back door, after honking the horn twice, by reaching in through the open window. Dutch remembered stopping in front of the wine shop. Hadn't the cabby honked his horn twice then?

"Franco, it's a setup." Dutch tried to reach out and stop Franco from getting out, but his muscles weren't working right for some reason.

Franco grunted as he slid towards the open door. "I gotta drag your ass out or you coming out on your own?" he asked.

The vinyl seat stuck to his flesh as he inched over to the open door, wishing whoever had done whatever to him had had the decency to dress him.

"Come on, convict-move your—"

THUMP! THUMP!

Dutch heard the sound, then saw the lieutenant's body fall to the ground. A coffee-stained smile, behind the barrel of a pistol, appeared, and he knew his luck had turned.

"Remember me, Dootch? I take no chances with you this time." The cabby motioned with the barrel for him to move.

Two men, each dressed in tight shorts and t-shirts, picked up Franco's body and took him to dock, then onto a boat.

"I like fat ones," the muscular Spaniard said.

Dutch smiled at the cabby. "I'm a little slow," he said. He was forced to use his arms and legs to slide across the seat, until finally he was at the door.

"I hear you was dead?" The cabby asked.

"I feel like I was." Though his left leg felt better, except for the bandage tape pulling hairs.

"You wish you was when Jorge's padre sees you."

"Oh, so it's gonna be that. Who the hell are you? What's your gig? Ripping off escaped convicts? What'd you do, track me down or something?" Dutch asked, testing his leg and standing up.

The cabby chuckled, but kept the gun on him. "Destiny," he replied, gesturing for Dutch to move to the dock.

The marina was a diverse area with all sorts of boats; fishing, rowing, tugs, sailing, cats, mini-barges, speedboats, gondolas, and two large hydrofoils further out. Beyond the maze of floating wooden docks, was another marina which held larger, more expensive, yachts, that were too big to fit this close to shore.

The boat, whose motor was running, that they were walking toward was an ancient twenty-foot fishing boat, painted aquamarine, and dubbed "*Orca 5*."

"Got a pair of pants or something?" Dutch asked as they walked onto the wood planks of the dock, no longer on land.

"You can wear fat man's clothes—" A laugh. "I don't think he'll need his clothes on this sea cruise.

"What?"

"You see, you see, now come on." The cabby suddenly became stern, and gripped Dutch's tricep to hurry him over the edge.

Dutch heard the men shouting, and saw a black limousine coming into the marina parking lot, where the cab had parked, and then, like some repetitive karma, things went black.

"Señor Giuseppe." Mister Pee bowed.

"Mister Pee." Señor Giuseppe returned the gesture.

"I have a yacht being fueled. Please bring your men," Mister Pee informed him.

Serena slipped out of the car and into her wheelchair, after hearing Señor Giuseppe and the Chinese man talk about a yacht. She saw a Chinese man standing at the end of a floating platform, where larger boats picked up passengers. That's where she started to roll while Señor Giuseppe and the other men were busy. No way were they going to keep her from getting on the yacht and going after her love.

The fear spread through her body, made her hands slip on the wheels, as she pushed herself onto the floating docks. The smell of the sea was thick and intimidating, not like on the cliffs, where the wind mixed and cleansed much of the sea's baser scents. The smell here seemed to rise up from the calm waters, letting her know that beneath the surface something much more dangerous existed, waited, stalked. It brought back not-so-distant memories, from which her fears stemmed, and she could only imagine how her love felt, already out upon the dark seas...

He looked down at the beautiful woman, who wore only a thin hospital gown, and was sweating and breathing hard from the exertion and effort it must have took to get up the ramps and out to this dock. He wondered if his boss knew.

"You coming?" he asked in English.

"I must." She looked up at the man, then heard the rumble of large motors, and saw the white shadow slipping towards them.

"My name is Dee Di-like D-D." He put out his hand, and she shook it.

"Serena—like Serene with an uh at the end. Nice to meet you."

A rope flew towards them, and before it hit her Dee Di picked it out of the air, and quickly tied it off, as the motors reversed. The boat slid to a stop against the old rubber tires with a short squeak.

A man jumped off the yacht's deck, flying the ten feet, and landed lightly onto the wood deck, simultaneously securing a line.

"Hey! You coming too?" He smiled at her.

"Could you carry me aboard?" Serena asked, at the same time wondering if Dee Di would say anything.

"Sure—let's go!" The bundle of energy folded out a ladder from the deck, turned to her. "Put your arms around my neck, naked lady." He laughed then bent down so she could hop on.

As the ship's mate carried her onto the deck of the yacht, she rethought her bravery for a moment, remembering the ocean she'd treaded in a time long ago, escaping one demon while running into another, much more personal, beast. Again, she could sense it below, waiting, a shadow following her everywhere. But there was no hesitation or panic, just a lump in her throat, and the feel of the universe guiding her towards him.

"Thank you," she told the man who flashed her a smile and bounded out of the spacious room.

The lounge-like room was thirty feet long and twenty feet wide, ceiling mirrored, and the floor a thick beige shag. Against the stern wall was a big screen television, while a cherry wood bar sat against the opposite bow wall, backed by more mirrors. There were four long couches and six easy chairs, all thick with pillows and deep cushions, and glass tables within easy reach. The walls, besides the mirrored portions, were wood paneled—with a dark ebony wood—so that everything stood out against it. There were five paintings, two of which she knew very well. Tinted windows ringed the room, and she looked from the dark seas awaiting to Señor Giuseppe, the slender Chinese man, and eight or more men coming down the ramp towards the yacht. All were armed except Señor Giuseppe and the Chinese man.

"What's she doing aboard?" Mister Pee said, more than a little perturbed. He looked at Serena, who sat at the far end of the nearest couch, pulling the short hospital gown to her knees.

She matched his stare, while Señor Giuseppe leaned over and whispered something to Mister Pee, who smiled brightly, and bowed graciously.

He put out his hand. "I'm deeply sorry, Miss Repetto. I did not realize you were the artist whose lovely paintings I buy to decorate so many of my humble belongings." He kissed her hand when she outstretched her own. "I hope you accept my apology—we are all very stressed."

"Of course, since you have such good taste." She smiled. "Would you happen to have any clothes?"

Mister Pee snapped his fingers and a nearby servant went to a door and disappeared. "You may call me Mister Pee, if you like."

The boat grumbled to life and slowly left the docks. They had to maintain a slow and constant speed until the big boat cleared the marina. Due to the yachts size there was only one way out, which was down a main thoroughfare. This took five minutes just to clear the marina, check for incoming barges or tankers, until they could throttle up both of the 1500-horsepower diesel engines.

She sensed a few of the soldiers looking at her bare legs, and she subconsciously pulled the hem down further, not to mention the thin material was nearly see-through.

Her hopes for clothes lifted when the servant returned, but instead went to Mister Pee, who shook his head and turned to her from his seat.

"I'm sorry, but all the closets were emptied for refurbishing just yesterday. However, I'm informed that there are towels, if you'd like a few?"

"I guess I'll just have to be a man," she tried to joke.

"That would be very impossible indeed—would you care for a drink?"

A MEMORY OF FOREVER

"Seven Up? Ginger ale? My stomach's a little queasy," she asked.

She watched Mister Pee look at the black-tied bartender, who had come out of hiding, and was now pouring drinks she swore he could not have heard her order. Then he was handing her the drink, as well as one for Mister Pee, and Señor Giuseppe.

A man in a white uniform came into the room.

"Mister Pee, we have the *Orca 5* on radar—one and a half miles to the west, heading for Corsica, or the Med. We'll catch him in twenty minutes or less at our current speed."

"Thank you, Captain, proceed." Mister Pee waved him off with a hand.

"Well, I guess we'd better huddle up," Señor Giuseppe said, plopping down in a chair next to Serena. *I'm not comfortable with her being here any more than Mister Pee, but after the story she'd told me, how can I stop her. If it is her destiny?* He knew he would have hell to pay if she were hurt.

Serena was glad for Señor Giuseppe's nearness, and she listened to the men making war plans, but she was captivated, drawn, to the blackness outside of the boat's lighted aura. It beckoned and called to her, but so did someone else.

She shut her eyes and listened for him, silently calling her lover, letting Julius know she was coming; "I'm coming, my love." She willed her thoughts to him.

19

On the High Seas...Again

"Squeal like a Pig!" Raymond, six feet tall, weighing over two hundred and fifty pounds, yelled.

His ninety-pound brother Felix applied the crude electrodes that were actually a pair of jumper cables, which were attached to an outlet on a clankety old generator.

BUZZZZHHHHH!

"Ahhhheeeeeee," Franco screamed, and continued screaming.

Felix laughed in a high-pitched giggle.

Raymond brought the whip down on the fat man's bare backside. The carbon fiber fishing rod struck the blueberry flesh, which tensed upon impact, then rippled up and down Franco's trunk.

BUZZZZZZZZI II II II II II II IHH!

"AAAHHHHHHEEEEEEEEEEEEEEEE!"

"Squeal! Squeal like a pig!"

BUZZZZZZZZZZHHHHHHHHHHHHH!

"AAAAAAHHHHHHHHHEEEEEEEEEEEEEEE!"

"He's shit hisself!" Felix exclaimed with pleasure, and his high-pitched giggle.

"Grab the hose and spray him off!" Raymond ordered.

"You don't give the orders!"

Felix cringed as Raymond raised an arm to bitch-slap him.

"You do it and I'll let you go first," Raymond promised.

He felt one of the men touch him, while the other was talking in the Spanish he so despised, but at least they weren't frying him with the electrodes. Then he took that thought back as something touched him intimately. The whip cracked across his neck and shoulders, as he felt himself being violated.

Franco's eyes bulged, and he bit off the tip of his tongue, as he remembered how he had let the gangs rape the young fish who wouldn't become snitches, or do his biddings. The whip cracked.

Raymond poked the fat man, who was wedged between the piles of fishing nets, but there was no response. "You screw him to death, you idgit! You tell Papa who did it too!"

"No! You whip him to death! You!"

"No you!"

"No you!"

The two continued for a while.

"What, you no like fat man's clothes?" the cabby asked.

Dutch looked at the two-sizes-too-big pants and decided to stay with the hospital gown. He'd already surveyed his surrounds, on the bridge of the *Orca 5*, which was now struggling in the five- to ten-foot swells of the Tyrrhenian Sea. It seemed every surface of the bridge was eroded, worn, or scarred. The glass covering the gauges were smudged, and had to be tapped every so often.

He rubbed his neck, where the cabby had clobbered him with the butt of the hand gun, but there was no blood, and surprisingly, he didn't have a headache. The only ache he did have was the deep throbbing in his left leg. *What the hell is going on?* he wondered, as he looked out of the window to the deep blackness outside the filthy glass, and felt the pull of the sea below, its very essence drawing his attention, warning and beckoning at the same time.

The cabby, gun still at the ready, leaned against the ancient wood instrument panel, not seeming to care about where they were heading. He reached over and turned up the gas lantern, which swayed on a hook in the ceiling.

"You no like?"

Dutch threw him the pants, and grinned.

The cabby sniffed them, and "Whooeee'd" before balling them up. He opened the only door to the bridge and threw them out onto bow deck, where a ghost picked them up and took them to the sea.

The fishing boat crawled up a swell and slid down its back, the motors revving as the twin props cleared the surface for a moment. They were both forced to keep their own balance.

"We're in mid currents now," the cabby said, as if his and Dutch's fate were now forever sealed.

"So what's goin' on?" Dutch asked straight out, wondering where Franco was.

The cabby smiled proudly, thinking about telling the American, before speaking. "You have bad luck, Dootch, but I like you — I have many family — mostly drive Eurocabs, and rob a few tourists. We are Gypsies from Corsica —"

The *Orca 5* dropped ten feet instantly, and Dutch thought about making an attack, grabbing the door frame for balance, but the cabby smiled knowingly at him, the gun still in his hand, and pointed at Dutch's gut.

Once the boat came out of the bowl, the cabby adjusted the wheel, and continued, "We aren't assassins or killers. No, we earn an honest living — we take only cameras, traveler's checks, camera's, jewelry, you know." He waited for Dutch to approve, but only got a nod, which seemed to be enough. "But you mess things up — you and your Chinese friends. You kill my sister's son, and my uncle's son —"

"I didn't touch him! I mean, if you want revenge, why don't you get the guys who really killed your cousins —"

The cabby laughed. "We will, in time, but you pay for both when we get to Corsica."

"I have a lot of money!" Dutch tried.

"You escaped convict—you have not even a penny, I checked." The cabby looked him up and down, then laughed. "Look at you'self."

Raymond, back in his shorts, stumbled onto the bridge, barely fitting through the door. He was contrite and apologetic, even before the words left his mouth.

The cabby seemed to know that he had done something bad. "What did you do?" The question inevitable.

"I think the fat man died," he told the cabby in a quiet manner.

Dutch watched as the older, and much smaller cabby made to strike the big muscular man, who flinched away, and raised his hands to ward off the blow that never fell.

"No pay for you! Throw the body overboard!" The cabby spat in disgust. "Go!" he ordered.

Dutch watched for an opening, figuring his only chance would be to seize the gun from the cabby, and force him to turn the boat inland. The only other method of escape would be to jump overboard, but there wasn't a chance in hell he was jumping into the middle of the rolling ocean.

His fear of water was overpowering, and his gut was balled into a tight fist, but he knew she was counting on him to come out of this alive. He must survive, if only for her, because he knew she, too, would die. This would not be how he ended his days, not after finding her, and not after having viewed such a golden glimmer of their future when she was in his arms.

Raymond and Felix threw Franco's bulk onto the foredeck, then stomped up the steps, and were about to throw the lieutenant overboard when the cabby screamed and cursed and cut the engine.

Dutch wondered what this was about as he tried to keep his balance, after nearly falling forward.

"You idiots! Stupidi, stupidi!" The cabby continued to berate them in Spanish, until they moved the body to the other side of the boat.

Dutch smiled as both men strayed away from the cabby's waving fists, and leaned forward to see Franco's jiggling flesh as they lifted him up. He saw the welts laid across Franco's body, the blood smears around his ass and thighs, and he knew what had gone on below deck. He'd seen a few rape victims in prison, left in the showers, naked—the young and weak, whom the predators had taken advantage of, but Franco was a proud man whose manhood had been stripped and taken in a fashion more violent than he'd ever seen. For all his evil, he was still a human being, and Dutch felt sad for him; "Poor bastard," he whispered. He watched the body go overboard, and—

Lights blinded them, a loud air horn blew, and then a tall white ghost rammed the boat, as if it had come out of the ocean swell. Raymond shouted and tried to push the steel hull off of his father's fishing boat. Wood splintered, and the *Orca 5* groaned under the weight of the yacht's hull, which had rode up onto the bow. He pushed and shouted in a high-pitched voice, knowing he would be taking the blame for this as well, before he took one, two, three bullets and fell back into the nets.

Dutch saw the cabby jump the nets, and the dead body, and knew what his plan was. He limped to the door and put his weight against it. The glass window shattered, and he felt the barrel of the gun against his temple, then strong fingers in his short hair.

"Shit," Dutch muttered, as the cabby pulled him out of the bridge, gun to his head.

A spotlight shone directly upon them, even as shots were being exchanged between Felix and the men on the yacht.

He realized her presence just beyond the dark windows, and the glare of spotlights, just as his left leg buckled and he was looking at the sea between the two hulls. Dutch heard a cannon's boom in his head and felt a searing heat against his left ear, and then he was falling overboard, into the cold black liquid of the open sea—

Serena searched the small boat with her eyes, as soon as the spotlights had lit it up. Even before she saw a skinny man drag him at gunpoint out of the bridge, she knew he had been standing there behind the grimy windows. Now she shuddered, her face against the cold glass, as the man held the gun against Julius' head. Then a swell lifted the bow of the yacht, blocking her view, and she heard a shot that was much different than the constant automatic gunfire. When the yacht slipped down off of the bow of the fishing boat, and she was able to see, Julius was gone, the cabby shooting bullets into the water, before his body started to dance and twitch as bullets began slapping him around. She was already dragging herself to the door, then out into the cold air, searching the water, while the skinny gypsy was finishing his dance macabre.

Bullets were still flying from the holdout aboard the *Orca 5*, but it wouldn't be long, as the projectiles were literally ripping apart the fishing boat's wooden surfaces.

Señor Giuseppe saw her out of the corner of his eye as she went overboard.

"Noooo!" Señor Giuseppe shouted after her, moving forward, then being thrown backward as the *Orca 5* exploded with a whoompf, and threw off a concussion wave of gas so hot that it sucked the oxygen from the air around him and the other men.

He was struggling to hold his breath, and swim towards the bright orange glow off to his right, which had let him know that he was indeed swimming for the surface. He saw the lights of the yacht in the same direction, but they were getting smaller and smaller.

He broke the choppy surface and came up out of the water. A swell raised him up even higher, and he sucked oxygen greedily and slapped his hands on the surface. He went under for a second, then bobbed back up.

When he was comfortable in his ability to tread water, he began swimming back towards the lights of the yacht, which were at least a hundred yards away, he guessed. His intuitive mind, and memory, started to prey on his thoughts, forcing him into silent prayer. He concentrated on moving and kicking, keeping his heart pumping and his core temperature warm—

She screamed as she bumped her head into something, until she realized it was him.

"It's me, Swan!" he shouted, then grabbed her naked form and held her tight to his own.

"My love," she whispered in his ear, clinging to his body, at the same time kicking her feet to stay afloat, but so wanting to wrap her legs around his trunk.

"Swanlake, my love," he said into her ear, holding her tight, feeling the stress leave his body. A new energy infused his cells, and his soul, and gave him a stronger constitution to survive. "Thank thee, Oh Lord." He kissed her on the mouth, even as the waves lapped and threatened them.

He felt something. Behind and beneath him. It had rubbed the backs of his calves, and then he saw Swanlake's eyes open, and she started to scream.

The palm of a hand struck Swanlake in the forehead, knocking her away from Dutch, as the arm of the crazed thing wrapped tight around his neck from behind. A gurgling snarl, and she saw Julius slip beneath the surface. A swell lifted her gently and set her back down, then she felt a coarse skin brush the bottom of her feet, and she began shivering with fear, tucking her legs tight against her bottom.

"Julius! Julius! Dutch!" she shouted into the darkness.

There was no answer, not even the splashes of a struggle.

Dutch knew whose deadly grip it was. He had felt it once before, ten thousand miles away, in another, much drier hell. He bit into the fleshy forearm, but there was no reaction, even as he tore off flesh. They were both falling down and down, until something much larger than the two of them went by so close that Dutch's skin was instantly given a painful rash.

Franco's insanity broke, and a clear thought entered his brain, making him forget the humiliation and pain in favor of a greater fear.

Dutch felt the hold loosen, and he pushed away and swam for the surface. It was not as far above as he thought—

"Swan!" he shouted the moment he could. "Swan?"

"Over here! Over here!"

He swam to her and she to him, met, and clung to each other, kissing, trying to regroup once again.

He pulled away. "It's here, my love," he whispered to her in the darkness, wishing the yacht would come this way.

"I know," she answered. "Just hold me tight, my love."

"Giovanni—" Franco growled in the dark, five meters away. "It's coming for us, boy!" A fearful laugh. "Where you at, boy?"

"Shhh, my love. Don't say anything," she whispered into his ear.

"Where's that girlie at? I'll take care of her too."

They both felt the pressure wave of a submarine-sized monster passing below them, and then heard Franco begin to scream and shout.

"Ahh—Get away, get away, aahee!" he screamed in a high-pitched voice.

Dutch held her shivering form against his own, and lifted her legs so she would not be taken first this time. He vowed to himself that he would die before she, this time. "Wrap your legs around my waist, my love."

She did as he asked. "How is it with thee, my love?"

"I am alive and with thee," he said in perfect Italian, "and we shall forever be, thee and me, hand in hand, in the dark and in the glow, we shall be together, like two heads on a pillow."

"I have our pillow," she whispered in his ear, trembling as something swam by their bodies in the dark, bumping them roughly.

"Fret not, my love, they will come soon." He prayed for the yacht to see the direction of the current and come for them.

She clung to him, pressing every inch of her flesh against his, wishing he was inside of her, even now, when her mind was trying to combat the urge to scream and scream and scream.

He felt her fears and apprehension as she pressed against him tighter and tighter. "Shhh, maybe it will leave us this time," he lied.

Franco screamed nearby, letting them know he was still alive, still a threat, albeit a very small one in comparison. It seemed to be playing a game with them; Inni-mini-miny-moe. While the boat, getting closer, searched out the swells with its great spotlight.

The light crossed over them, then came back, and Serena waved her hands in the air. Dutch saw it looking at him as it passed by in an agonizingly slow drift, as if it knew the light would allow Dutch to see it, to recognize it. A chill ran down his spine as he recalled the scars and gouges on the white-shark's mammoth-sized head, and stared into the depths of the black pearl. He swore it smiled back at him, with its eye, a recognition of sorts, then with a flick of the tail it was gone.

"Hold fast, my love." He was trembling, but tried not to show it.

"I will always hold fast to thee, my love." There was a hint of a smile in her voice. She was happy, now in the light, warmed by his flesh and within range of his voice, and able to speak to his intelligence. What more could she ask for?

"Is that a smile on your beautiful face?" he asked, trying to block out the panicked screams, and sounds of terror that Franco was making somewhere behind him.

"It just might be," she teased, embracing and forgetting the fear. "I have waited all my life for him, Lord, let us live this time."

They heard the boats engines reversing, and more lights fell upon them. Dutch saw the love in her eyes, and behind her the gray back of the beast, then the tall dorsal fin, seven feet high, which blocked out the searchlights, as if they were in some nightmarish eclipse.

Dutch held her tight and turned her away from the beast, placing his body between it and her, though he didn't think it would matter. Its head was as big as a full size van. They would be but tidbits in its belly. He prayed the men on the yacht would recognize the danger and hurry. The lights were indeed coming closer, just as—

It had him around the upper thighs, saw blades digging in, when it could have sucked his body all the way down into its pinkish-white throat, instead taking Franco's gurgling, screaming body into the dark waters reddened by blood.

He heard Franco's voice, high-pitched, screaming in unrelenting terror, then a gurgle, and it was quiet except for the shouts from the crew aboard the yacht.

A rope ladder came overboard, as the white hull slid close by, and she grabbed it and someone yanked her up out of the water. Señor Giuseppe hauled her naked form up and over the rail and wrapped her in a thick blanket, even as she struggled to turn and make sure Dutch was safely aboard—"Hurry! Get him out!" she shouted with authority. They all knew something was down there, had seen the ragged gray sail cross in front of Dutch and Serena, which had caused many to rethink their ocean swims and fishing trips. Now it was paramount that the rope ladder be thrown perfectly, as the current instantly began taking Dutch away from the boat again.

He grabbed the rope out of the air, thankful for the rising swell beneath him. Dutch wrapped it around his arm as Señor Giuseppe and another large Italian began dragging him through the water.

Dutch saw it coming out of the corner of his right eye, knowing it would reach him before he could reach the yacht. Franco's large upper torso burst out of the water, rushing at him, the large dorsal fin of the puppeteer behind him. He locked eyes with the insane man, who smiled and reached for him, intent—whether his or the beast's—on dragging him to a watery grave.

A single shot was fired, and Dutch saw a dot appear above Franco's left brow. The rope tightened around his wrist, nearly pulling his shoulder out of its socket, but he watched the great beast before him, chasing him, as it tossed Franco's body down its gullet, then flicked its tail and came for his legs.

He heard and felt the bullets going by him, but the pressure wave beneath him told him that it was too late. Dutch looked up and found her beautiful face, mouth open, screaming in the ugly emotion of fear, and then it was under him and the lights of the boat blurred and faded, as a warm breath of putrid air surrounded his lower body, and he concentrated on holding fast—

20

CHI

"He's lost too much!" Doctor Woo muttered to herself, knowing that her own future relied on this man living. She gathered her "chi" and brought it out of her, into her hands, which moved slowly over his chest and heart and head; the vital organs, which needed her inner strength to survive this dangerous time. Blood was being added to his own supply, but she didn't know if it was too late. She'd had to reclose the wound first and that had taken longer than the first time, because she wasn't in the hospital, or in an operating room. She breathed out and concentrated, pushing her warming force into his cool body.

The BP was still too low, heart not fast enough—

Mister Pee walked into the small doctor's office, which had been arranged for surgery, and looked at Doctor Woo's attempts to master her force.

"Have you done everything medically possible, Doctor Woo?"

"Yes, it is up to him now." She bowed as her superior ordered her out with a gesture of his hands.

"Uhhmmmmm—" Mister Pee shut his eyes, placed his hands together over Dutch's body, and rubbed them together ten times. A rumble came from his throat, deep and yet soothing, like a building purr. Then a hiss through his teeth, his body temperature rising five degrees, but directed to his palms.

This new perception—of days long withered away, whose truth could never be exactly and fully described with even the most precise scientific analysis—and understanding, with all its gifts and odd comparisons, beauty and ugliness, love and hate, fog and smog, life and death, could not distract her from the inner voice, which prayed and begged to the omniscience above; "Let us be together this time, please don't take us away from each other." And on and on the prayer went, in silence, amidst the tension of the room.

Señor Giuseppe expected the worst when Doctor Woo came out of the small room. He perked up, waited for the small woman, who looked too young to be a doctor, then slowly relaxed when she said nothing. He watched her walk into the women's bathroom, and wondered what was going on inside the examination room, which they'd used to operate on Dutch's wound. He didn't know if he should go in and help Mister Pee, or stay here, helpless, listening to Serena's silent sobs, or prayers, which sounded alike to him. His thumbs met and separated, met and separated.

A MEMORY OF FOREVER

He felt the sunlight upon his skin, warming his outer body, and inner organs, comforting him and lending to him a power, a bar to cling to; rather, he sensed life had not left him completely. The dark shadows slowly disappeared, the ghostly voices (some in languages he did not understand but felt akin to) fading to an earthly hum. Amidst this conundrum of comings and goings—of spiritual and aural—he could smell specific meals of long ago, from times when he was a child in America, before his father died, their days clear in his mind; the day before his first day of school; a weekend with the entire family, his father cooking lamb on the grill out back; five days before he died (His father cooked all the meals in their household, up to the day he died). Finally, it was pain that brought him from the surreal into the real.

Mister Pee did not hear Dutch moan in pain, in realization of the sensation now that he was back among the living, his state being one of deep meditation, his bodily force, his "chi," being directed downward into the body, heating and causing expansion, and therefore, life. In his mind his hands were fire, his force so strong that he had only keep his hands near Dutch's flesh. A silent hum seemed to emanate from him, like the flickering of a candle in absolute silence. Finally he connected, became the dying man, his aura slipping into the organs, and was able to further add to the strength he imbued into his friend. He felt his own heartbeat matching that of Dutch's, and was able to stir the weaker heart into activity, even as the scientific infusion—of blood and medicine—did its job—

Dutch opened his eyes.

Mister Pee's eyes opened, intuitive senses taking over, telling him he was being watched. The mechanism so ingrained from past experience that it even invaded his deepest meditations. He felt Dutch, in the spiritual sense, slip away from him.

He couldn't help but begin the long track downward, his eyes slowly falling, his neck bending: *Please let my legs be there*, he thought.

"They are still there, Dutch," Mister Pee smiled down at him.

His second thought. "Is she okay?" It was a hoarse whisper. Dutch felt Mister Pee's hand upon his arm, unnaturally hot, and began to understand the warm infusion of life he'd felt in the dark shadows of the dying. As blood began to fill his veins and arteries, he began to feel the forgotten sensations; PAIN! CRAMPS!

"I will send Doctor Woo in, my friend, and tell your friends that you are alive." He turned to walk out—"Mister Pee," Dutch started. "I felt you inside…within me…thank you."

"You owe me.

Dutch smiled and put his head back onto the pillow, just now realizing that he was completely naked. He heard a scream outside the room, the timber and voice familiar. He pulled the white cotton sheet underneath him over his lower half, settling for this, as he heard footsteps coming towards the door, running for the door—

"Dutch—Julius!" Serena screamed happily as she burst through the door and ran to his side. Nobody questioned her about walking.

"What shall we call each other, my love?" Dutch asked, barely able to lift his arm, but managing to touch her face and accept her kiss.

"No, no, no," Doctor Woo said in a quiet manner. "No smooching now—he needs rest."

Serena felt the woman's grip on her arm, and allowed herself to be led away, now that she knew he would live, and they would be together. She felt her knees buckle, then Señor Giuseppe was holding her up.

"You again?" Dutch whispered, once they were alone.

"I apologize, but I had to kill you to save your life."

"I guess I should be grateful, so thanks for killing me," he said in a weak voice.

"Shh, you really do need rest now." Doctor Woo patted his hand, then began checking his vitals.

21

Three Weeks Later

"And in other news, reports from Italian officials have determined that the body of escaped convict, Dutch Giovanni, was accidently cremated while waiting to be shipped to the United States."

The female host looked up at the monitor, and smiled, before delivering her next lines. "Now if that was conspicuous, we have a similar report that is related to that story. FBI Agent Dawn Carroll, seen here in this photograph, who was also the agent in charge of investigating Lieutenant Paul Franco's whereabouts, has disappeared as well. If you remember last week's top story, about Arizona Department of Corrections officials harvesting organs from inmates and selling them to the rich, or to high ranking officials, it makes you wonder what else is going on in this investigation—"

"—sounds fishy, Disell," the male host cut in as planned. "On another front, the corpse of a big-mouth shark weighing ten tons was found on the coast of Florida. Inside the thirty-foot beast, which was supposed to be extinct, was the body of five people, yet to be identified—"

"Oh God, that's gross..." the female host interjected, as the music came in to setup their commercial.

She watched her mother's tears falling; a consequence of her newly delivered message.

"Mama, I have—" Serena paused. "I need to be with him." There was no other explanation to the gravitational yearning, the force that attracted her to Julius. What could she say that wouldn't be excused by others as love, when it was more than love. It was the pinnacle of all things that hold two different species (man and woman) in that constant longing to be within each other's presence, which even now begged her attention.

"I know; I know, it's just losing both of you at the same time is so hard, my daughter," she urged understanding.

Serena hugged her mother, felt the sobs hiccup against her ears, and the wet cheek pressed against her own. It broke her heart to hear her mother cry, and she being the cause of it, or at least half of it, her own tears falling.

The horn honked outside.

"Mama, I have to go now, Aunt Cassy is here to keep you company and you know I'll visit. Mama?" Serena hoped her mother understood, and approved.

"Okay, okay," her mother backed away, not hostile, but in a manner that meant that her sobbing was done and now it was time to wish her daughter the best and send her off with good spirits. "You go ahead with your life, my dearest daughter. I'll see you at the wedding, right? And you'll call often?"

"Of course, Mama, you know that. I'm not leaving the country or anything." She smiled and kissed her mother on the cheek. "I love you, so please take care of yourself for me."

"Tell Dutch—oh—I mean, tell Fabio I said hello."

"Dutch will be delighted to hear that," Serena whispered.

"Be happy." She smiled for her daughter's sake, trying to hold back the flood that would come soon enough.

"Thank you, Mama. Don't be sad...okay..." Serena still wasn't satisfied, but knew that her mother was strong enough to get through this period of sadness, until, maybe, she found another.

"I'll walk you out. Here, let me get one of the bags." Her mother cheered up, and helped her carry out her luggage, trying to present a happier facade, than that of the last three weeks.

Serena wished Aunt Cassy goodbye, thanking her for staying in Genoa to keep her mother company, though she knew it was no trouble. Then she got into the black Mercedes, where one of Señor Giuseppe's drivers had been waiting to take her home.

Home, Serena smiled, thinking of how she would pass the time in this backseat until she could be with him. She flexed her thigh muscles, and calf muscles, which she'd been exercising vigorously for the past three weeks, when she had time. Between her father's funeral, and the move to the villa north of Naples, and Julius, she had little time for anything else. There wasn't anything else that she wanted to do.

"Stop the car, Federico." Claudia's shop was open, and Serena wanted to say goodbye. She had a special surprise for her.

The gift shop was empty, as usual, with Claudia behind the counter, reading a romance novel. When the bell dinged, the older woman looked up, then beamed a bright smile, with a little start of a scream.

"Serena! God, I thought I'd never see you again!" As she ran forward, tears falling, she saw the big covered painting.

Serena hugged the woman awkwardly, still having a little problem with her own balance, especially under the weight of another, or in positions she wasn't accustomed to; for instance, holding a thirty-six-by-twenty-four-inch oil painting, trying not to drop it, while being hugged to death.

"Okay, okay, Claudia! I miss you too, but I might fall," she laughingly spoke.

Claudia stepped back and smiled, her hands still on Serena's cheeks. "God, but you are so beautiful, more than before, and you're really walking. Thank God. I read about it in the newspaper, but I didn't really—well—"

"I brought you a going-away gift, and a promise to come visit when I am in town." Serena handed her the covered painting. "Please wait till I leave to look at it. I hope you like it."

"Oh, thank you." She hugged her again, leaning the painting against the wall. "I'll miss you each day, Serena."

"Thanks for being there for all these years, and for keeping my spirits up," Serena referred to instances that Claudia could not know of, nor understand how she had helped.

"Do you have time for coffee, or dinner?"

"I'm leaving straight away, but you're invited to the wedding in October."

"I can't wait to meet your man...Oh, Serena, I will truly miss your company." Tears fell. "You have my address, and you can send me yours when you get home, okay. Write me."

"I promise."

Claudia watched her friend leave, then turned to the painting with curiosity. She picked it up and untied the knot of twine holding on the brown paper covering. As the painting came into view, she had to step back.

"It's me," a whisper, tears falling from her eyes. "It's really me..."

HERCULENIUM, PRESENT DAY

HE WAS WORRIED, but he knew she was safe, even as the sun dipped into the sea and he was still alone in their new home. Eager. Waiting. His hands ached from pounding nails and screwing screws for the past two weeks.

Their new home was like the one they knew before, whether by coincidence, or by fate. A large kitchen with a connecting dining room, one main hallway that led to three bedrooms —one of which was being turned into a nursery —and two bathrooms, a small study and library, and a large living room. The floors were all red clay tiles, sealed, and polished to a high gloss. Hanging greenery Swan's touch permeated the house with sights and scents, which softly imbibed the senses with a feeling: homeliness and privacy. *Rather like a bumblebee in a sweet-smelling flower, without all the buzzing around and worker-bee mentality,* Julius thought to himself.

He'd felt guilty about taking another identity, like some invasive spirit or body-snatcher, which his conscience did not sit well with. However, he'd realized with some thought, and conversation with

Swan, that he was also his Dutch-self, as much as he was his Julius-self. There was no violent stripping of another's reality, or of the baser and higher qualities, but an invitation to reckon and bring together the selves. To place the dual memories into line, and work to secure those distant memories he still couldn't quite place, but which came upon him each day.

His only sadness was that he couldn't see his family, which he believed would have helped him to reconcile with the guilt. But Mister Pee had said he might be able to work something out in a couple of years, and that gave him some hope. He would love to see Salvatore and his wife.

He felt guilty for being allowed to love Swan, not dissimilar to the guilt felt by the survivors of horrific plane crashes. *I should have died and gone on like everyone else, but for the Grace of God. Why have we been allowed this joyous opportunity, to be granted the warmth of reunification with true love? Not in the meaningless sense of samsara, birth and rebirth, but the continuation with the conscious knowledge of previous lives, previous places, and most importantly, previous love.*

Indeed, Swan and I can speak the near secret language, long forgotten by present-day linguists, and often in the throes of passion, we revert to this language.

Maybe tonight we'll be speaking in that long-lost language, he thought, surveying the full moon, the burning candles that surrounded the quilts and cushions he'd laid out on the patio, near the soft light of the blue pool. *If only she'd get here soon,* Julius hoped, and leaned back against the cushions....

Swanlake felt her heart quicken as she approached the gate, and dark house beyond. A flickering light came from the side of the house near the walkway that led to the pool and patio. The warm breeze carried the scents of the forest around them, which were alighted with the golden flicker of the candles. She followed a trail of rose petals she spied upon entering the gates, and found her surprise at the end of the trail.

She took off her shoes and quietly stepped onto the quilt, where he lay sleeping, a peaceful smile on his lips. She slipped off her skirt and blouse, and everything else, until she was as naked as Julius was. She sidled up close to his body, feeling the heat emanating from his tanned skin, then traced her fingers down his chest, through his soft mat, then down across his belly, and finally to his manhood, which was soft and pliant in her hands. She loved to explore his body while he was sleeping, as she did now. Her lips kissed soft flesh, and blew across the dark-brown jungle, until glistening rain drops appeared, which she drank to quench her thirst. Then took him fully into herself, using her tongue and throat and lungs, a hot flush burning her lower belly, wetting the thatch between her legs. His prickly hair tickled her nose. She breathed him into her core, suddenly needing him awake inside of her, enveloping her whole body with the fire that he always started. But she wanted to taste him first, and her hand was finding new places on its own. Worlds began to spin away, along with their memories, and she was only there and now with him, the warm steel rubbing the deepest areas of her throat. Then she slowed and released him, until her man's tool became soft again. She blew on the spit-slicked flesh, which was like hot lava just cooled by water, but still pulsing with that inner fire that was ready to burst forth at any moment. She explored the rod-shaped flesh, and its bulbous mushroom, maybe eight inches or more, with her tongue and lips and breath, until it grew and grew. Blood filled it once again. Fire danced in her eyes, her fingers danced between her thighs, and this time she didn't wait. She took him all the way into her throat, nibbling on the base of his staff, delighting and rubbing her nose in his curly hairs, her lungs sucking him harder and longer, willing his juices to wet her lips and fill her. Her own orgasm was building to a higher plateau, a soft climb to another heavenly cloud, which burst forth with thunder and lightning when she felt two large fingers enter her newly opened folds. It was more than she could take, her lips releasing momentarily as she forgot what she was doing in the moment of explicit and extreme pleasure. She felt his fingers in her hair, guiding her up and down, as he spat jets of hot lava into her shaking body. Two fingers stretched her softest flesh, preparing the way. She shook again at the thought of what was to come.

She played him again, until he was hard and rigid, but he stalled her demands with his hunger for her body. He rolled her onto her back.

"What are you doing now?" she asked curiously, as cold champagne brought out a delighted exclamation, and then he was upon her like a hungry lion. Tongue scooping out the flesh of the honeydew, squeezing and probing. Her eyes sparkled, and she could not close her mouth for the moans and yelps that continued forth.

When he was done, seemingly hours later, she lay back exhausted and ready for him, needing him so badly that she was grabbing at his flesh, pulling him onto her glowing body, begging to be plundered.

"I love you," he whispered to her, hypnotized by the fires that danced in her eyes, as he lowered himself between her ivory pillars.

She felt him lift her legs, then spread them, so that the tops of her knees were on each side of his face, her legs dangling over his shoulders. She loved this sensation, completely vulnerable, but oh, so exquisitely in his capable hands, her fields ready to be plowed again and again.

"And you are my only, forever but would you please stop teasing me and—oh, Julius!" she exclaimed as he thrust his spike deep into her gold vein. "Do it—do it—all of it, my love!"

She was so tight; it was hard for him to keep himself from instantly spewing his seed inside of her, which was why she'd sucked him off once before. He knew she was learning, and remembering, how to make love. He stared into those blue skies, and they enveloped him, as he drove into her gently at first.

She felt him stiffen and grow larger than she'd ever felt him, and the thought and sensation brought an explosion into her belly. Even as she feared his plunging and pulling, she loved it, longed for it to continue. Her muscles tightened around him, his rock hard flesh hot and unforgiving, in that perfect unison of man and woman.

"JULIUS!" "SWAN!" They both cried in unison. Muscles twitched and spasmed. The world disappeared momentarily, then it changed—

She felt herself flipping over, and his beautiful shaft was somehow going even deeper and with a new sensation, his balls slapping against her mons, his hands rough around her breasts, fingers clamping hard nipples, with each thrust pulling them.

He felt himself staying hard, excited by her acquiescence, and new sensations, new depths, his cock seemingly bigger than ever before, if that was physiologically possible. Their bodies, in that position, fit perfectly, each time his hips slapping into her rounded ass cheeks, then pulling out and grasping her breasts to pull her to him even as he plunged into her, so that they met, hard and violent, his sword stabbing deeper and deeper into her. He told her, leaning in to his thrusts, pulling her back, that he loved her. Over and over he drove his manhood into her womanhood. When he let go of her left breast, she felt his hand snake down between her legs, her mouth open, saliva dripping onto the material of the quilt unconsciously, his fingers toying with her belly button, then soft fingernail scratches in her pubic hair, pulling and letting go in time with each thrust and then her right, one hand between her legs, the other full of silky yellow hair, he began to thrust harder into her, which was upon request of she beneath him. For a long while both continued—

—she was on her hands and knees, with him licking the salty perspiration off of her spine and doing several other things with his fingers and hands that pleased her too much, once again, as she began to steadily and fiercely articulate, while the coup de grace was in sight; "Yes, Julius! Keep fucking me! Yes, yes, yes, yes!"

Then, as he spewed himself into her, his literal gene pool, he thrust himself too hard into her and then collapsed, with him atop of her steaming body.

"I think I forgot who I was, my lover," Swanlake whispered into his face, breathing in his breath.

"That wouldn't be the first time...for either of us."

"Ouu, don't pull out, lover," she begged, knowing that it wasn't him, but the human body.

"You keep squeezing those muscles and you'll get more of this," Julius warned.

"Oh, you think I can't take this?"

"I just don't want to over—do it, with—you know—you being pregnant and all," he added gently,

She touched the side of his face, and kissed him soft and long, before speaking. "I can go all night, if you can, my love."

And so they did.

22

THE ROMAN

THE PECULIAR SHAPE of Piazza del Herculenium was due to the canalization and diversion of rainwaters on an irregular and bare ground, shaped like a semi-amphitheater, where the hills, on which these ruins of upper Herculenium sat and came together. One rutted road skewered the center; an ancient interstate led, from hither to dither, yet beyond the findings of today's archaeologists. Surrounding the site, which may have encompassed four or five football fields, was a very pleasant landscape, rich in green fields of olive trees, vineyards, and cypresses. The ground within the site had been lowered, and from it, the ancient homes and ghosts of pre-79AD sprouted. There were one-room, two-room, and many-roomed villas, all built up from the same pinkish-brown brick, preserved by the fiery ash cloud of two eruptions.

"Blasted Vesuvius," an angry whisper from within the darkness.

Then he spied her walking down the road, which led up into the more expensive villas and haciendas, and he put down his tools and smoothed out his uniform. From within a dark one-room hut he watched, gathering her familiarity, wondering if it could be her; the dream woman who had resisted him.

Her blonde hair was pulled back into a ponytail, slightly off-center, and her clothes were all very casual, as if she'd thrown them on. His eyes followed her into the store.

An ache began as he grew hard thinking of redemption, and conquest. As the sores opened, the infected skin cracked and bled, and he cursed the doctor and his salve, never once blaming himself for not taking the medications, or applying the salves.

Having just returned from Somalia, where he'd been stationed with the UN peacekeeping forces, there was no time for such trivial matters, for he had seen—revealed to him in the terrified face of a starving black girl he had raped (one of many)—himself, here in these ruins. He was finding things that his other self, from the ancient times, had knowledge of. He had no time to continue seeing the doctors or buying medications, nor anything else, for he was going to be rich. Once he found the pouch of diamonds, that his aunt and uncle of long ago had hidden within the home he was now digging in. But the riches, the soon-to-be found wealth, were gone, vanished in the glimmer of the silky blonde hair he knew intimately—

"Ciao." Serena smiled and picked up her sack of food for the next two days. "Buona sera." Then she pushed the door open.

The old shopkeeper smiled a toothless smile, never having moved anything else, save for two fingers on the cash register, which were even now poised over the worn out keys, though the store was empty.

Serena paused to look out over the archaeological site, which was on a lower plane than the one she now stood upon. She could see into the alleys and crevices and into the center, all of it looking very familiar to her. Then she walked down a small trail, and onto the rutted main road, and walked into the realm of ghosts.

The thickets of trees and forest bushes were all wild on this upper hill, and blocked the view from the Herculenium archaeological site, or the small family run store, where Julius knew Swan had gone to buy food for breakfast. In two weeks the power company would run a line up to their villa, but until then, they'd have to buy their perishables at Graziano's market.

A twig snapped in the bushes nearby.

"Hello?"

Something is wrong, a voice told him. *Swanlake is in danger*, the voice continued, and he began to walk faster, careful of the ruts. He felt a presence in the hedge of thick bushes that lined the winding dirt road, but it wasn't threatening him. It seemed to be urging him on, faster—

"Doh!" The ground accepted his body, with a hard embrace that rocked his senses for a moment. "Shit!" He felt blood dripping off his brow, rolling down his nostrils, like a fly walking on his skin. Julius swiped it and stood back up, cursing his clumsiness.

He walked and swiped, walked and swiped, no longer paying attention to the snapping twigs on the other side of the hedge, but hoping in the back of his mind that it wasn't a pack of wolves or some other predator. He hadn't had any time to explore the area, with all the construction he was doing on the villa that Mister Pee had signed over to them, in exchange for two of Swan's paintings. They'd planned to search the forest, but had been too busy working and discovering each other, emotionally and physically.

She wanted to walk through the bowels of the ancient town, reunite some of her suspicions with some of her intuitions, find things that she knew were near, far, here or there. When they had a phone service, she wanted to see what it would take to get her permission to dig around in the site.

She turned down a small alleyway that seemed familiar; *yes*, she thought, *the Farinis lived down this pathway.* Up a couple of steps and she could once again see the horizon, and the buildings below her. To the South lay the Tyrrhenian Sea, majestic, vast, stretching to the visible horizon, and within that haze of far away, she swore she could see Sardinia and Sicily. The sun was now high, bright, and in the air she could smell the cypress, oak, uncut grasses, and the bloom of the newly opened flowers.

Yet, her thoughts were filled with her love, and she felt the weight of the groceries, and she wished he were here with her now. They could talk, search, and figure out things together; it was her favorite pastime. They would sit for hours, talking in an old dialect only they could understand, putting together memories. Sometimes he would write them down, and sometimes they would both let them float away. They learned that there may have been another time when they had had a chance to reunite, in the sixth or seventh century, somewhere on the Emerald Isle. They were still digging into the seemingly endless well of memories, which each of them carried in their heads. They were far from discovering and ferreting out all the details, but that was to come. She stepped down, looking at the nooks and crannies, but found the dark squares in the sunbaked walls a little spooky, as if someone were watching her from behind the windows.

"*Buon giorno*," Darius said from behind.

Startled, she turned and backed away, then slowly regained her composure. "You startled me." There was something familiar about this soldier; the attitude of his green eyes.

"Please, forgive me. I'm Darius Carutto—my uncle lives down the road, and works this site." He gestured, with a look, to the entire archaeological site. "They say that this was Herculenium."

"I thought it was on the Southern side of Vesuvius?" Swan questioned. "Your uncle is an archaeologist?" A hope forming.

"No, there's actual proof that this was the original town, where Herculenium originated, and that they had another village near the coast—a sort of summer and winter home thing. Very interesting. But there are pictures and scrolls—would you like to see them? I know where my uncle hid them, for further study—"

"Oh, I wouldn't want to disturb it—I have to get home anyways—"

"Well, I was actually thinking about digging around if I could."

"Good, follow me." He started to walk towards the site, hoping that her curiosity would urge her to follow. Darius had learned much in this new world; you had to do things under cover of darkness, or at least out of sight. One couldn't just grab a woman and rape her in broad daylight. But the begging cry inside him, some sense of fate blackened by desire, cried for him to just snatch her up and strip the clothes off her little body, and take her. He felt himself growing hard at the thought of what was to come, a painful sensation due to the sores and scabs on his penis. He itched and waited for the sound of her footsteps.

"How long has your uncle been an archaeologist?" Swan asked, giving in to her curiosity.

Darius smiled, the spider sensing delicate tugs on the web, and then he spoke. "Forever."

They passed the first low walls of the smaller homes, which had been the first to be excavated. There were makeshift roofs covering the lava encrusted bodies, frozen in terror.

Swan looked away. She knew the house, and the family, who were nothing more than statues now. It nearly made her cry, for the daughter, Marisa Montello, had been one of her best friends...so long ago.

"I'll tell you what," Darius started. "I'll show you and you can come back and visit the site, and you can talk to my uncle and come back some other time." He paused, then added, "I'll be leaving the country tomorrow, but I'll let my uncle know your name."

"That's very generous." But she didn't like where they were heading, a dark doorway at the end of the alley. It looked like a cavern. "Listen, I have to get back with the eggs and milk..." She noticed something familiar in his stride, and it was beginning to dawn on her. The green eyes, powerful legs, purposeful stride. *The Roman*, a voice cried. She had to get back to Julius.

A pleasant breeze dried the sweat on his brow, and the blood had stopped flowing down his face. The market was just ahead—

"*JULIUS!*" A scream echoed within the maze of walls and streets and half-homes, and frightened him down to the narrow.

The Roman had somehow stepped in behind her, and put her in a hammer-lock. His powerful forearm crushed her wind pipe. She kicked at him, but her legs were still too weak to do any real damage. Finally, as stars began to appear in her eyes, her fist connected with his groin and the devil relaxed his hold enough for her to fall forward and stumble towards the doorway of the excavated villa.

He was on her again, grabbing her left ankle and dragging her into the tarp-roofed room. He tossed her into the dark corner.

"You've gotten much prettier, whore," his real self said. "I know you remember…"

Even in the dark she could see the sheen of sweat on his forehead, and a menacing glow in his dark eyes. She got to her feet, and stood in a defensive position, while trying to breathe in the dusty air of the small room. There was only one way out. Past him.

"Oh yeah, I like it when they fight me…it's better than a cold fish just laying there," he taunted her, edging closer.

"*JULIUS!*" she screamed, and charged at him, screaming like a crazed and cornered banshee. She nearly escaped.

He punched her in the solar plexus, and she collapsed, gasping for air, as he kicked her over on her back and undid his pants.

"Please don't," Swan begged.

A MEMORY OF FOREVER

Swan's desperate cries of terror caused a chill to run up his spine, as he ran down the alley towards a dark doorway where he hoped she had been taken. He saw the groceries, strewn about on the hard-pack dirt walkway, and knew he was heading in the right direction.

Julius took out the gift given him by Señor Giuseppe, and pressed the button. He heard a man's growls as he shot through the doorway.

Red rage blinded him as he saw Swan's bare legs kicking at the giant of a man. He saw the man's intent, and Swan's frightened eyes. *Outrageous!* He put the gift into the man's back. Once, twice, thrice, and then he lost count.

Strong hands grabbed him by his right arm, and Julius spun, before he recognized the eyes, and the expression on the face. He dropped the knife and turned to Swan, who shot into his arms and hugged him tightly.

"Shhh, We are together now, my love—forever." He kissed her dirty brow, and lifted her face to his. "He is dead and gone." But there was something in her expression.

"I know this man." Swanlake shivered in his grip as she looked down at the dead Roman soldier, his security guard clothes now bloody. "He was the kidnapper from the death squads, who tried to—" She sobbed, and he held her tighter.

"Swanlake? Julius?" A familiar voice beckoned them.

They each turned, but it was Swan who put a name to the face. "Papa?"

"My Swan," the older man said, then looked at the scene. "Come, let us leave this place now."

After much hugging and kissing and greeting and questions, Julius looked towards the market.

"I have some friends who will dispose of the body. I have to use the phone."

"Have you learned nothing of these times?" Alexander chided, and pulled out a cellular phone from a pant pocket.

"Oh, Papa, how did you…"

"It's not just me, either." Alexander saw his daughter's eyes widen with joy. "Your mother lives as well…"

Julius accepted the jumping Swan in his arms as she exclaimed with delight and then just as fast jumped out of his arms and began to run up the road.

"I must get cleaned up," Swanlake shouted back.

They watched her disappear around the bend, not without some trepidation, but unwilling to block her newfound joy after such a near tragedy.

"Do you remember how to make paper?" Alexander asked, putting his arm around Julius' shoulder.

"As well as before."

"Then you'll begin your apprenticeship anew."

Julius laughed in agreement. "Yes, I may as well."

Exhausted, but emotionally brimming with joy, they lay in each other's arms.

"Each night we shall be," she whispered into Julius' ear, then smiled.

"Forever together thee and me…" he answered in the ancient language, and turned his head on the large pillow to stare into those blue eyes afire.

"We are blessed, my love," Swan said, snuggling closer.

"That's because our love is true," Julius responded.

"Do you think there are others?"

"I'd guess there are…I'd bet there are." And he took her to another world….

Printed in the United States
31115LVS00004B/295